"The rapid-fire [...] series keeps the adventure passionate.... Fans will fall in love with Tyler's latest sexy alpha male, Nick Westfall."
—*RT Book Reviews*

"A story full of hope, recovering from a harrowing trauma, and of finding love again. Sheer brilliance."
—Romance Junkies

"Never a dull moment . . . full of suspense, action, and romance. I loved the fascinating world full of captivating characters that J. D. Tyler has created. I couldn't put it down. 5 Stars, Top Pick!"   —Night Owl Reviews

Cole's Redemption

"Tyler delivers once again with the fun fifth installment of her Alpha Pack series. . . . Fast-paced and passionate adventure is a hallmark of Tyler's writing."
—*RT Book Reviews*

"What's not to love? All in all, a very satisfying, sexy read."   —Pretty Sassy Cool

"Oh, I do love a good SEALs-turned-kick-ass-shifters story and this one . . . fits the bill."   —The Book Swarm

"A sensual blend of military and paranormal romance."
—That's What I'm Talking About

continued . . .

Hunter's Heart

"Rapid-fire . . . red-hot." — *Publishers Weekly*

"Fast-paced with a great sense of adventure, as only sexy psychic Navy SEALs turned wolf shifters can provide . . . a particularly hot read." — *RT Book Reviews*

"Amazing characters, wonderful drama . . . hot and to die for. Make sure you have a cool drink close at hand. . . . Final word on this book: Get It Right Now!" — Dark Faerie Tales

Black Moon

"I loved every single minute of [*Black Moon*], every event, and every twist. This book was action-packed and smexy-packed. You will fall in love with Kalen if you weren't already." — Under the Covers

"Intense romance and danger. . . . Werewolves and Marines are a heady combination, making the men of the Alpha Pack exciting and passionate." — *RT Book Reviews*

Savage Awakening

"In a genre with werewolves aplenty, *Savage Awakening* leads the herd with its strong character development and intensity. . . . It's hard not to fall in love with the Alpha Pack." — *RT Book Reviews*

"Fans of great paranormal romance should absolutely read this book, as well as book one; I know they'll become series fans like me if not already."
—The Book Vixen

Primal Law

"With *Primal Law*, J. D. Tyler has created a whole squad of yummy shifter heroes whom readers will fall head over heels for.... I can't wait for Tyler's next Alpha Pack adventure!"
—*New York Times* bestselling author Angela Knight

"Tyler has set up an intriguing premise for her series, which promises plenty of action, treachery, and scorchingly hot sex."
—*RT Book Reviews*

"Sizzling and interesting, *Primal Law* pays homage to Lora Leigh's Breed series while forging its own paths. The characters are likable, and the work speeds along."
—Fresh Fiction

"In a genre where the paranormal is intense, J. D. Tyler may just be a force to be reckoned with. The book kept me riveted from start to finish." —Night Owl Reviews

Also by J. D. Tyler

Chase
THE
DARKNESS

AN ALPHA PACK NOVEL

J. D. TYLER

A SIGNET ECLIPSE BOOK

SIGNET ECLIPSE
Published by New American Library,
an imprint of Penguin Random House LLC
375 Hudson Street, New York, New York 10014

This book is an original publication of New American Library.

First Printing, August 2015

Copyright © J. D. Tyler, 2015
Excerpt from *Primal Law* copyright © J. D. Tyler, 2011
Penguin Random House supports copyright. Copyright fuels creativity, encourages diverse voices, promotes free speech, and creates a vibrant culture. Thank you for buying an authorized edition of this book and for complying with copyright laws by not reproducing, scanning, or distributing any part of it in any form without permission. You are supporting writers and allowing Penguin Random House to continue to publish books for every reader.

Signet Eclipse and the Signet Eclipse colophon are trademarks of Penguin Random House LLC.

For more information about Penguin Random House, visit penguinrandomhouse
.com.

ISBN 978-0-451-46692-1

Printed in the United States of America
10 9 8 7 6 5 4 3 2 1

PUBLISHER'S NOTE
This is a work of fiction. Names, characters, places, and incidents either are the product of the author's imagination or are used fictitiously, and any resemblance to actual persons, living or dead, business establishments, events, or locales is entirely coincidental.

If you purchased this book without a cover you should be aware that this book is stolen property. It was reported as "unsold and destroyed" to the publisher and neither the author nor the publisher has received any payment for this "stripped book."

Penguin
Random
House

To my granny Ladine Howard, who loved nothing more than to curl up with a glass of iced tea and a steamy romance novel. I hope there are lots of both in Heaven.

Because you weathered every hardship life threw at you and proved yourself a survivor, just like our hero, Micah's story is for you.

I love you and miss you so very much.

Until we meet again.

One

Every night, Micah Chase battled the monsters in his dreams.

The ones responsible for his captivity and torture. The ones who did terrible things to him—forced him to do things—that made him wish he was dead. And each day, he awoke to the increasing reality that the nightmares about his hellish time in captivity weren't simply products of a tormented and cracked mind.

They were *memories*.

Worms, churning up the rot in his soul, filling him with self-loathing. Hatred. Yeah, he'd liked it much better back when he couldn't remember a fucking thing.

Pushing himself out of bed, he walked into the bathroom, feeling far older than his twenty-nine years. The Alpha Pack had been called out yesterday to eliminate a nest of goblins—how the *holy fucking hell* had those little bastards gotten through the portal from the Unseelie realm, anyways?—and his body was covered in scratches and bruises from their nasty little claws and teeth. He should've healed by now.

That he hadn't was cause for yet another worry in a very long list of them.

In the bathroom, he studied his ruined face in the mirror. He'd taken his good looks for granted once. Before he had been tortured like a lab rat, made to scream in agony and beg for death. The dark eyes that stared back were dull, hollow with pain and mental exhaustion. Dark brown hair, once shiny and full, hung to his shoulders, limp and lifeless as his gaze. But it was the sight of his face that hurt most of all.

The left side was perfect. A reminder of how truly naive he'd once been to the evil in the world, to what one being was capable of doing to another. The left side, however, was a mess of scars, like melted candle wax had been poured from his forehead to run down over his brow, then down his cheek and neck. In reality it had been molten silver, splashed onto his face as he'd been held down, screaming.

"You'll do what you're told next time, dirty wolf! Isn't that right?"

"No! Stop, please!"

"He still hasn't learned." Eyes burning with manic light, Dr. Bowman flicked a hand at an assistant. "Again."

Shaking his head to clear the horrid scene from his brain, Micah gripped the sink and thought bitterly how books and movies didn't always get it right. While he'd healed, his wolf shifter's DNA hadn't been able to rid him of the terrible scars.

But maybe it was fitting that the outside matched the inside.

Ignoring the throbbing in his head, he turned on the water in the shower and let it get hot before stepping into the stall. For a few minutes he stood and enjoyed the spray beating down, soothing his tired, abused muscles. It did little to ease the pain in his head, however. In fact, the throb ramped up to a sharp stab behind his left eye that left him breathless, and warmth gushed from his nose.

"Shit."

He swiped his hand underneath his nose, then stared at the blood. There was more this time, the bleeding heavier. It would stop, though. Always did.

Tilting his head back, he let the spray wash the blood away until the flow ceased. Then he finished his shower and stepped out, toweling off. In the bedroom, he dressed in jeans and a plain black T-shirt, then pulled on his black boots, sliding his big knife into the right one. Typically he went light on weapons when he and the guys weren't out on a call. But he couldn't always shift into his wolf, especially in public, and it never hurt to be prepared.

As he straightened, his gaze found the small pill bottle resting on the dresser. He hated being dependent on that shit, so leaving it behind should be easy. Right? Yet the very thought of being in town, out in the field, or even across the compound, and not having it when the demons closed in? God, the idea made his hands shake and his heart race. Made him sweat.

Taking myst was like wrapping himself in a soft, warm blanket, chasing away the cold. The darkness. The stuff cocooned him in a layer of *I-don't-give-a-fuck*, at least for a few blessed hours. Sweet relief.

Hating himself, he snatched the bottle with a curse and opened the lid, downed a couple pills, dry-swallowing them. Then he shoved the container into his front jeans pocket. Sucking in a deep breath, he let it out slowly and waited. Gradually, the medicine took effect and he felt the turmoil in his mind ease. His muscles relaxed, tension bleeding away.

There would be a price, though. Always was.

Leaving his quarters, he walked into the hallway and

shut the door behind him. Everyone was probably at breakfast by now. The thought of eating made his stomach twist, but he didn't want to be alone. Besides, acting normal, sticking to his routine, kept his buddies and his sister, Rowan, off his back. Mostly.

Fake it till you make it.

His boots shuffled on the carpeted floor as he made his way to his destination. Outside the dining room, he paused. The aromas of pancakes, bacon, and syrup simultaneously made his stomach rumble and stirred a flutter of nausea that rose in his throat. He was so hungry, he could have eaten a half-cooked goblin, but the side effects of the medicine prevented him from consuming much without getting sick. Another misery to add to the growing list.

"You gonna go eat or just stand there sniffing the air?"

Turning, he managed a grin for Nick Westfall, the Alpha Pack's commander, and tried to ignore how the expression pulled strangely at the ruined side of his face. His boss was with his new mate, Calla Shaw, and the vampire princess was glowing. Nick appeared as proud and happy as any man would, being the reason for that glow—and the baby in her belly, which was several weeks along. Lucky bastard.

"Good morning," Micah said, nodding to them both. "Princess, you look more beautiful every time I see you. How're you feeling?"

"Thank you." She smiled as her mate tugged her into his side possessively. "Other than some morning sickness when I first wake up, I'm doing well."

"I'm glad to hear it. After you?" Stepping aside, he gestured for Nick and Calla to enter the dining room first. His attempt to avoid further conversation wasn't as subtle as he'd thought, and Nick kissed his mate on the lips, hanging back.

"Go on ahead, sweetheart. I'll be right there."

"Okay." She threw Micah a look of sympathy before proceeding inside.

Once she was gone, Micah tried to head Nick off. "I'm fine, so there's no need to start in on me again. Really."

"Is that so?" Nick's sharp blue gaze pierced him like an ice pick. "I suppose that's why your eyes are blood-shot and have circles under them so dark—it looks like you haven't slept in a month. Or why your hands are shaking."

Suddenly self-conscious, he looked away, fisting his hands to still them. "I'm okay, Nick. Just a little tired. The meds are helping."

"From where I'm standing, I have to disagree." The other man's frown deepened. "But I realize now isn't the time or place to get into a discussion. I want to talk to you after breakfast, in my office."

Fucking fantastic. The commander was just concerned. Logically, Micah knew that, but it still sucked to be sin-gled out and pinned down. Unreasonable anger churned in his gut, but he managed to nod. "Sure."

Appearing satisfied with Micah's answer, the com-mander left him. Taking a deep breath to steady his nerves, Micah walked into the dining room and cast about for a good place to sit. For damn sure not with his boss. He didn't want to give the Seer more opportunity than necessary to poke around in his biz.

At one table, he spotted Noah Brooks, Sanctuary's head nurse, sitting with Phoenix Monroe, one of Micah's Pack bros. Noah was a smaller guy, slim, with short, messy blond hair and big blue eyes that he currently had trained on the tall, lithe man who would be his Bondmate—if only the dumbass would cooperate. But Nix refused to meet his mate halfway, had made it pretty clear to his teammates how uncomfortable he felt having a male for a mate, and it was obviously killing poor Noah and driving a wedge between the two. It took the anger already boiling in Micah's blood and amplified it a few notches.

If I had someone who looks at me the way Noah looks at Nix? I'd jump for joy. Who cares if he's a dude?

Self-consciously Micah touched his face. Yeah, like that would ever happen now.

Also sitting at the table were his sister and her mate, Aric Savage. As much as he wanted to sit down and find out what the hell was going on with Nix lately, he wanted to get grilled by Rowan even less. But it was too late. She'd already spotted him and was smiling, waving him over. With a sigh, he resigned himself to enduring the nosy woman's scrutiny.

Taking a seat, he nodded a greeting to the group in general. "Hey, what's up?"

"Morning," Rowan said brightly, eyeing him. She was annoyingly fresh-faced and alert this morning, long dark brown hair pulled back into a neat ponytail. "Did you sleep well?"

"Yep," he lied, reaching for the pancakes. "Like a baby on tranquilizers."

"That's funny, 'cause you sure don't look like you did. In fact, you look terrible."

He snapped before he thought to filter his mouth. "Why'd you ask the question when you already knew the answer? Or do you just enjoy giving me shit?"

Rowan frowned. "Jesus, Micah, ease up."

Across from him, Aric shifted in his seat, a low growl of warning rumbling from his chest. No doubt Micah had pissed off the man, and the wolf within, something fierce.

Inside Micah, his brown wolf stirred and growled right back, unwilling to back down.

The redhead's voice was low and even as he spoke. "Your sister is just worried about you, like all of us are. No need to bite her head off."

The men glared at each other and the moment stretched taut. But when he saw Rowan exchange a tense glance with Nix, and Noah's eyes widen with trepidation, his anger popped like a soap bubble. The sun was barely up and he was already ruining people's day.

"I'm sorry." Guilt snaked through Micah. Remorse. He tried to soften his tone as he met his sister's concerned gaze. "I just get tired of everybody analyzing my every move, that's all. I'm fine."

She didn't believe him any more than he believed himself, but she wasn't going to push the issue in front of their friends. He didn't know if that made him feel better or not, especially when he caught Noah and Nix exchanging worried looks of their own.

Nope, he still felt like crap.

He got busy filling his plate, knowing he wouldn't be able to eat half of it. Too late, he realized he should've taken less so the leftover amount wouldn't be as noticeable. Still, he ate what he could, chewing slowly, willing the food to settle. The bacon, tasty as it was, sat like a greasy rock in his stomach, and he gave up on it after one piece.

Hoping to lighten the mood at the table, he addressed Noah. "So, how are things going over at Sanctuary?"

His question had the desired result, the nurse's face breaking out in a big smile. Aside from Phoenix, the younger man's job at the new building in the Pack's compound helping to heal and rehabilitate injured and sick paranormal beings was his favorite subject.

"It's going pretty good," Noah said with enthusiasm. "The recreation room on the top floor is done, and it looks awesome. We had a big-screen TV installed, and some big comfy chairs, books, magazines, and a couple of game tables, too. There's also a juice bar, and some light workout equipment in another area."

Noah was so animated, Micah couldn't help but smile. "Wow. Sounds like you've all put in a lot of thought and work into the place."

"We have. The new recreation area was needed for our patients who've healed enough that they need more to occupy themselves outside their rooms. It's been a hit so far."

"I'll bet. Speaking of healing, how's that tiger shifter who came in not long ago? What's his name? He was pretty bad off."

Noah's expression sobered. "Leonidis. He's still in rough shape. His family is taking turns staying at Sanctuary to be near him. He may make it, but we're not sure yet about a full recovery."

"Damn." Micah shook his head. "I could never be a doctor or nurse. I admire what you guys are doing over there, putting broken guys like me back together."

"You're not broken," Noah said softly.

Uh-oh. Here came the unwanted sympathy.

"Nah, you're just cracked," Nix put in, breaking the awkward moment before it could fully form.

Micah chuckled, and the others visibly relaxed, appearing relieved. Christ, did they really think he was that freaking fragile? "Cracked and superglued so tight I'm a damn work of art. Right, Noah?"

The nurse shook his head, but his lips were turned up in a small smile edged with concern. "Right."

Quickly Micah took two last bites of his pancakes. Then, pushing his plate away, he stood, pasting on a cheerful grin. "Well, this has been fun. Gotta go check on my bike, so I'll see you guys later."

The others issued a round of good-byes, but Aric watched him with a narrow-eyed stare. Nothing got past the redheaded wolf, but he didn't challenge Micah's excuse as he turned to leave. As he started toward the exit, Micah saw that Nick was still finishing up breakfast and talking with his mate, so maybe he'd get some time to himself before the meeting with the commander.

On the heels of that thought, a loud tone pulsed through the air, startling everyone into silence. Micah halted briefly, his current troubles blown away like so much dust, for the time being. The alarm meant only one thing—the Alpha Pack had to take to the air, fast. No time for a team briefing. Nick would receive a call from his boss, General Jarrod Grant, stating the emergency situation that needed to be handled and the location. The commander had already risen from his seat and was on the move, putting his cell phone to his ear.

Micah, for one, couldn't wait for the fight. Adrenaline coursed through his blood like fire.

He took off after Nick, his Pack brothers following suit. There was no time to dash back to their quarters. They ran outside, across the driveway, straight for the huge hangar that housed their land vehicles and aircraft to find their standby pilots already firing up two of the Hueys. Aric would pilot the third.

Some of the team armed themselves with weapons from the secure storage unit in the hangar, but aside from his knife, Micah didn't bother. Honestly, his wolf was much stronger than his human half in a fight. And unlike most of the others, his particular Psy gift as a Dreamwalker wouldn't help anyone much in battle— unless all the combatants suddenly fell asleep.

Not damn likely. Snorting to himself, he climbed onto

Aric's copter. If the man was flying, he couldn't give Micah shit. Of course there was his sister to deal with, along with Sorcerer/Necromancer/black panther Kalen Black, Channeler/gray wolf Ryon Hunter, Hammer—aka former FBI agent John Ryder—and a watchful Nick.

The commander pulled out his cell phone, answering an incoming call with a greeting loud enough to be heard over the engine and whirling blades. "Jarrod, what's going on?" After a brief conversation, he ended the call and keyed the handheld radio that would send his voice through their headsets.

"Got a bad situation fifty miles north, a panicked family under siege by what they described to the dispatcher at the sheriff's office as *large beasts with wings*." He let that sink in as the copter lifted into the air through the portal in the hangar's roof, and several of the team cursed.

Micah almost choked. "Demons?"

"Demons are my best guess," Nick confirmed for the benefit of those listening on units in the other helicopters. "We haven't fought anything this lethal in a while. They're going to make the goblins look like poodles. You guys ready?"

A chorus of *Fuck yeah* and *We got this* chimed in through the headsets, and Micah grinned in spite of the sliver of fear that send shards of ice sliding into his blood. Some things never changed. The Pack never backed down from an enemy. *Never*.

"Watch the fangs and claws," Nick went on. "Their venom can be deadly, even for shifters. Go for the kill, fast. Don't listen to anything they might say, or engage in a verbal confrontation. Let the bastards get into your head, and you're fucked. They love to take slaves to the Underworld almost as much as they love to kill—which is probably why the family they're trying to get to isn't dead yet. They're toying with the poor people, but they won't wait much longer."

Micah shuddered. Of all the horrors never to experience, aside from his own kidnapping and torture, being taken to the Underworld and subjected to whims of demons were right among the top five. According to legend, the demons answered to Hades. Was that even true? Another item to add to the list.

Let's not find out.

Across from Micah, Kalen and John were talking. Glancing next to him at Rowan, he was disconcerted to find her observing him worriedly. Shaking his head to stave off any questions or lectures, he looked across to Ryon to find the man staring at him. Or, not *at* Micah, exactly. More like, glancing *around* him.

"Man, what are you looking at?" he growled.

The other man stilled for a few moments, eyes glazing over, which was creepy as hell. Then he met Micah's gaze and simply said, "Later."

"What?"

"I'll talk to you about it later."

"What the fuck is that supposed to mean?" A suspicion struck him. "You seein' dead people again? Around *me*?"

Ryon's grim silence was answer enough.

"Who are they?" Rowan demanded, startled.

"Seriously, fuck that shit. Tell 'em to buzz off."

Ryon just sighed and turned his gaze out the open side of the Huey. "Doesn't work that way. Wish it did." He refused to say more, and silence descended between the three of them.

"Go on, fly away," Micah hissed to the spirits or whatever was hovering near him. Of course, he couldn't sense them, but that didn't mean it bothered him any less.

Ryon knew they were there, and that was good enough evidence for him. What the fuck did they want?

Ryon gave a negative shake of his head to indicate that hadn't worked to send away the spirits, and went back to watching the forest whiz past below them.

Well, Micah's friend didn't seem too concerned, so apparently there was no immediate danger. Putting it out of his mind for now, he closed his eyes and mentally prepared himself for the coming battle.

Demons were big bastards. Shut out their voices. Get underneath them. Avoid sharp objects. Go for a quick kill, head and heart. Easy. Like taking a Sunday stroll.

Okay, maybe not that simple. But Micah couldn't deny he was looking forward to the fight. Anticipation began to pump through him the closer they got to their destination, and by the time the Hueys landed in a meadow surrounded by mountains, his mind was totally focused on the job.

As soon as they were clear to move around, his sister and John bailed from the helicopter without looking back. With their particular Psy gifts—Rowan was a Dreamwalker and Hammer a Tracer—they would fight better in human form, with weapons, like when they had been in law enforcement. Kalen's panther was lethal, but his skills as a Sorcerer were essential in a battle against such a formidable enemy, so he remained dressed in his dark jeans and long leather duster. Micah, Nick, and Aric shed their clothes quickly and shifted into their wolf forms.

Nick, a large white wolf, led them about a hundred yards from the helicopters. Jaxon Law, RetroCog/Timebender/gray wolf and the Pack's second in command, strode quickly to the head of the group in human form to stand with Nick and John. Jax was an imposing figure, tall and muscular with short black hair and a neat goatee.

He was a son of a bitch in a fight, too, no matter what form he chose.

"Listen up," Jax called out. Then he pointed over the meadow to the north. "The homestead is just over the rise, about a mile and a half away. Unless the demons are stone deaf, they heard the copters, which means we need to strike fast. Hopefully the noise distracted them and bought the family some time, but that and landing closer meant sacrificing the element of surprise. Hit those fuckers fast and hard! Let's go!"

Handing the enemy advance warning of your arrival? Not optimal. But sometimes there was no help for it, and you did what you had to do. They took off, their pace quickly eating up the distance. About a half mile from the place, the team's human sniper, A. J. Stone, set up on a ridge. It was always damned comforting to know A.J. was out there, ready to pick off the enemy sneaking up behind them.

As they raced down the slope, a large, sprawling log cabin came into view. Nestled in the hills, surrounded by trees with the mountains rising majestically around it, the scene should've been breathtaking.

But to the terrified family inside, their haven had become a nightmare. Their screams could be heard clearly through the broken windows and bashed-in front door, even if Micah hadn't possessed a wolf shifter's enhanced hearing.

Pouring on the speed, Nick cleared the threshold of the front door ahead of them, Micah right behind him. The sight that greeted them should've terrified him, but there was no time to be afraid.

The demon standing in the living room splintering the sofa like a matchstick whirled to face them, a grin full of yellowed teeth spreading across its broad gray face. It took up the whole space at nearly seven feet tall, leathery wings spanning some twenty feet wide. Long, razor-sharp claws tipped the big, almost-humanlike hands and feet, and its chest was broad.

"Greetings, fools," it said pleasantly. Then it tossed the sofa aside and launched itself at Nick. The fight was on.

More demons materialized seemingly from nowhere, and the team had all they could handle.

"Micah, look out!"

John's shout came just in time to keep Micah from losing his head. Turning, he ducked, avoiding the demon's claws but losing a tuft of fur in the process. *Shit, that was close!*

Snarling, Micah rushed the creature, going straight for the throat. The demon wasn't going down so easily, however. Though it stumbled backward, it managed to grab him and fling his body across the room and into the wall. He hit hard enough to crack the plaster, which rained on him as he fell to the floor. Stunned for a moment, he shook himself off and went in for round two.

On this second charge, he changed tactics. The demon was prepared for him to jump again and go for the throat. Instead, he hurtled himself at the creature's legs. In a flash, he sank his fangs into the vulnerable thigh muscle—and ripped out the demon's hamstring. Screeching in pain, the bastard fell hard, writhing.

Got you now, fucker. Micah swiftly tore out its throat, and as the demon gurgled helplessly, Micah shifted into his half-man, half-wolf form. Then he used his own sharp claws like knives, plunging them into the creature's chest and ripping out its black heart. The beast died, eyes glazing, surprise still etched on its ugly mug.

He didn't get to savor his victory. A hard blow took him in the side, and he rolled a few feet. A new demon attacked, and he used the hamstringing method again, with success. Dispatched the enemy. And again, on another. The Pack was winning the battle, and hopefully they'd find the family—who'd stopped screaming—alive, safe, and barricaded in the basement.

Just as he finished taking the heart of another demon beneath him, Rowan screamed from somewhere behind him. "Micah!"

Still in half-form, he turned—

"Ungh." Blinking, breath stolen away, it took him a couple of heartbeats to register the demon towering over him, smirking in triumph.

"Die, wolf."

The claws of one of the beast's hands were buried in Micah's chest. The strange, cold burn of the venom was spreading through his limbs, his lungs, making it hard to breathe. He tried to lift his arm, to swipe his claws at the creature, but couldn't. The demon laughed and dug the talons deeper.

"Micah! No!"

A loud *bang* sounded. And the demon fell away in a shower of blood, brain matter, and bone. The claws were torn from Micah's chest, and he sank to his knees, gasping. Unable to retain his shift, he returned to human form and stared at the blood gushing from the grisly wound to stream down his abdomen.

"Shit," he wheezed.

The instant he toppled to the floor, hands were on him. The noise of the waning battle faded into the background. Suddenly he was on his back with Zander Cole, the Pack's Healer, beside him dressed in fatigues and a dark T-shirt. Tucking his gun into his waist band, Zan placed a hand over the bleeding wound.

"Steady," he said in a quiet, soothing voice. "We'll get you fixed up in no time."

"Yeah. Thanks." Micah's next breath was strangled in his chest, as though a fist was crushing the life out of him. "Hurry."

Zan closed his eyes and stilled. Micah was in too much pain to look down and watch what he was doing, but a warm glow began to seep into his chest. Gentle waves lapped at the agony, wearing it away gradually. His breath came easier, and he began to relax. Thank God for the Healer, or he might not have survived the trip back to the compound.

"I want you to stay still, okay?" Zan was frowning slightly, trying not to show his worry.

"Why? I feel a lot better."

"I'd just rather you take it easy until we get you back and let the doctors examine you."

Nick crouched at Micah's side, back in human form, a borrowed coat wrapped around him. "House is secure. Family is safe. Kalen is wiping the demons from their memories and replacing them with poachers who broke in, looking for money and weapons."

"Would poachers do that?"

"It was the best he could do in a pinch," Nick said wryly. "Sheriff Deveraux is here, too. We're letting them take over the scene."

Sheriff Jesse Deveraux was a big, mean-tempered asshole. And a good ally to the Pack. He was one of the few humans outside the compound to know about the paranormal world and the Alpha Pack's role in it. Grumpy or not, he was also an honest man, and a good guy to have on your side.

"So, basically, we were never here," Micah said.

"You got it." The commander eyed him, then glanced at Zan. A look passed between him and the Healer before he addressed Micah again. "You going to be okay?"

"Yeah." He wasn't sure that was totally true, but that's what he was going with. Clearly neither of the men was convinced.

Nick patted his shoulder. "You'll do as Zan says. Like I told you, a demon's venom is nothing to fuck with. Zan healed the worst of the wound, but you're going to feel like shit for a couple of days. Stay put while I send somebody for a stretcher."

Micah opened his mouth to protest, but a glare from the boss cut it short. "Fine."

With a sigh, he closed his eyes and drifted, ignoring the activity around him. Jeez, he was tired. Someone covered him with a blanket. Rowan stroked his hair and whispered, "I love you, you jerk," which made him smile as he murmured the sentiment to his sister in return.

A few minutes later, he heard Nick, Zan, and Rowan talking some distance away and realized they were discussing him. He probably should've alerted them to the fact that he was awake.

Nah, screw that. He wanted to know what they were so uptight about that they weren't saying to his face.

"What is it?" Rowan asked, voice quiet.

Zan answered. "I'm concerned about some anomalies I detected while I was healing your brother."

"Anomalies? What do you mean? Like tumors or something?" Alarm tinged her questions.

"Not like a disease, but more of a sense that something isn't right inside his body. The healing was more difficult than it should've been and—"

"But Nick said that demon venom is deadly, so of course something wasn't right. Besides, it wasn't so long ago that your healing abilities weren't up to speed. Maybe you're still having some trouble."

Zan didn't seem to take offense to that suggestion,

but he was insistent. "I assure you, my healing is right on target again. The cells in Micah's body weren't knitting as quickly as they should have been, even after a demon attack. They needed a lot of coaxing to re-form, more than usual for one of us. I just think it bears watching, that's all."

"All right." She sighed, her tension palpable. "Thanks, my friend. I appreciate it."

"Don't thank me. I want to see him well as much as anyone."

Humiliation crept through Micah. He loved them for caring, but hated being a burden. Hated lying flat on his back when he was supposed to be stronger than his problems. A protector. But at the moment, it didn't matter that he loathed his situation, because his body was doing its job. Shutting down, forcing him to rest whether he wanted to or not.

Exhaustion claimed him. And in seeped the nightmares.

"Bring him this way."

Micah stumbled along the dim corridor, held between the two big guards. Fear clogged this throat. He knew where they were going. What they were going to do to him this time?

He'd resisted so far. Each time, the doctor upped the stakes. Pushed his mind and body further. Withheld food and water. Tortured him nearly beyond endurance, What more could they do to him? Nothing but kill him. That would be a blessed relief.

In the dark chamber, there were two shifters waiting. Unkempt hair hung over their round, frightened eyes, and their bodies were unwashed. One was chained on a concrete slab over a drain. The other, bolted to the stone wall, faced his companion, spread-eagle.

This was a new game their captors were playing. A chill

of trepidation raced along his spine as he watched Dr. Bowman stride forward, a small smile on his face.

"Ah, Micah. Welcome. Let me introduce you to Parker and Tyler. Parker is there," Dr. Bowman said, pointing to the shifter positioned over the drain.

Dread grew in Micah's chest, settling like a lead weight. Whatever game Bowman was playing, it didn't bode well for any of them. Especially when the doc and his goons had always referred to their captives by number—until now. He had a terrible suspicion that Bowman had moved on to the next stage of his plan to turn him into a killing machine, someone who wouldn't let personal details like names interfere with his objective.

He had no idea at the time how right he was.

"Micah," Bowman went on pleasantly, "it's time for you to earn your keep. Your strength will make you one of my top enforcers. You're going to teach Parker his place in the hierarchy among shifters."

"Teach him, how?" Micah asked cautiously.

"Starting with this."

With a flick of Dr. Bowman's hand, a guard stepped forward, holding a bullwhip. The guard presented it to Micah, who stood staring at it as though it was a venomous snake.

"You . . . you want me to whip him with that?"

"Yes, and you will."

Glaring at the doctor in hatred, he spat, "What makes you think for one second I'll do what you say?"

"This."

Another guard stepped from the shadows, dragging a slender woman with long, thin blond hair. No, not a woman. The female shifter was barely more than a girl, perhaps not even twenty years old. She cried out piteously as the guard slapped her hand onto a wooden block and grabbed an ax.

"You comply, or she loses body parts. One by one."
Bowman smiled.

Bile burned Micah's throat, and black rage consumed his heart. But he grabbed the whip and let the coils unfurl.

And he turned to Parker, regret tearing at his soul.

Two

"Jacee, where's my fuckin' beer? Did ya have ta grow the damn hops first?"

Jacee Buchanan groaned, dodging patrons while balancing her tray of drinks, and resisted the urge to dump the whole thing right on top of Clyde's stupid head. She hated the exaggerated way he drew out the pronunciation of her name—Jaay-*CEEE*—making it more singsong-y the drunker he got.

"I'm coming, you shithead!"

Clyde and his friends hooted as she made her way over. If he and his buddies hadn't been regulars, she could have gotten in trouble with her boss for talking to a customer like that, but the fact was they ate up the attention. It was a weird sort of ritual they had going, and it worked for them. Yeah, they were annoying, but harmless. And they tipped well.

As she handed out the drinks, Clyde attempted, as always, to pull her into his ample lap. Like always, she laughingly avoided his advances while pretending to be

the tiniest bit flattered, a fine art all bartenders and serv-
ers had to master or else they wouldn't get far in that job.

"Shorthanded again tonight, honey?" Clyde asked
loudly, above the blaring country music.

"Yep. Had another server call in sick. You know how
it goes."

As a bartender—or mixologist, as some of the fancier
city types preferred to be called these days—that's really where she wanted to be. Behind the bar, creating
drinks. More and more often, it seemed she got stuck
pulling double duty, both mixing and serving. She had
nothing against hard work. Hell, she'd been working all
her life, never had it easy. But doing the jobs of two
people sucked.

"Just tell the boss you're done for the night and hang
out with us."

She winked. "You know it doesn't work like that. Jack
would have my hide."

Same old. Every time they came in. But they were a
friendly bunch, so she let it ride. After passing out their
drinks, she tucked the round tray under her arm and
started back toward the bar. Just as she did, a group that
never failed to attract a ton of attention came through
the entrance of the Cross-eyed Grizzly.

Especially hers.

The men were from that top secret compound in the
Shoshone National Forest all the locals believed to be a
plain old research facility. Jacee knew better. These men
were, in fact, a black ops team of wolf shifters—and one
panther—whose job it was to protect civilians from all
sorts of paranormal predators. With any luck, humans
would never find out about the evil things that went
bump in the night.

Jacee knew about the Alpha Pack for a couple of
good reasons. One, she wasn't human. And two, Jax Law

was a former lover of hers. She kept her eyes and ears open, and it paid off. Selene, Zander's mate, was the only one of the Pack who had a clue that Jacee was a coyote shifter—even Jax didn't know—and that's the way Jacee wanted to keep it.

A few months ago, when Selene had first arrived in town, she'd somehow made Jacee as a coyote right off the bat and had kept her secret in exchange for information. Whatever the she-wolf's problem had been, it had obviously worked out. She seemed happy, holding her mate's hand as they walked with the group to a large table in one corner.

For one fleeting moment, Jacee envied them. They were a pack and they had one another, whereas Jacee had nobody. Loneliness swelled in her breast for her long-dead family, but she ruthlessly squashed it before it could drown her. There was no sense in going down that road again. She was alone. No changing that fact.

She was just glad Jax and his mate, Kira, weren't here tonight. Not that she'd been in love with the wolf, but it still hurt to see the happiness on their faces.

Just as she started to turn away, one of the team caught her eye. *He* was here again. The tall, leanly muscled man with the scarred face and shoulder-length dark brown hair. He didn't show up with them often, but when he did, she found it difficult to take her eyes off him. There was just something arresting about him that stopped her in her tracks every time. Made her pulse race. Her palms sweat.

He'd been beautiful, once. Like he could've graced magazine covers if he'd wanted. But to her, he was still gorgeous despite the ruined left side of his face. What drew her the most, though, was the deep well of sadness in his big brown eyes. She wondered what pain ate at his insides.

And she wondered if that was what drove him to reach into his pocket now and then and pop the pills when he thought nobody was looking.

Could a wolf shifter become an addict? Was that possible?

Snapping out of her musings, Jacee approached the table. As she did, it occurred to her that she'd never actually waited on their group when *he'd* been with them before. Last time he'd come in, she'd been behind the bar. She gladly took the opportunity to study him close up as she went around and took their orders, and found he was even more striking than from a distance. His injury only added to the mystery of the man and wolf. In her world, battle scars were honorable. They added rather than detracted from his powerful aura.

Finally, it was his turn. Jacee stopped next to him, leaned over slightly and smiled down at him as he looked up and met her gaze—and the room tilted under her boots.

The man smelled absolutely amazing. Like fresh pine, rain, and man, all rolled into one tantalizing scent that awakened her coyote with a little growl and shot a bolt of arousal from her brain to her toes. And every sensitive place in between. *What the hell?*

"Wh-what would you like to drink?" she stammered. His eyes had widened as he stared back, and the unmistakable scent of arousal wafting from him told her that she wasn't alone in whatever was happening between them.

"Crown and Coke, please." His voice was low and smoky, sending shivers along her spine. That chocolate gaze raked her from head to toe and back up again. From the heat there, he liked what he saw as well.

"Coming right up." Turning, she nearly tripped in her haste to put some distance between herself and the alluring wolf.

"Damn, Micah," one of the guys ribbed, "what'd you say to Jacee?"

Glancing over her shoulder, she saw the handsome wolf smile a little, shaking his head. *Micah*. God, what a great name. Hurrying, she filled their drink orders and loaded up her tray. As quickly as possible without spilling a drop, she returned to their table and handed out the drinks, trying not to act as though she was watching Micah.

Hell, who was she kidding? She was watching, and so was he, and they were both doing a lousy job of pretending otherwise.

"Can I get you guys anything else?" She half expected the stupid comments a lot of the other patrons made, but from this group it was refreshingly absent most of the time. Aside from some harmless flirting, they didn't bother her much. Maybe that had to do as much with her former fling with Jax as anything, but she was glad.

She also noticed that Micah refrained from making any of the usual tasteless jokes. For some reason, she would've felt really let down if he had. To her relief, he simply looked her straight in the eye and said, "I'm good for now. Thanks."

Forcing her mind back to her job, she filled more orders. A commotion at the door caught her attention, and she frowned as she spotted a foursome she'd hoped would never dirty the place again. Especially since Jack had thrown them out last time the ringleader of the sorry band of bikers had tried to push her into joining him out back for a little "fun."

Looking around for her coworker, she saw Julie was busy on the other side of the room. Damn. With a sigh, she resigned herself to several hours of putting up with the jerk. Too bad his good looks were wasted on his shitty personality. If she didn't know better, she'd swear he was a jackass shifter.

"Hey, Grant," she said, striving not to sound as if she'd like to let her coyote rip his face off. "What are you guys drinking tonight?"

Leaning back in his chair, the biker crossed his arms over his chest and gave her a cocky grin. "Can't I just have you, honey? You'd taste better on my tongue than any beer."

"Beer it is," she said brightly, ignoring his pass. "What about you all?"

After she filled their orders, the men settled down for a while. She was able to watch Micah, hopefully without him realizing it, and take care of her other customers, too. Unfortunately, as the first hour passed after their arrival, Grant and his buddies became drunk. And when Grant got wasted, he got sort of belligerent. He and his group weren't fun and harmless like Clyde and his friends.

"Come on, baby," Grant crooned, grabbing her wrist when she was making another trip to the bar. "Sit on Papa's lap and tell him all your troubles."

Jesus. "Let go, asshole." She was getting tired, and her charm was wearing off. From the corner of her eye, she spotted Jack scowling toward them, but she knew her boss was eyeing Grant and not angry with her.

Wresting free of Grant, she continued on her way.

Jacee hefted another tray of drinks on her shoulder and headed back across the room for a table on the other side of Grant's. As she walked past him, her foot caught on something, and she had a split second to register that Grant had stuck his boot out in her path. She'd been moving at a fast clip, and there was no catching herself.

With a cry, she went down hard, the crash of glasses and bottles loud in her ears. Shards went everywhere, and liquid splattered over the floor, her shirt, face, and arms. For a second she remained there, stunned. The cheerful noise in the room died, and then Jack started toward them. She was pushing herself up to give Grant a piece of her mind when an ominous growl reached her ears.

As someone helped her stand, she saw Micah crossing the room, long legs eating up the distance with quick strides. The expression on his face was murderous, and right then she was glad she wasn't Grant.

Micah reached the biker before Jack could, and grabbed the laughing man by his leather vest, spinning him around. The amusement died on his face immediately.

"Hey, what the fuck? I was just havin' some fun—"

Which was, apparently, the wrong thing to say. Micah gripped the front of Grant's shirt and unloaded his fist in the jerk's face. The biker's head snapped back, and Micah let him fall to the floor, gazing down on him with disgust. Grant was out cold.

Then her rescuer studied the faces of Grant's friends. "Anybody else feel like harassing Jacee or any of the ladies who work so hard to serve your sorry, drunk asses?"

A general round of denials ensued, in which the trio assured Micah and Jack, who'd arrived to survey the mess, that they had no idea Grant would go so far to screw with her just because she wouldn't "put out." Charming.

Jacee was only half listening to the douche bags, because her arm was throbbing, and she was wet, pissed, and embarrassed. But she was also intrigued by this man who'd jumped to her defense and was even angrier than Jacee. Standing straight and tall, glaring at Grant's buddies and the room in general, he looked every inch the dangerous predator she knew him to be.

He was magnificent.

Before she could thank him, he bent and hauled Grant to his feet. The biker was groggy, blinking at Jacee almost in surprise, like he couldn't quite grasp what had happened.

"Apologize to Jacee," Micah growled, "before I break your stupid neck."

"I—I'm sorry." Grant seemed to realize they had everyone's undivided attention, and his face reddened. "It was a joke that got out of hand. Again, I'm sorry, Jacee."

Lips pressed together, she nodded. That was the best she'd give him, and he seemed relieved, anyway. Micah grabbed him by the back of his vest and frog-marched him toward the door. Jacee followed to see what he'd do. When he reached the porch, he literally picked Grant up, holding the vest and the seat of his jeans, and *threw* him out onto the gravel driveway.

Grant landed with a thud and a curse, but quickly scrambled up and limped away, his friends following.

"Don't come back," Micah warned them. "You do, and next time I'll fuck you up."

Jacee's wicked little heart fluttered and melted a bit more.

Micah turned to her boss. "Jack, it's time for you to seriously consider hiring a bouncer. This shit is happening way too often. The rough customers are going to drive off the good ones, and one of your girls is going to wind up hurt." His eyes slid to Jacee as he said that, studying her in concern.

Jack laughed, the sound unhappy. "Yeah, I know. I don't suppose you'd want the job?"

"I've got one already," he said. "But thanks."

"Well, if you ever reconsider, even for part-time, let me know."

Micah nodded, then looked to Jacee. "You all right, ma'am?"

She smiled. "My mother was 'ma'am.' I'm just Jacee. But yeah, I'll do."

He smiled back, and even the way the scars pulled at that side of his face didn't affect how handsome he was to her. "Your arm is bleeding."

"It is?" Holding up her right arm, she finally noticed the cut on top of her forearm. It was a couple of inches long, and the bleeding was already slowing, thanks to her shifter healing. By tomorrow it would be a pink scar, but she'd have to keep a bandage on it for the rest of the week so as not to arouse suspicion. "Crap."

Jack cursed. "Let's get you inside, wash that out, and get a bandage on it." Without waiting for an answer, he strode back inside.

Micah wanted to help. He didn't have to say anything, but she could sense his anxiety, his reluctance to let her go. She gave him another smile. "Thanks for the rescue. Grant's an ass."

"He shouldn't be a problem again. If he is, let me know."

"I appreciate it, but Grant's not *your* problem."

"He is now," Micah said in a low voice, stepping closer. His scent drifted to her nose again, wrapping around her like a warm blanket.

His nearness was heady, intoxicating. What the hell was going on?

"Why do you say that?" she asked, a hint of nervousness creeping into her voice.

"Don't you feel something? God, you smell so good, like cherries and almonds."

"So do you," she murmured, "but like pine and rain."

Tentatively, he brushed a hand down her uninjured arm. "I know what you are."

That gave her a jolt, and she snapped her gaze up to his. "How?"

"Tonight, I finally scented you. My wolf knows, and don't tell me you didn't already know what I am. What my friends are, too."

She paused, then admitted, "Okay. I knew about you all. More than you realize."

He nodded. "I think I know what's happening between us, too. Don't you?"

"I . . . I'm not sure." But she was avoiding the subject, and they both knew it.

He didn't push further on that particular point, but the knowledge was in his kind brown eyes, the tilt of his smile. His face didn't seem as sad as it had earlier tonight, and she wasn't ready to examine why too closely.

"Okay," he said softly. "I'd like to see you again. I want to get to know you."

She blew out a breath and looked away from his arresting gaze. It was so hard to think with his scent and warmth enveloping her, calling to every cell in her body that was both female and shifter.

"A wolf and a coyote?"

"Why not?" he said.

"I doubt your friends will be thrilled."

"They're more than just my friends, they're my Alpha Pack brothers. But they don't get a vote."

"You say that now, but you might feel differently later." Right then, she knew she should come clean about her prior relationship with Jax. But she thought of the sadness she'd seen in his expression earlier and couldn't do it. On a primal level, she knew Micah was important to her, and she wasn't going to risk messing things up so soon.

No, she'd tell him in the future, when they knew each other better. Not yet.

"Come on, let's get that arm looked after."

Taking her hand, he led her inside. The patrons had quieted some, and a few had left because the hour had grown late. Someone had cleaned up the glass and alcohol from the floor, for which she was thankful. She was less thankful for the speculation and curiosity on the faces of Micah's teammates as he walked her toward the back, and she decided to pretend she didn't notice.

Just through the double swinging doors leading into the kitchen, to the left, was the office. The door beside the office was the staff restroom, complete with a first-aid kit. As they reached the restroom, Jack came out of the office.

"Oh, there you are. Need some help with that cut?"

"I've got her," Micah answered before she could open her mouth.

Jack hesitated. "When you're fixed up, fill out a workman's comp form and go home. It's slowing down now, so we're good." Then with a smirk, he turned back inside and shut the door.

In the restroom, Micah fished under the sink and brought out the plastic container with the supplies. While he worked, she admired the way his muscles moved under his T-shirt and snug jeans. How his brown hair fell around his face and to his shoulders. Damn, she had it bad.

He proved to be a gentle caregiver, dabbing alcohol on the wound to clean it, then dressing it with a square bandage and some medical tape.

"Thank you," Jacce said.

"You're welcome. I'll walk you out."

The man was patient, waiting while she gathered her purse from the office, quickly filled out the form, and told Jack good-bye. He was so solicitous of her as well, placing a broad hand on her back as they left and shielding her from his Pack's stares with his body until they were outside.

"Which car is yours?" he asked.

"Over there." She pointed to a silver Chevy pickup that had seen better days.

"Nice truck."

She shrugged. "It's fifteen years old, but it gets me around, on a good day."

"I'm a motorcycle guy myself."

"Yeah?" He pointed to a black Harley parked on the side of the building, a few yards away. "Nice."

"It gets me around."

He grinned at her, and she couldn't help but grin back. There was something about the man that called to her. It was more than the years of loneliness, of mourning her lost family, of yearning for the touch of another. It was the possibility of a man who might be hers to keep. What would that be like?

Their boots crunched on the asphalt as he walked her to the truck. At the driver's door, she turned to face him—and found herself gently pushed against the side of the vehicle with one of his hands braced on the roof above her head. His front was flush with hers, his body heat branding her like an iron.

Slowly, he lowered his head, giving her time to protest the kiss he was about to take. In answer, she wrapped her fingers in the soft hair at the back of his head and pulled his head the rest of the way down.

Explosive. That was his taste on her tongue, assaulting her senses. Hardening her nipples and making her sex ache. She couldn't have stopped her reaction to him any more than she could have halted a tidal wave, and she didn't want to. Her coyote growled in pleasure. Now she'd know his essence, his scent, anywhere. She knew what he was to her.

But she wouldn't use that name for him. It was too soon.

After exploring her mouth for several moments, he

pulled back and stared down at her, expression warm. "You taste so damn fine."

"You're pretty yummy yourself."

He sighed. "You are so getting the short end of the stick with me—"

"No. Stop right there." She glared at him. "If this is about your scars, save it. I don't care about those, except I hate that you had to get hurt. They don't make you any less attractive to me."

"Thanks," he said, sounding sincere. Reaching up to her face, he tucked a lock of hair behind her ear. "But I wasn't really talking about the scars. I've got baggage, Jacee. Loads of it."

"So do I. But we'll get to know each other and share the burden, right?"

Again with the sadness. She didn't like the look on him. "Right."

"I'm off tomorrow night," she told him, "in case you wanted to know."

That cheered him considerably. "I did, in fact. Can I get your contact info in my phone?"

"Sure."

He pulled out his cell, opened up his contacts page, and gave her the device. She typed in her first and last names, number, and address, then handed back the phone.

"There you go," she said, getting out her phone.

"Jacee Buchanan. I like your name."

"Good, 'cause it's the only one I've got." She winked. "What's your last name?"

"Chase."

"I like yours, too. Now call me."

He did, and she added his name to his number.

"Can I pick you up tomorrow afternoon, take you to dinner?" Micah asked.

Suddenly he looked a little unsure and so sweet she

kissed him again. Slowly. "Yes. A bit old-fashioned, are you?"

"Some, when it comes to treating a lady. Is that okay?"

"More than. What time?"

"Pick you up at six?"

"On that Harley?" She eyed it with some doubt.

He laughed. "No. I was going to drive my car, unless you *want* to ride the motorcycle to dinner."

"Well, maybe not this first time."

"That's what I thought. See you at six."

"Awesome."

Several leisurely kisses later, he let her go and strolled to the bike. She watched his ass sway in his jeans until he straddled the machine and started it with a throaty roar. Then she got into the truck and fired it up, wincing at the cough it gave as she followed Micah from the parking lot.

He turned left to head out of town, and she turned right to go home to her modest house in Cody. For the first time in many years, the idea of going home alone wasn't quite as terrible as before. She had a date with a sexy wolf.

And she planned to make the most of it.

Jacee tossed and turned, trying to sleep.

After one in the morning, and not much success on that front. She was exhausted after the drama on her shift, meeting Micah. Making that special discovery about him. It was too much, and it swirled around in her brain until she finally gave in.

Her dream started out innocently enough.

She was running through the Shoshone in coyote form, one of her favorite activities. The only thing she would've loved more would have been sharing the run with one of her Pack. Someone she loved. Cared for. Anyone. Running alone was a lonely feeling, but she tried to concen-

trate on the joy of being alive. Of feeling the earth under her paws and the wind in her face.

As she ran, she came to a stream and paused to drink. In the water, another image joined hers, and when she jerked up her head, there stood a gorgeous brown wolf. His coat was full and shiny, his chest broad, legs long. The only interruption to his beauty was the scarring visible on one side of his face.

Even in her dream, she knew this wolf—Micah.

She yipped at him happily and took off. With a re-sounding bark, he ran after her. He chased her through brush, over logs, across a meadow. She was pretty certain he could've caught her anytime, but the fun was in their togetherness, not who won.

Finally he did catch up, and pounced. He sent them rolling across the grass and leaves, nipping playfully, pinning her underneath his bulk. At no time did she feel threatened. Instead, just incredibly filled with joy, as she hadn't been in ages. Their play was a balm to her soul.

And then it changed.

Over her, the wolf stilled. His body rippled and length-ened, and seamlessly he changed to his half-form. He was a more powerful version of Micah, with fangs and claws, fur covering his chest, arms, torso, and legs. And his cock and balls, too.

Arousal swamped her, and she changed as well with a thought. While stronger than her human form, her half-form was much smaller than his. She reveled in his power as he spread her legs, reached between them to rub her sex. He parted her folds, dipping his fingers inside to fuck her with them, and she whimpered, raising her hips to en-courage him.

He'd stop if she wanted. No question. She felt safe with him, and so she didn't want him to end things. Spreading her legs wider, she pulled his head down, loving his chuckle as he fastened his mouth to her and started to lick. God, that preternaturally long tongue was magic, stroking her core and driving her wild. He laved and sucked her clit until she thought she'd go mad.

And then she exploded into a thousand shards of light, calling his name.

Jacee awakened with a start, heart pounding. Sex throbbing in the aftermath of a powerful orgasm. Wait. She'd only dreamed that, right?

Looking down at herself, she saw that she was flat on her back, naked. Her legs were spread and her sex was wet. Just as though Micah really had been there, pleasuring her with his mouth. But that wasn't possible. She was alone.

It was a hell of a long time before sleep claimed her again.

This time, she didn't dream.

Three

Micah felt like a complete shit.

Last night had gone so well. He'd been drawn to Jacee for weeks now and hadn't known why—until she'd gotten close and his wolf had scented the delicious aroma of cherries and almonds. He'd begun to suspect. And then he'd gotten a taste of her when they'd kissed, and his wolf knew.

Jacee was his mate.

The idea was stunning. Frightening and exciting. Could a broken man like him actually have something to offer a mate? Surely she was getting ripped off. Bondmates had no say in the matter, because biology ensured that once they met, they would either mate—or sicken and die without each other. Some choice for Jacee.

And then he'd totally invaded her privacy after they'd gone home for the evening. He'd already ruined things by using his ability as a Dreamwalker to take advantage of her. She no doubt thought her sexy dream was just that—a dream. His conscience, however, wouldn't allow her to go on believing a lie. Not a good way to start a *real* relationship. If that's in fact what he hoped to have, biology or not.

Picking up the bottle from his dresser, he shook out two pills and downed them with a day-old bottle of water. On second thought, he shook out two more, swallowed those as well, and braced his hands on the edge of the dresser, trying to calm the building chaos in his brain before it got too bad. Gradually, he began to relax.

But there was the nosebleed and the headache to deal with before he could venture from his quarters.

Half an hour later, feeling almost like himself, he left his apartment and ventured into the hallway. Not even the slightest bit hungry, he decided to head for the hangar and tinker with his motorcycle for a while. It had been idling a little rough lately, so maybe—

Someone slammed into his shoulder, hard. Inside, his wolf leapt into attack mode.

Moving fast, he grabbed the body and threw it against the wall. Distantly, he heard a frightened cry as he pinned the man with one arm and extended his claws on the other hand. His fangs lengthened as he buried his fingers in his captive's hair, yanked back his head to expose his throat—

"Micah! What the fuck?"

Enemy. End him.

"Let him go!"

Someone hit him from the side, knocking him away from his prey, and they went down in a tangle of limbs. The enemy on top of him was bigger, stronger. He needed to get free. Or shift. Yes, his wolf could defeat the man who was fighting him.

"Micah, get ahold of yourself!" A blow to the side of his head sent his brain reeling, scattering his thoughts.

The red haze of anger lifted, and his wolf retreated.

The sight that greeted him at first filled him with confusion. Then horror.

Noah was leaning against the wall, breathing hard, eyes wide as he stared at Micah. The shirt of his blue nurse's scrubs was torn, dots of red bleeding through the fabric where Micah had scratched him.

"Oh, my God. Noah, I'm so sorry."

"Hey, um, it's okay." Noah tried a shaky smile. "Guess I need to watch where I'm going."

"No," John said, climbing off Micah to scowl down at him. "It's not okay. You attacked a staff member without cause or provocation. You lost control."

Which was the precise moment Phoenix walked up, and Nick was with him. Awesome.

"What?" Nix said, taking in the scene.

Micah pushed to his feet. "Look, I said I'm sorry. It won't happen again."

Nick's expression was like a gathering storm getting ready to unleash. "What won't happen? Did you actually *attack* Noah?"

"Yes, but he ran into me," he tried to explain. "Or we ran into each other, and my wolf thought—"

"My office. *Now*."

Fucking shit. Nodding, Micah could only watch miserably as the commander stalked off in the direction of his office, John following. Turning, he started to apologize to Noah again. But before he could take a step, Nix got between them, getting right in his face.

"Touch him again, ever, and I'll kill you. Brother or not," he said quietly. He was dead serious.

"I said I was sorry, and I am."

"Get yourself together, Micah. We all see how you're suffering, but you're a time bomb ready to go off, and we don't know what to do."

"I'm dealing with my issues the best I know how." he paused, anger rising again. "What about you? How are you dealing with yours? That mating thing coming along just peachy?"

"That's not any of your goddamn business," Nix growled.

"Nope, but looks like you'd better make it yours. Sooner rather than later." He jerked his chin to where Noah was disappearing down the hallway.

Nix cursed and took off after Noah.

Micah stood in the hallway for a moment, collecting himself. He'd fucked up. Bad. He'd apologize to Noah again, later, without an audience, and make sure the man knew he was sincere. First, he had to appease his boss.

When he reached the office, he knocked once before slipping inside. Nick was sitting behind his desk, papers in hand. Setting them down, expression hard, he gestured for Micah to sit. Nerves assailed Micah but he schooled himself to appear calm in the face of the commander's quiet anger.

"What the actual fuck was that out there? You lost control and attacked Noah in the middle of the hallway. *Noah*, who's half your size and wouldn't hurt a fly." His jaw clenched and his blue eyes were like steel. "Talk to me."

"I don't know. I was walking along, and I was deep in thought, so when he ran into me I guess I just reacted."

"Snapped."

It sounded terrible, put like that. "I don't think I really would've hurt him."

"We don't know that because John stopped you before you could do any harm." His frown deepened. "Is Mac still counseling you?"

Dr. Mackenzie Grant worked in Sanctuary, with Dr. Melina Mallory, Noah, and the others. She was also Kalen's mate, and the daughter of General Jarrod Grant. In short, a woman not to be fucked with.

"Some. I'm seeing her this afternoon."

"Good. You'll tell her about this incident or I will. If Noah hasn't already, that is."

"Yes, sir."

"The pills. How many are you taking?"

He should've expected the question, but it still caught him off guard. "Mac prescribed one in the morning and one at night."

"No. How many are you *actually taking*? Don't even *think* of lying to me."

"I . . ." Micah scoured his brain for an excuse, but came up with nothing. Except the truth. "Ten or twelve a day," he said with shame. "The doses don't seem to last as long as when I first started taking them."

"Have you discussed this with Mac?"

"No."

"Do that today also. Have her change the dosage, or the meds, or whatever she decides, but do not keep her in the dark about what's going on. Same goes for me. If you're having problems, you come to me and Mac. We depend on you, and so does your team. Is that understood?"

"Yes, sir."

Nick's expression softened some. "I'm only coming down on you because I care, dammit. Do you remember the vision I told you about a few weeks ago?"

"How could I forget?" he muttered.

Nick leaned forward. "It's going to come to pass if you keep this up. You're going to *die*. I know Jacee is your mate, and you'll leave her alone and grieving. I don't know how else to impress on you how serious I am."

A shudder snaked through Micah. He knew better than to question a Seer as powerful as Nick. But he couldn't help asking, "What makes you so sure there's any way to change my fate, anyhow?"

"Is that why you're being so reckless with your health?

You can't change your future, so fuck it? Because if I caused that by telling you—"

"No! You didn't. I swear that's not the way I feel. I'm just asking, honest."

The commander relaxed some, sitting back in his chair. "I know 'anything is possible' sounds trite, but it's true. I'll tell you something I told Jax once. The decisions people make are like pinballs, sending each outcome in a new direction. Every decision you make affects something or someone else in a thousand different ways. Even yourself. If you know something you're doing is self-destructive, it's *not* too late to change."

"Until it *is* too late."

"Exactly." The meeting obviously concluded, Nick stood. "I'll get a full report from Mac after your session."

"Yes, sir."

"Remember, we're here to help you. Call on me anytime, and I know the same goes for any of the Pack."

"I'll remember."

After shaking Nick's hand, Micah left and went to the hangar, where he killed a couple of hours tuning his motorcycle, lost in troubled thought. Inevitably, his mind went to Jacee. What the hell was he thinking, pursuing her when his personal life was such a clusterfuck? He should call and cancel their date.

At the idea, his wolf howled in protest and his guts churned. As soon as his shifter counterpart had scented and recognized her, ignoring her wasn't even an option. Not that he really wanted to, but his crap was the last thing she needed in her life.

Which means you need to clean it up, fool.

The first step to doing that was to speak honestly with Mac. With a sigh, he wiped his hands on the grease rag and tossed it next to his bike. Then he headed for Sanctuary.

Over the past few months, a connecting corridor that

ran between the main compound and the new building had been completed. The worry in doing so had been keeping the recovering patients with serious issues out of the main building, but the Pack had installed security measures to ensure no one could get through the doors but staff. Punching in his access code, Micah waited until he heard the click of the lock disengaging, opened the door, and stepped through.

His boots echoed strangely on the tile, giving him the disconcerting impression he was going to his own execution. Which was stupid, since the doctors were trying to help him. After another security checkpoint, he turned down another corridor toward Mac's office.

In the lobby area outside the doctors' offices and exam rooms, Noah was standing with a clipboard in hand, looking over some papers. Micah swallowed his pride and stepped up to him, not blaming the other man for eyeing him warily.

"Hey, I want to apologize again for what I did earlier. I snapped," he admitted. "I'm not sure why I lost control, but I'm going to talk to Mac about it."

"You'll be honest with her?"

"Yes."

The wariness faded, and Noah smiled a little. "Fair enough. I accept."

"Are you all right?" Micah gestured to Noah's chest. The nurse had put on a new shirt, hiding the cuts.

"Yeah, it was just a couple of scratches."

He rolled his eyes. "Tell that to Nix. He threatened to kill me if I ever touched you again."

Noah blinked. "Seriously? That's funny, considering *he* won't touch me at all."

Oh, boy. "Listen, I'm no expert on much of anything where relationship stuff is concerned. But give him time, man. He thought he was straight all his life, you know?"

"And then I came along," Noah agreed miserably. "Sometimes he's so sweet, and the rest of the time he acts like I have the plague."

Micah searched for a way to give the guy some perspective. "Say, imagine if you'd suddenly found out your Bondmate was a woman, and you're *gay*. You never thought you were wired to have sex with her, but your wolf can't stay away and you gotta boldly go where your little gay self hasn't gone before." Noah made a horrified face, and Micah laughed. "See? So give the poor bastard a break—you feel me?"

The nurse bit his lip and then nodded. "Okay, I'll try harder, for Nix."

"You're doing fine. Just be patient." Micah glanced toward Mac's office. "I'm late. Guess I'd better get in there." Micah offered the other man his hand, and they shook.

"Good luck."

At the door to Mac's office, Micah knocked. It was partly open, and he heard her call for him to come inside. He stepped in, closing the door behind him, unsure what to expect. She greeted him with her usual warm smile and pushed a lock of curly brown hair behind one ear.

"Micah. Sit down and tell me what's been going on with you lately."

"Have you spoken with Nick?"

"Should I have?"

Then he guessed the answer was no. He shrugged when inside he felt anything but nonchalant. "I'm having some trouble with my meds."

Her face grew serious. "What seems to be the problem?"

"The doses are lasting for shorter and shorter periods of time, and I'm getting more and more . . . anxious. Easily upset. I'm taking more pills than I should," he admitted. "And, frankly, I'm craving them."

"I see." She frowned. "Myst isn't supposed to be a habit-forming drug. How long is the benefit lasting with each dose?"

"Maybe two hours."

"That makes it seem hardly worth taking. Have you noticed any side effects?"

"Nosebleeds, sudden migraines, and mood swings. I, um, lost control and attacked Noah in the main building a couple of hours ago," he said quietly, shame heating his cheeks.

Mac's brows rose. "He didn't mention it to me when he came in."

"He said it was only a few scratches, but still. I can't quite believe I lost it like that."

The doc sat back in her chair and studied him for a moment. "Okay, one of two things is happening. Either myst is not compatible with your system, thus the nasty side effects, or you're simply becoming inured to it and it's not working anymore. Either way, those aren't ideal scenarios. I'm going to order some blood drawn, run a few tests just to make sure nothing strange shows up. Zan stopped by after the demon attack and mentioned he thought he detected some sort of anomaly in your blood, so it's best to look."

Fantastic. "Okay."

"How are you feeling, by the way? How's your chest?"

"Sore, but healing."

"All right. In the meantime, I want you to wean yourself off the meds gradually. Think you can do that?"

"I can try." Knowing how bad his need for the drug had gotten, though, he had his fears. "Why not just go cold turkey?"

"I'd like to save that as a last resort. Even then you'd do that here, under supervision."

"Like detox."

"Yes. Stopping a drug suddenly can be dangerous because the body's reactions can vary so greatly to the shock of withdrawal. We just don't know enough about myst yet for me to allow you to detox on your own."

"Fair enough." Though he hated the idea of being placed in a hospital room. Maybe locked up for his own good, and others'. "I'll try the weaning-off method."

"I think that's wise."

"No other shifters have experienced problems with the drug except me?"

"None at our facility, but I'll make some calls. We definitely have a few patients using myst, and you can bet we'll be keeping a closer eye on them. It could be you're one of the few unlucky shifters whose body isn't taking well to the drug." She lifted a sheaf of paper and studied some notes in his file. "We'll continue counseling, though, and hopefully you won't need another drug to help you cope. You've come a long way since you were first rescued."

"Yeah."

Mac paused. "Something else is eating at you. What is it?"

He stared at her. "How do you know?"

"You have a tell."

"I do?" He tried to think what gave him away and came up with nothing. "What is it?"

Her lips curved up. "If I told, you'd stop doing it and ruin my powers of observation."

"Damn."

She sobered. "So, what's wrong?"

"It's not that it's something that's *wrong* per se, but . . . I've met my Bondmate."

"You—your *mate*!" For the first time since he'd walked in, a huge, genuine smile spread across her face. "Micah, that's wonderful, isn't it?"

"Yes, absolutely. But it would be even more awesome if I wasn't a drug-addicted head case! What if I hurt her like I almost did Noah this morning?"

If he did, he'd die. Just take himself out, quick and easy.

"We'll make sure to get you well so that doesn't happen," she reassured him. "Besides, your wolf is wired to be even more protective of his mate than you are. I don't think you'll have to worry."

"I hope not." He rubbed the back of his neck.

"Who is she?"

"One of the bartenders down at the Grizzly. Her name's Jacee Buchanan."

"Jacee?" Mac got a funny look on her face.

"Yeah, why? You know her?"

"I've met her a few times when we've been in there. But no, I don't really know her."

Something in her tone gave him pause. "You don't like her."

"No, it's not that at all. Believe me."

"But?"

Mac sighed. "Let's just say her presence will make things a little more interesting around here for a while."

"What does that mean? How so? Wait—is it because she's a coyote?"

"No, that's not it, either. I'm afraid you'll have to ask Jacee," Mac said. "It's really not my place to say anything."

"That's not fair, since you brought it up," he muttered.

"I wanted to give you a heads-up, but I'm not jumping in the middle," she said firmly. "Now, back to you. Any more nightmares lately?"

When Mac made up her mind, there was no changing it. So he gave in and told her about the most recent nightmare, of being forced to torture the two eagle shifters. How he didn't have a choice, or Bowman's lackey would've chopped the female into pieces. Hell, he might have anyway, later on. Micah had no idea what had become of her, or any of them except Aric, who'd been rescued with him.

"The last time we spoke, you were convinced these dreams are actually repressed memories. Do you still feel that way?"

He nodded. "More than ever. I haven't had any new memories while I'm awake, only when sleeping, but I feel like they're *right there*, you know? As if the door's already open a crack and soon they're going to all come back."

"If you're feeling so strongly, it's probably just a matter of time before they *do* come back. The question is, how are you going to be able to handle all of those memories swamping you *if* they all return at the same time?" She studied him closely.

He knew that look and could already guess what she was thinking. Micah was a ticking bomb, especially given his bad reaction to his antidepressant. The physical symptoms, and now the attack on Noah. On top of all that, he might remember the entirety of his months in captivity at any moment.

She was reconsidering the wisdom of hospitalizing him and not waiting for that bomb inside his head to go off, detonating not only himself but everyone in his kill zone.

"Doc," he said, hating the pleading in his voice, "give me a chance to beat this on my own. You said yourself I've made good progress. I know it's all coming to a head, but I can't be locked up. My mate is out there, and she's going to need me."

His wolf whined just thinking about staring at four padded walls and being separated from his mate while he went completely insane. Got sick and died.

"We can bring her here to you, when the need for you two to mate becomes an issue." But even she wasn't happy with that plan any more than he was. It was obvious from her quiet voice and somber expression.

"And lock her up, too? No. I won't have my mate become a prisoner when none of this is her fault. She deserves better. *Please*, Mac, I'm asking you not just as my doctor, but as my friend. Let me try to handle this first."

She sighed. "You *would* have to pull the friend card."

"I just want a chance. If I can't deal, I'll check myself in."

"That's just it—you might not be able to if it comes to that." She fell silent, thinking.

Micah waited, deciding not to push further and risk having the doc dig her heels in. He did his best to appear compliant and harmless, accepting of whatever fate she doled out rather than quietly losing his mind.

Finally she gave a small laugh. "Relax. I'm still going to let you try to wean off the pills on your own, and we'll continue counseling."

"Thanks," he said with gratitude.

"But one more incident like your attack on Noah and you'll find yourself a guest here for a while."

"Got it. I'll do my best not to let anyone down."

"It's not about letting us down," she said gently. "It's about getting you well. Concentrate on that and the rest will fall into place."

"I will. Thanks."

They talked for a few more minutes. Then Micah stood and bid her good-bye. Noah was waiting to take him to an exam room, where he drew the blood samples and checked Micah's vitals.

"That's it. You're ready to go," Noah said, gathering the vials of blood. Before Micah could open his mouth, the nurse held up a hand. "And don't apologize again. Let's forget it and move on."

"Okay. Thanks." Smiling, he clapped Noah on the shoulder and took his leave. Belatedly, he wondered if that would count as "touching" the nurse in Nix's eyes. He sure hoped not.

Making his way back to the main building, he pulled out his cell phone and gave in to temptation.

Hey, it's Micah. You busy? he texted.

A few seconds later, Jacee's reply came through. *Nope. Just came in from the garden. About to shower.*

You have a garden? What kind?

I do. I like making things grow. I have tomatoes, cucumbers, squash, and two types of peas.

Micah grinned. He liked the idea of Jacee digging around in the dirt, babying her little plants. *Wow, I can't even grow a cactus! I'm impressed.*

Don't be too impressed. I killed my row of corn last year. Ha!

Warmth spread through him. He also liked that she could laugh at herself. *I thought you lived in town.*

I do. It's just a small garden. I only need enough for me, and the rest I put up in jars and give as gifts.

An uneasy feeling stirred inside him, and he struggled with how to respond. *Well, you might not want to give all the rest away now. . . .*

True. I may have a hungry wolf at my door very soon. ;)

The uneasy lump dissipated and he grinned to himself. *I have a feeling you're right.* He paused. *So, are we still on for tonight?*

You bet, but why don't you let me make you dinner instead of going out?

Was there anything not to like about this woman? *Next time. I don't want you working on our first date— let me treat you. Then maybe we'll go for a run later.*

Okay, that sounds great.

Cool, see you soon. Looking forward to it. :)

Me too. ;)

"What in the ever-loving hell are you grinning about?" Aric drawled, stopping next to Micah in the hallway close to the recreation room. "Who are you texting?"

"None of your biz, bro-in-law. Take a hike, literally."

"Is it that Jacee chick? The one you went all Mike Tyson on that asshole for last night?"

"What of it? Buzz off, Aric," he said, getting annoyed at the derision in the other man's tone.

"Come on, you hooking up with her now or something? I thought you had better taste than to get involved with that ho."

Micah's wolf roared to the surface, straining to be set free. White-hot anger sent the blood to his head, fangs and claws shooting forth. Only Mac's promise to lock him up if he lost control again kept him from wiping the floor with the redheaded wolf. Yeah, mauling his own brother-in-law would accomplish that, quick.

"Jacee is my mate," he said in a low, deadly voice. It was quite possible he'd never seen Aric pale that fast or look so sick.

"I — Say what, now? Your mate?" Aric looked around, clearly stunned. "Shit."

Micah snarled, "Is it so fucking shocking that I could possibly have a Bondmate, especially a woman as gorgeous as her? Say what's on your mind."

"No, man." Aric shook his head and ran a hand through his hair. When he met Micah's angry gaze again, his words and expression were sincere. "You know me better than that. So what if you have scars? Nobody who matters will care about those."

"Okay. Does this have to do with whatever Mac knows about Jacee that she won't tell me?"

The other man held up a hand. "Listen. I do not want to get in the middle of this. I'm sorry for what I said about Jacee, all right? I had no idea she was your mate."

"That shouldn't matter. You have no right to talk like that about somebody, especially calling her a ho when you don't really know her. I thought you were better than that." Slowly he forced his wolf to recede. It wasn't easy, his anger was so volcanic.

Aric winced and had the grace to look contrite. "You're right. Judging people isn't fair, and I should know better. I just want to point out that you don't know her either yet."

"Aric," he warned.

"That's all I'm going to say. Except you're my brother and I care about you."

The jerk would have to go and say something nice. "Thanks, but I can take care of myself."

"Sure. Peace out. See you later."

Frowning, Micah watched Aric go. Apparently, his friends had a preconceived opinion about Jacee that was less than complimentary. That pissed him off more than a little. They hadn't even given her a chance. All things considered, he'd play things closer to the vest when it came to telling the others about Jacee. At least until he could figure out what they were freaking out about—or Jacee told him herself.

After checking the time on his phone, he sighed. Hours to go before he could pick her up. Might as well make himself useful.

He couldn't help but note the spring in his step, which hadn't been there before.

Nick rubbed his eyes, tired.

Keeping a compound full of testosterone-driven shifters busy and out of trouble was more work that it seemed worth some days. Some more than others. Today he simply wanted to go back to the quarters he shared with Calla, take a long shower, and hit the bed early. Not like him at all.

But the visions were coming more frequently and in greater detail. Especially the one he'd seen moments ago and was still recovering from. The terrible one he'd warned Micah about. Closing his eyes, he thought back to recall every single thing, out of necessity.

Micah and Jacee Buchanan faced off in an unfamiliar bedroom. "What the fuck is this, Micah?" she shouted, shaking a small bottle in her fist. The contents rattled ominously between the couple. "You told me you'd stopped using! You lied to me, to your team!"

"Jacee, please—"

"Please, what? Give you another chance, and another, while I wait for the day one of your brothers comes to tell me you're dead of an overdose? Or were gutted by the enemy because you were stoned during a fight?"

"No," he denied, voice tight. "That won't happen."

"You need to go." Looking defeated, she turned her back on him. "Now."

"Baby, please. Don't throw me away. I'll get help. I'll quit. Anything—"

"Now, Micah."

She meant it. Micah had no right to stay, no grounds to defend himself. Taking a breath, he said, "I love you. That won't change, ever. I'm always here if you need me or change your mind."

Numbly, he walked past her and out the bedroom door. Kept going, all the way outside to his motorcycle, where he sat and stared at her house for long moments. A tear trailed down his face, and he wiped it away with his sleeve. Trying to keep it together.

Failing.

Cranking the bike, Micah sped away from the house. From the loss tearing out his insides. He ran from his ruined life, the destruction of his hopes and dreams. With the Pack, with his mate.

And so he didn't see the shifter with the huge wings swoop down from the sky, talons extended, intent clear. Nick couldn't scream. Couldn't warn Micah of the danger.

The creature hit Micah from the side, hard, knocking him from the speeding motorcycle. Micah went airborne, flying through the air for awful seconds—until he slammed headfirst into a tree. Falling to the ground in a crumpled heap, head at an unnatural angle, he stared into the sky. Struggled to breathe.

And then stopped, brown eyes fixing on a point he could no longer see.

And that wasn't all. Another vision hummed at the edge of Nick's awareness and slid slowly into his consciousness like a snake through tall grass.

A predator watched from the shadows, seething with ha-

tred. He was careful, keeping himself hidden. Always hiding in the shadows. No one could see what he'd become.

But the one who'd done this would pay. He would see. And he would die.

Nick stood, shaking off the exhaustion. Micah's fate hadn't changed, but it would. It had to. He hadn't lost one of his men yet.

And he damn well wasn't going to start now.

Four

A real date.

Almost giddy, Jacee dug through her small closet and discarded one top after another. She felt like a silly teenager, trying to find the perfect thing to wear in order to please Micah, when deep down she sensed he wouldn't care. Even if he wasn't scarred, she didn't believe he'd be hung up on appearances.

But she still wanted to please him, and twenty minutes later, she finally settled on a short-sleeved blue blouse that contrasted nicely with her dark hair. Then, wanting to show that she owned more than just the jeans and cowboy boots she wore at the bar, she pulled on a pair of breezy black capris and slipped her feet into a pair of black sandals.

In the tiny bathroom, she put on minimal makeup, not nearly as much as she wore at the Grizzly. She stared at herself for a few minutes, fretting over that some. Again with the appearances. But the Jacee who flirted and made nice with the customers at the bar, who wore tight jeans, low-cut tops, and heavier war paint, wasn't who she really was on her own time.

No, she was a simple girl. She liked to think of herself as a nice person who wanted someone to see the real her. Not the made-up slut a lot of folks no doubt believed her to be. Especially Jax and his buddies.

That thought made her cringe. Even more, the idea of what Micah would think or do when he found out that his future mate used to sleep with one of his Pack made her sick to her stomach. She had harbored some feelings for Jax at one time, so it hadn't been just sex on her part. But it had been on his, and he'd never made any promises. She'd known their brief fling couldn't last, and yet she'd let it go on until he met his mate.

Who knew how long she would've continued to cling to a man she'd *known* wasn't hers? Until she finally met Micah, which it turned out was inevitable. God, that was what embarrassed her more than anything. To realize how lonely she'd been, so much so that she'd been willing to sacrifice her self-respect to stave it off, even for just a while.

Micah would understand. She hoped.

Enough of that. Tonight was about new beginnings, and it seemed both of them deserved to be happy. Leaving her hair loose, she left the bathroom and made sure she had her small cross-body purse, wallet, and keys ready to go.

A few seconds later, she heard an engine and the crunch of tires on the driveway out front. Peeking out through the blinds, she was surprised to see a sleek black two-door Mercedes coup parked there. The driver's door opened, and Micah got out and stood—and Jacee's mouth watered.

He wore dark jeans, which hugged his thighs and sex like a glove. An emerald green button-down shirt emphasized his strong shoulders and chest; it was tucked in, showing off his trim waist. Dark coffee-colored hair fell in layers to his collar and around his handsome face. Yes, handsome to her even with the scars. She wondered if he wore his hair longer to obscure some of it or if he just preferred the style.

As he started up the steps to her porch, she went to the door and flung it open before he even got the chance to knock or ring the bell.

He smiled, happiness lighting his eyes. "You look beautiful."

"Thanks," she said. "You look gorgeous yourself. Want to come in?"

"Sure."

Stepping inside, he immediately gathered her in a hug. He felt so good and warm, she wrapped her arms around him, pressing her check against his shoulder. Just stood there getting the feel of his body against hers. And it felt pretty damn nice.

"Is this okay?" he asked.

"More than." She smiled. "You smell good."

"So do you."

"Mmm." Pulling back slightly, she tilted her face up for a kiss. He wasted no time giving her what she wanted.

His mouth was every bit as delicious as she remembered, but fresh and minty with a hint of toothpaste. Her tongue stroked his and he moaned, the vibration making her tingle all over. She found she liked being the cause of those sounds from him, and did it again.

Chuckling, he put a bit of space between them. "If you don't stop, we'll never make it to dinner."

"And your point is?" she teased.

"As tempting as it is to stay here and have dessert first, I want to prove I'm a nice guy. I'm not *just* out for your hot body." Grinning, he winked.

He looked so much like a mischievous boy, she laughed. "I already think you're a nice guy. But I am hungry, so shall we?"

"You bet."

They stepped outside, and she locked the house. Then he escorted her to the car, where he opened the passenger's door and helped her inside. It seemed chivalry wasn't totally dead, contrary to rumor, and she liked that. A lot.

Almost as though reading her mind, he said, "My mother raised me to treat a woman with respect. That means opening doors, paying the tab, running to get the car when it's pouring rain, bringing her soup in bed when she's sick—you name it. If any of this is going to be an issue, it's best to get it on the table now." He quirked a brow playfully at her as he backed out of her driveway.

"Well, we'll have to negotiate on you always paying the tab," she informed him pertly. "I work and I can pay, too. And I'll take care of my mate any way I see fit, when he's sick or not."

"Hmm. I can work with that."

As he turned off her street, he reached out with his right hand and held hers. That simple act sent a wave of joy through her so fierce, it was dizzying. How long had it been since she'd done something so pleasurable with a man that had nothing to do with getting naked? This touch was about companionship, getting to know each other. It was pure and good.

She had so desperately needed that in her life, and fate had sent Micah.

"So, does your mother live in Wyoming?" she asked.

He shook his head. "She lived in Los Angeles, California, where my sister, Rowan, was a cop with the LAPD. Mom passed away a few years ago from cancer."

"I'm so sorry." She squeezed his hand.

"Me, too. She was a great mother, did everything she could to raise me and Rowan up right. We lived in a barrio on the East Side and didn't have much, especially after our dad took off when we were little, but she gave us all she could."

"You grew up in a barrio?" She couldn't help being curious about his background.

He nodded. "Mom was a legal immigrant from Mexico. She met my dad in LA, and he moved in with her. He was a white man, good-looking, but looks couldn't save his wicked soul, she used to say. Guess she was right."

"Then you take after your mom, because I don't sense an ounce of bad in you."

He looked startled for a moment, then huffed a laugh. "I hope you're right."

That seemed like an odd response. What did he mean by that? Delving deeper would probably make things awkward at this early stage, however, so she let it drop.

They rode in comfortable silence the rest of the way to the restaurant, which was only a few short minutes. He parked in front of a nice steak-and-seafood place she'd seen only from the outside, and shut off the ignition.

"Is this all right?" he asked, turning to her. "I found it online, and the reviews were good. It's supposed to have great food with a higher-end menu, but not so fancy that you need to dress up or make reservations."

It struck her that he really wanted this evening to be nice and to make a good impression. She leaned in and gave him a soft kiss. "It's perfect. I can't wait to try it."

"That's good. I was afraid you'd already been here and maybe didn't like the place. But I wanted to surprise you."

"No worries."

They got out, and he held her hand as they walked inside. He gave the hostess his name, and they were immediately shown to a candlelit table in a secluded corner.

"I thought you didn't have to have reservations?" She studied him as he sat beside her.

"Right, but I wasn't leaving anything to chance."

That warmed her inside, and she melted. The waiter brought their menus and took their drink orders. He ordered a beer, while she asked for a glass of red wine. That decided, she focused on her man.

"So, I half expected you to drive up to my house on your Harley, plop me on the back, whisk me into the sunset, and enjoy burgers and beers on a patio somewhere."

"Oh, we'll do that. Don't you worry. Probably more often than not, because I don't eat like this every night, I'm sorry to say."

"That sure clashes with the image of the Mercedes. That's a 'steak every night' kind of car if I ever saw one."

"Isn't it? I don't live very high on the hog, though. I just love the car. Bought it with my settlement money from the Navy."

"You were in the Navy?"

"I was a SEAL," he confirmed. Looking around, he lowered his voice and met her gaze again. "Like a lot of my team was, before we were turned."

That part was a shock. Quickly, she, too, made sure nobody was in their vicinity to overhear. "You're not a born wolf?" she whispered.

"Nope. There are only two-natural born ones at the compound—Nick Westfall, my commander, and his daughter, Selene."

"I've met Selene, when she first came to town." Time for a confession. "She wasn't a happy camper back then, and she realized what I am. I didn't want anyone to know, and she knew that, too. She put some pressure on me to tell her what I'd heard about your team. So I told her what I knew, which wasn't much."

Micah's eyes widened, and he whistled softly. "Wow. What did you learn about us?"

"I have great hearing, and you know why. I'd picked up pieces of your conversations at the Grizzly and put them together enough to find out that you guys weren't running any kind of regular research facility, and your team is black ops of some sort. And that you're wolves, and Kalen is a panther."

"Thanks for telling me."

"Your commander won't be happy when he finds out."

Micah laughed, and the reason soon became clear. "He might know already. He's not just a born wolf. He's a rare white breed, and a PreCog."

She gaped at him. "You're kidding."

"No. His white coat signifies his status among his kind as a Seer. So, basically, he knows stuff. Sometimes stuff we don't *want* him to know."

That made her laugh. The waiter brought their drinks and took their order. Jacee went for a filet mignon and Micah asked for a big ribeye, both with salads and baked potatoes. Her stomach rumbled just thinking about the meal, but the real feast was right in front of her eyes.

Micah told her some about growing up, and she was surprised to find out that he was actually two years younger than his sister, Rowan. Jacee had trouble thinking of him as the "little" brother when the fine specimen of a man with her was anything but small. As he related tales of him and Rowan getting into trouble in the barrio as teens, she enjoyed observing his expression and his mannerisms when he spoke. He was so animated and funny.

"Rowan was always much more of a hellion than me," he asserted smugly. "It's a wonder she turned out to be a cop. Mama was sure she'd end up in juvie, especially after she stole twenty packages of hot dogs from the grocery store."

"But you were the perfect child?"

"Of course!"

"I'll bet. What the heck did she do with that many packages of hot dogs?"

"Did you know you can draw on a hot dog with a Sharpie?"

"Um, no," she said with a giggle.

"Well, you can. Rowan had me help her draw googly faces on all the wieners, and then we stuck them in all the neighbors' mailboxes and on their front porches."

"Oh, my God! Didn't you get in trouble, too?"

"Sure, I did. But I didn't know she'd stolen them, even though Mama smacked me in the head and yelled at me to use my brain, and where the hell did I *think* she'd gotten two hundred wieners?"

Jacee snickered. The image was pretty humorous. "How did she get them out of the store?"

"She didn't. She pinched them off the delivery truck in the alley behind the store after the guy ducked inside for a few minutes. Mama was so pissed, she marched us down there and made Rowan confess, and me, too, for my part in the escapade. We had to scrub floors and stock shelves for a week to pay for the defiled dogs."

Jacee couldn't help but laugh out loud, and the waiter arrived at that moment with their food. He gave them an indulgent smile, served up, and after seeing if they needed anything else, disappeared. They ate companionably, and she basked in being near Micah. At one point she noticed he didn't seem to be eating as much as he should, but she didn't think more of it because he seemed fine.

They chatted for the rest of their meal, and if Micah

had noticed that she hadn't divulged any history about her family, he didn't mention it. She was grateful. She loved her family still, but talking about them was hard. Emotional. And she didn't want anything to spoil this lovely dinner.

They each had another drink and sipped for a while, but declined dessert, being too full. After they were done, he paid the tab, as promised, refusing to allow her to even get the tip. Even Jax, as nice a man as he was, had never bought her a meal. Never paid her much attention. She was beginning to adore Micah.

Outside, he helped her into the car again, and they were soon on their way. He drove in silence for a few minutes, and she noted they were headed out of town, in the direction of his compound. Night had fallen, and the sky was clear, twinkling with stars.

"You still up for that run? Or, if you're too full, we can just walk."

"A run sounds great, actually." Her coyote yipped in agreement. "I need to burn off all that energy from that great food."

"I know the perfect place. We won't go all the way to the compound, but we'll go for our run in an area not too far from it. There're other places we can go, but for miles around our facility, the land is warded."

She peered at his profile in the darkness. "Warded?"

"By a protection spell. Kalen is a Sorcerer and Necromancer. He's quite powerful, and he placed a ward around the grounds a while back when we were having trouble with an Unseelie King and his Sluagh. And before you ask, the Sluagh are fallen Seelie who went over to the dark side, so to speak. They used to be beautiful Fae, then chose to 'fall' and serve the evil Unseelie, and so their beauty was taken from them. They become mindless drones, their only purpose to do what the Unseelie king says—which is usually to maim and kill."

She shuddered. "That's horrible. Those things aren't around anymore, I hope."

"No. The ones the Pack didn't kill were sent back across the plane, into their own world. Hopefully never to cross again. Especially since Kalen killed their previous king, Malik."

"Holy crap. Kalen must be all kinds of badass to kill an Unseelie king."

"Yeah. He gets his power honest—Malik was his father."

"Damn! Shades of Luke and Darth, anyone?"

"For real. Not only that, Kalen has a half brother at the compound as well. His name is Sariel, nicknamed Blue, and he's the former Seelie prince who was cast out because the court found out Malik was his father, too. Fortunately for us, while extremely powerful, both of Malik's sons are inherently good. They're only bad when they need to be. Hopefully Kalen's son, Kai, will follow in their footsteps and take after them, not his grandfather."

"Oh? How old is Kai?"

"Only a couple of months. Cute little bugger, too. His mother is Kalen's mate, Dr. Mackenzie Grant. He's got his Uncle Blue wrapped around his little finger, and Blue absolutely *hates* handing him over to the new nanny when they're all busy working."

"I'll bet. Gosh, that's an interesting group you live with."

"You have no idea."

It occurred to her then that she would get to know all of his friends, too. Micah was her mate, and it was probable that she'd have to go to live on the compound with him eventually. That thought gave her a sudden jolt. Leave her home, her garden? She'd worked so hard for the things she had.

But they were just *things*. Objects. Nothing could replace a mate and that precious bond.

The Shoshone rose around them, the trees dark sentries against the sky. To a human, perhaps the sight might have been creepy, but her coyote was right at home and itching to run in the moonlight. Micah steered the car down a secluded road for a couple of miles, then pulled over into a turnabout and parked.

"The car will be fine here," he said. "I've come here before on my way home from town."

They got out of the vehicle and stretched their legs, and she contemplated stripping in front of him to shift. Would he think her too bold? Among her old pack, nakedness was normal. Not that they had been nudists, but when they'd been shifting, it was no big deal. Both forms were as natural as breathing.

"We'll walk into the woods before we undress," he said. "I doubt anyone will come along except maybe a deputy. I don't think Sheriff Deveraux would be too happy to find us standing around in the buff."

"Then Jesse would demand an explanation as to why we were naked outside the car rather than inside, making out."

"Oh, he knows what we are. He just wouldn't be happy about finding us naked."

"He does? Since when?" That was news. Jesse Deveraux came into the Grizzly all the time, and she'd never gotten wind that he knew exactly what the Pack was or what they did.

"Since the Sluagh were attacking a bunch of local families and the sheriff saw shit he shouldn't have. So

Nick decided it would be good to have an ally inside local law enforcement, and the man has come in pretty handy, even if he is a grumpy bastard."

"He is that, for sure. Sexy but an asshole."

Micah frowned. "You think Jesse is sexy?"

Grinning, she pressed against him. "He can't hold a candle to you, so don't sweat it."

They kissed slowly, which got her motor revved and ready to go. He tasted so good, she sincerely hoped to sample much more of him soon. Backing away, she took his hand and let him lead them into the forest.

After walking for a ways, he stopped next to a fallen log and began to undress, not bothering to turn away. That settled the question of whether they were going to stand on ceremony, and so she did the same. Unashamedly, they watched each other.

His shirt went first, and she admired his chest, sprinkled with a fine dusting of dark hair. He was toned and fit, not too bulky, his abs flat. On his right biceps was a gorgeous tattoo of a wolf's head, and it rippled with his muscle.

Here and there she noted scars, some thin and long as though they'd been made by a whip or knife, some puckered and round as though by silver bullets or burns. But they were a warrior's scars, and she admired him for them.

One baseball-sized scar on his chest looked recent and far too near his heart. "What happened there?"

"We had to battle some demons the other day. One almost got the best of me."

"Are you all right?"

"A little tender, but I'm fine."

When he pushed down his jeans, she saw that he'd gone commando, and her pulse sped up some. Here was a mouthwatering specimen of manhood. His thighs were long and muscled, athletic, his calves nicely shaped. *And his cock, oh, my God.*

His staff, quiescent against his thighs and nestled atop an impressive set of balls, was fairly large even in that state. Under her scrutiny it began to awaken, and plumped some. While erect, it surely had to be a good eight inches. She had a fleeting moment of doubt, but knew he'd fit inside her. Mates were meant for each other.

"Have you looked your fill?" His lips quirked up.

"Not nearly. You?" By now her clothes were off as well, and she wondered what he thought of her body. Her figure was slim, but her breasts were on the lush side.

"Not even close, because, Christ, you're beautiful." Reaching out, he took her hand.

Her heart did a slow turn in her chest. "Thanks. So are you."

"Guys aren't beautiful," he said, looking away and shaking his head as though suddenly shy. "Or at least this one isn't. Come on, let's run."

Before she could protest his words, he stepped back and shifted. Dropping to his hands and knees, he let the change flow gracefully, reshaping his limbs and face, growing a luxurious brown coat and a full bushy tail. When he was done, he was a good-sized brown wolf, half again bigger than her coyote.

"You're wrong," she whispered. "You're gorgeous."

Then she let the change take her as well, and her coyote finally got to come out and play. His wolf trotted over and greeted her with a happy bark, sniffing and nuzzling all over her face. Then with another bark, he took off, glancing back, clearly indicating for her to follow.

She ran after him, exhilaration coursing through her blood. Joy. Especially in running with another. It had been so long since she'd enjoyed companionship of any kind, and her family had been gone for years. And now to feel the wind in her face and the earth under her paws alongside the wolf who would be her Bondmate?

Heaven. Pure and simple.

With his more powerful legs, she knew he could likely outrun her if he wanted, taunting her with his greater strength. Yet he made sure to keep his pace steady so she could run by his side. His actions toward her as a shifter said a lot about what kind of mate he'd be in human form as well.

They finally came to a small brook and stopped for a drink. After satisfying their thirst, they took off again. Once Micah flushed out a rabbit that had been hiding and looked to her in question, but she merely shook her head. This one could go free tonight—she was still stuffed from earlier. With a bark, he sped off again.

She wished they could communicate telepathically, but it wouldn't be long. After they bonded, they'd be able to speak in each other's heads and feel the other's emotions. It was a definite perk of having a mate, though her mother had sometimes complained good-naturedly that it gave her father far too many ways to pry.

Shutting off the sad memories before they could form, she concentrated on the rest of their run. When they ended up in a pretty clearing farther down the stream, Micah stopped and shifted back to human form, then sat down on a soft patch of grass and held out his hand to her. Following suit, she shifted back also and took his hand, sitting next to him.

Putting an arm around her, he pulled her close. She snuggled into his chest, inhaling his scent, stronger than before with just a pleasant hint of manly sweat from their exercise. But damn, he wasn't even breathing hard.

"I like this," he murmured. "Never thought I'd have this. Not even close."

"Why? Because of your scars?" Reaching up, she stroked his cheek. His reply was quiet.

"Yes, but not the ones on the outside."

The words seared her heart. "Oh, Micah, who hurt you?"

For a long moment he was silent. Finally he said, "Remember Malik?"

"The Unseelie king."

"Yes. For a while, he posed as a human billionaire and ran a company called Lifeline Technologies. Most of the company was legit, but it was also a front for a more sinister operation. Malik and a rich human, Orson Chappell, were kidnapping humans and shifters of all types, and sending them to labs all over the country. In those labs, the subjects were experimented on, their DNA messed with, spliced, whatever."

"God, that's horrible."

"It gets worse. Dr. Gene Bowman was in charge of the actual testing of the subjects, and a more evil man never lived."

"He's dead now?" she interrupted.

"Very, along with the other two. Anyway, Bowman's goal for them all was to create a breed of super-shifter soldier who would basically be invincible in battle, yet could be controlled by his master to do his bidding." Micah gave a sad laugh. "I was kidnapped in an ambush during an Alpha Pack mission, and they thought I was dead until they got a tip that I might be alive and being held hostage in one of those labs."

"Thank God they found you."

"Yeah. Some other Pack members were taken during that same ambush, and they got me back, plus Aric, who'd been kidnapped later and tossed in with me. They also recovered Phoenix Monroe from a different lab."

"He's the one who's supposed to be Noah's Bondmate, but it's not going very well with them?"

"Yeah. You've met them?"

"They've been in the Grizzly a couple of times with the group."

"Oh. I keep forgetting you've met almost all of us."

"So, this," she said, touching his cheek again. "What happened?"

"Bowman had me strapped down and poured molten silver on my face. Even Zander, our Healer, can't fix it, and he can heal damn near anything."

"I'm so sorry."

"Like I said, it's not really my face that bothers me, as much as I'd like for it to be healed."

"It's what the damage represents," she guessed. "The power Bowman wielded over you to keep you under control."

"You *do* understand," he said hoarsely, gazing into her eyes. "I hate what he did to me, but I hate that he forced me to comply even more. I hate that I was used in every possible way, and that they made me, in turn, harm innocent shifters."

"But you had no choice. I can see that in your eyes and hear it in your voice."

"There was always a choice." Bitterness crept into his tone. "I could've let them kill a poor girl by refusing to hurt two eagle shifters. I could've let the guards tear apart a young boy, had I not allowed the guards to use my body for their desires. Some choice."

My God. "You did what you had to, Micah. They threatened weaker shifters, knowing your protective instinct would come to the fore, that you would never allow them to be hurt when the stronger ones could take the abuse. They tried to condition you, and they failed."

"Did they? I hope so."

"They did."

"Can I touch you?" he asked softly. "Nobody has laid

their hands on me since those horrible days, and I haven't wanted to touch anyone else. Until now."

Wrapping her arms around his neck, she kissed his lips. "Yes, please."

"I won't claim you tonight, as much as I want to. It's too soon, and there's more you need to know about me." His eyes were dark pools of need.

"Same here. But I do want you, so much."

"You have me."

With that, he laid her back on the spongy grass and levered his body slightly over hers. She loved the weight and feel of him, the tickle of his chest hair, the heat of his lengthening shaft on her belly. His hair fell forward to envelop his face, so sexy in the moonlight; he reminded her of some pagan god come to claim her as his own.

Bending, he kissed his way down her jaw, neck, and collarbone. He continued on to her breasts, lavishing attention on one peak, which had hardened to a tight little point. His tongue flicked it, sending shards of delight straight to her sex. She wriggled under him, palms splayed on his back.

His muscles flexed under her hands, and she found his smooth skin was interrupted by more long scars. She wanted to kiss each of them, to love the bad memories away and leave him with nothing but good.

Continuing his journey, his tongue blazed a path down her stomach as his hand slid between her thighs. She parted for him and he explored, rubbing the folds, dipping his fingers inside, and spreading the moisture. Heat spiraled through her sex to her limbs and she moaned, wanting him.

"I'm ready. Please, Micah."

"I've got you, baby."

Carefully, he positioned himself between her open

thighs and brought the head of his cock to her opening. Then he pushed gently inside, moving slightly in and out, deeper each time, until fully seated.

"Sweet Christ, you feel so good," he breathed, gathering her close.

"So do you." She clutched at him, moving her hips.

In answer, he began to pump, slowly at first. She reveled in the delicious sensation, the scent of her mate wrapped around her, making love to her. His strength, his passion. All of that hidden behind a wall of sadness now broken down, she hoped for good.

His walls weren't the only ones crumbling, she realized. Sex before had been a cold, passionless act without a real connection, and she hadn't even known. But now . . .

Making love with Micah was like a burst of glorious color after being locked in a dark, lonely basement. A swell of emotion nearly overwhelmed her, and she held on tight, kissing his face and neck as he moved inside her.

Their tempo increased and she met him without stopping, hanging on to him as though she'd never let go. Her desire spiked higher, climax so close, and from his moans, his hips driving into her, his was near as well.

"Come for me, mate," he growled.

A few more thrusts of his cock, and she did exactly that, crying out as her orgasm shook her to the core. Micah followed right after, hugging her to his chest, peppering her hair with kisses. When the last of his release was finished, he rolled to his back and carried her with him, settling her on top of him.

Snuggling in comfortably, she sighed. "It's never been like that."

"Never?" He held her tighter.

"No. Sex without the closeness of a mate just isn't the same."

"True." He paused. "I've never felt that either, until now, and I'm not sure how I lived without it."

"With any luck, neither of us will have to go back to that existence again."

Her mate's wonderful scent filling her nose, she drifted. And they didn't move again for a long time.

Five

Micah shivered as Jacee traced her fingers over the scar that the demon had left on his chest. "I could've lost you before I even knew who you were to me."

"But you didn't, and I'm here." *For now. How long can I last? If the real monsters don't get me, the ones in my head just might.*

"I'm glad."

"Me, too." He played with her hair. "So tell me about your family. Do they live around here?"

She was silent for so long, he didn't think she'd answer. He was about to tell her to forget the question when she finally spoke up.

"They're dead. My whole clan was destroyed by Hunters a few years ago."

"Oh, honey." He squeezed her tight, his heart going out to her. To lose one's family was devastating, a shifter without a pack even more so. "I'm sorry."

"I escaped for the dumbest reason ever. I was spending the night in town at a human school friend's house and wasn't even there for the slaughter. Nobody knew about me or ever came after me."

"That's not dumb at all," he disagreed. "You were extremely lucky."

"I felt guilty for years because my parents didn't approve of my having a friend outside the clan. But I'd begged for weeks to stay over at Marcy's. Finally they gave in, and that night they all died. Or so I was told, but I was never able to see the bodies since there wasn't much left, and it was deemed too traumatic for me. My friend's parents fostered me, helped me through everything. Got me through school."

"I'm glad you had them."

"Me, too."

"Did you have siblings?"

"One younger sister, Faith. She'd be nineteen now."

"Where did your pack live?"

"In Texas, the hill country near San Antonio. I moved here three years after high school graduation and got my bartender's license, and I've been here ever since."

"Well, I'm sorry about your family, but I'm glad you're here now. I don't mean that to sound selfish."

"I know what you mean, and I'm glad I'm here, too." He felt her smile against his chest, and then she shivered. "Cold?"

"Just getting a little cool. No fur coat in this form, you know."

"I guess we should head back," he said with real regret. "Early day tomorrow for me."

"More demon hunting?"

"God, I hope not! The Pack has a meeting and then some training exercises. After that, Nick will probably have us wash the SUVs since that hasn't been done in a while."

"Sounds more fun than serving drunks."

"Thought you like your job?"

"Most days," she said. "But sometimes it does get old."

"Well, once we're mated you can do whatever you want. Stay there and tend bar, work at the compound, or go back to school and learn something else. The choice is yours."

Propping herself up on his chest, she stared at him. "You'd support me if I wanted to go back to school?"

"Why not? I'd like that a hell of a lot more than you being at the Grizzly every night serving guys like that asshole Grant. But like I said, it's your deal."

"You won't try to use your influence as my mate to make me quit my job later on?"

"No," he said firmly. "I'd never do that to you."

"Thank you. I have thought of trying to do something else, but there's never been enough money or time. I spend my days surviving, mostly."

"Well, no more of that. My mate will do what she wants."

She seemed so happy about that, it made him a bit sad that life hadn't treated her the best for the last few years. She had struggled, but she wasn't the sort to complain. He admired how she put her head down and simply did what had to be done.

With reluctance, he parted from her and prepared to leave. This spot would always be special to him, and to her, too, he hoped. There would never be another first time. But he prayed there would be many more. He still hadn't confessed his problem and that worried him, but tonight hadn't been the right time to spring his heavy crap on her.

Please let her understand.

They shifted back into their animal forms, and Micah admired her coyote once more. Real wild coyotes tended to be thin and scrawny, half-starved and not attractive. But Jacee's smaller body was filled out, her coat shiny and plush. She was a perfect example of her species, and he had no clue why her kind was looked down upon in the shifter world. It didn't make sense to him, but that sort of thing never did.

When they reached the spot where they'd left their clothing, they got dressed again, then walked back to his car. He kissed her soundly, then helped her inside. Once behind the wheel, he drove her home as slowly as possible, not wanting the night to end.

They made out in her driveway for a while, and when he couldn't put it off any longer, he walked her to the door. "Good-bye, for now."

She hesitated. "You can stay if you want."

"I want to take you up on that, believe me. But I think you need your space to process everything," he said ruefully. "I'm not going to rush you."

"You are quite a man, Micah Chase." She beamed at him, then gave him a long hug. When she finally pulled back, she said, "I'll talk to you tomorrow?"

"Count on it."

His wolf was howling piteously as he drove away from her house, and he agreed. The last thing he wanted to do was leave, but he knew he'd made the right decision. He didn't want to rush her any more than the mating urge would necessitate. He wanted her happy. Comfortable. If that meant moving at her pace, so be it.

The hour was late, or early, depending on one's viewpoint, when he arrived back at the compound. Only a couple of the Pack were up and about in the hallways, and he said good night to John and Sariel as he passed by. He didn't think those two ever slept.

But he did, deeply.

And blessedly without nightmares, for the first time in weeks.

It was a damned shame the peace didn't last.

A buzzing on Micah's nightstand woke him at oh-fuck-thirty, and he blinked blearily at the offending cell phone, trying to assemble his tired brain into some sort of order. The damn racket stopped, and he almost fell back asleep—until it started again.

"For shit's sake," he grumbled, fumbling for the stupid thing. His greeting was less than pleasant. "What do you fucking want?" There were a couple of beats of silence.

"You, in my office," Nick's deceptively calm voice told him.

Ah, crap. "Sorry, boss. Didn't know it was you. Did we move up the meeting?"

"No, it's still at eight. Something else has come up, though, so get dressed and come straight here."

"Got it, be there ASAP."

After hanging up, he checked the time on his phone and groaned. Barely past seven. What in the ever-loving hell was so important they had to meet before the meeting? Had some of his tests come back? No, it was too soon. Plus, Mac would've called instead.

Speculation would get him nowhere. Jumping in the shower, he made it quick. No way was he meeting the commander smelling like hours-old sex and his mate. After dressing in jeans and a T-shirt, then pulling on his shitkickers, he started off for Nick's office.

Once there, he was surprised to find Sheriff Deveraux waiting with Nick. The two men stood, offering their hands, which he shook. Then Nick gestured for him to take the second empty seat across from the sheriff.

"Somebody want to tell me what's going on?" Micah looked between the two men, but their faces were unreadable.

Deveraux spoke first, his tone gruff but not hostile. Yet. With the sheriff, you never knew when that could change. "Hello, Micah. I'm here on business, unfortunately. There was a woman murdered at a campsite last night just a few miles from here."

"Oh, wow. I'm sorry to hear that. But what does that have to do with me?"

"Where were you last night and into this morning, between ten p.m. and three a.m.?"

His eyes widened. "Are you serious? What is this? Am I a suspect?"

"Just answer the question, Micah," Nick said.

"I was with my mate! I mean, we haven't bonded yet, but she's my mate and we were together the whole time. I took her to dinner, and then we went for a run in the woods not far from here."

The sheriff glanced at Nick. "That explains why your car was spotted by one of my deputies last night, parked on Dublin Road. Will she back up your story?"

"Of course. She has no reason not to. But why are you tagging me for this?" he asked in confusion. And then horribly, he knew, and he gaped at Nick. "Jesus Christ. This is because of what happened with Noah? You think I snapped. You honestly think I could kill an innocent woman?" That hurt more than he could have believed possible.

"No, not really," Nick denied, shaking his head. "But when Jesse came to me this morning about your car being spotted, I had to ask."

The sheriff spoke up. "It does look pretty suspicious, the woman being torn up and you being a wolf. You were the only one on staff who was away from the compound during those hours."

"But I'm far from the only predator out there, paranormal or otherwise, Sheriff," Micah said grimly. "I didn't do this."

"Then you won't mind if I have some tests run on the inside of your car."

"Unbelievable." Micah ran a hand through his hair. "Do you have a warrant?"

"I can get one."

"On what grounds? You know what? Fine, test the car. I've got nothing to hide. But for what it's worth, John and Sariel can vouch for what time I came home and what condition I was in. I said good night to both of them, together."

"All right." The sheriff nodded. "Let's get them into another room."

Micah stopped himself from rolling his eyes, just barely. He knew Jesse was just doing his job, but it still upset him to have anyone think he could murder an innocent woman. And while the sheriff was wasting his time here, a killer was going free. That didn't sit well, either.

Nick called John and Sariel into a different room in the office area. Then he and Deveraux went and talked to them while Micah waited. A few minutes later the men returned and the sheriff spoke.

"They said you came home a bit after three, as you said. They also reported that you smelled of the outdoors, sex, and of a certain local female—not the murder victim. They would've scented blood on you, and there wasn't any."

"That's because I'm telling the truth," Micah said, tired.

"I believe you, but I'm going to test the car now just to rule it out. Once a question has been raised, it's best to follow through."

"I understand." He did. It just sucked.

Deveraux slid a file off Nick's desk and opened it, retrieving a few photos. "Do you recognize the woman in these pictures?"

Micah took them and studied them closely. The first two were of a smiling blond woman of about thirty-five, candid shots taken in front of a lake. The rest were of the murder scene, showing the poor woman's gruesome demise. His stomach lurched, though he'd seen many atrocities in the last few years. It wasn't something he thought he'd ever get used to.

"No, I've never seen her around before. Tourist?"

"Probably. She was camping alone, which is unusual. No ID, but it was likely stolen."

"I hope you find her family, give them some closure. And the bastard who did that to her, too."

"Thanks. Me, too."

By the time he left, Deveraux seemed satisfied that Micah was not his perp, not that he'd ever really believed it deep down. But he had to follow up his lead on the car, and once Micah had gotten over the shock of being questioned, he couldn't blame the man.

Micah was tired, but once that was over, there was no time to go back to his quarters and get more sleep. Worse, he was edgy, anxious. He hadn't taken his nighttime dose of myst because of his date with Jacee, and he'd forgotten to take it when he got home before falling into bed. Now he was jonesing, bad.

Ducking around a corner, he held up his hands. They were shaking, his heart racing, and he felt as if he was on the verge of a panic attack. Quickly, he dug in his front pocket and extracted the bottle, removing one pill and dry-swallowing it. Just one. His morning dose, and not one pill more. He had to wean himself off or end up in that damn hospital room.

The dose took the edge off, but not nearly enough. The meeting about fighting groups of rogue vampires, demons, goblins, and such was almost more than he could stand. They'd fought those beasts a thousand times, and he couldn't fathom why they had to talk *every* fucking thing to death.

"Why don't we form a knitting club and have raffle baskets, too," he muttered, rubbing his eyes.

"I'm sorry, *what*?" Nick's voice from the front of the conference room was irritated.

"Raffle baskets," Micah said loudly. "Why don't we have fuckin' raffle baskets? It'll make these meetings more fun! The women can bake cookies, too."

What the fuck am I saying? Shoot me now!

"Hey, I don't bake, asswipe," his sister shot back. "Bake 'em yourself and we'll eat 'em."

Several of the team snickered, and he looked up to find Nick glaring. "Sorry, boss."

"As I was saying . . . ," Nick went on, shooting looks Micah's way now and then.

Micah tuned him out anyway, because nothing short of a miracle was going to get him to pay attention today. He was a walking disaster, and struggling to hide it. When the meeting was over, he skipped training and went straight back to his quarters. He'd hear about it later, but he *had* to have more sleep.

As soon as his head hit the pillow, he was out. His dreams were shadowy. Uneasy. He was searching everywhere, never quite finding what he was looking for. And something was stalking him. Remaining just out of sight, waiting for the chance to strike. Finally, at some point, the dreams quieted and he slept better.

A knocking noise woke him some time later. Squinting, he saw that it was past noon. He'd missed lunch, and he still wasn't that hungry. He thought about not answering the door, but the determination of the person on the other side was greater than his will to ignore it. He answered.

And immediately wish he'd resisted. Rowan marched inside, and from the look on her face, this was not a conversation he wanted to have.

"Nick is seriously pissed at you."

"What's new lately?"

"You mouth off during the meeting and disrespect him in front of everyone? Then you have the gall not to show up for training? What's wrong with you?"

"I wasn't feeling well. I needed sleep." That much was true.

"Okay, even so. What about this morning? Raffles and cookies, for cryin' out loud. Have you lost your mind?"

"Probably."

"I'm being serious here!"

"Me, too."

Taking his hand, she led him over to the sofa and sat him down. As soon as he saw her expression soften and her prickly side retreat behind genuine concern, he knew he was toast. They were going to have *a talk*, and nothing would dissuade his sister until he gave in.

"I'm scared, little brother. You're the only biological family I have left, and I love you." She squeezed his hand. "Tell me what's going on with the meds. What did Mac say?"

"Does everyone know my business?"

"No. But I'm your sister, and I reserve the right to poke my nose in whether you like it or not. Tell me, please."

It was the quiet *please* that got him. A demanding sister he could ignore, but not that tearful worry. "Damn.

Might as well let you in on everything, since chances are you'll find out anyway." He blew out a breath. "Mac is having me wean myself off the myst."

"But that's good, right? You don't want to be on it forever."

"It's good that I'm getting off of it, but not the reason why. In my case, my system isn't handling the drug very well. I have to get clear of it."

Alarm had her sitting up poker-straight, fear in her eyes. "What do you mean? What's going on?"

"You've noticed the mood swings? Like when I jumped on Noah, and today at the meeting?"

"Who hasn't?"

"Exactly. You know that's not me, sis. I don't know if I can blame it all on the drug, but I feel like it's eating at me, making me so edgy I can't think, corroding my grip on my control every single day. The pills are giving me nosebleeds and headaches, too. Tanking my appetite."

Easing free of her grip, he stood and paced his living room as he continued. "But I'm addicted to them. They're not supposed to be habit-forming for shifters, but myst is a new drug, so obviously the doctors don't know everything. Maybe it's because of whatever Gene Bowman did to me in his lab, fucking with my blood and shit. Zan spotted something strange, remember?"

"Oh, Micah."

For a few seconds, he thought she'd actually cry, and Rowan never cried. He didn't think he could take that if she did. But she held in the tears, likely for his sake.

"What happens if you can't wean yourself off them?" she asked.

He sighed. "Mac will admit me to Sanctuary until my body is clear of the drug."

"Then what? Will you be able to cope with your nightmares and the memories returning?"

"I think so, eventually. I *am* better, and something's happened that will definitely speed along my healing."

"Really? What's that?"

"I've met my Bondmate." He smiled at his sister, hoping at least *one* person would be happy for him when she found out who his mate was.

Rowan shot to her feet. "Really? Oh, my God!" Rushing over, she swept him up in a bone-crushing hug. "That's great news! Who's the lucky lady?"

"It's Jacee."

"Jacee?"

"The bartender from the Grizzly."

There went the ecstatic smile. Just fell right off her face to drop like a rock at their feet. "She's your mate? Oh, no. Micah, really?"

"Okay, that's it," he said, anger replacing the optimism of moments before. "You're going to tell me why the hell I keep getting that reaction about Jacee, and I'm not going to take no for an answer."

"Wait. You told other people before you told me?" She had the gall to look wounded.

"That's just the way it happened. I was going to tell you as soon as possible, but it's been sudden for me, and I'm still processing the idea myself. Now, what's the deal with the weird reactions I'm getting? Out with it."

"You might want to be sitting for this."

"I'll stand, thanks."

"Promise you won't get upset."

"Began every horrible conversation *ever*. Rowan, I swear—"

"Jacee had a lover before you," she said carefully. "They weren't serious or anything, before you flip your shit, bro."

Inside him, his wolf growled, but he forced the beast

down. "So? Most people have been with someone by the time they're in their twenties, sis. That's normal."

"Yeah, well, keep that in mind when I tell you the guy was Jax." She watched him, waiting for the explosion.

Jax. "Our Jax?"

"You know another one?"

He tried to grasp the image of Jax and Jacee. His *mate* and his *Pack brother*. Together. Meeting for a rendezvous, fucking like a pair of horny animals, which was exactly what they had been at the time. And was sorry he did.

His breathing was harsh, his wolf howling in rage. His fangs burst through his gums, claws through his fingertips.

"Micah! It's in the past," Rowan said, raising her voice and grabbing his shirt. "It happened while you were in captivity and was over between them as soon as Jax met Kira."

"I'm going to fucking kill him." His voice wasn't even human anymore.

"Get hold of yourself! Mac will put you in solitary!"

Distantly, he understood that. But the penalty for losing it was a fading concept once his beast took over. Jax Law had touched his mate. Fucked her. There was no force on earth that was going to stop him from making the wolf pay for that transgression.

Turning, he shook off his sister's hold and bolted for the door. Her shout followed, as well as the thud of her boots behind him, but she wasn't nearly fast enough to catch him. Bursting through his door so hard it came off its hinges and smashed into the wall, he sped down the hall, looking for his target. He had no care for the startled looks the other pack members and staff gave him as he ran past, sniffing out the other wolf.

Where was he? At last he caught a fresh whiff of Jax's scent and trailed it to the recreation room. He barely spared a glance to note that some were eating their lunches and watching television in there, others playing games. He looked only at Jax, who was playing Ping-Pong with John and laughing, having a grand time.

The arrogant, whoring son of a bitch.

At that exact moment, Aric glanced up from his video game. "Micah? What the hell?" Then, "Oh, shit. Someone told him."

Aric threw down the game controller and shot to his feet, body tense.

"Yeah, Rowan, who has bigger balls than anyone in this room," he growled. He fixed his murderous gaze on Jax, who finally looked up at him and frowned in confusion. "Bigger than yours, you piece of Sluagh shit."

Jax's eyes widened. "What the hell are you talking about?"

"You have to ask?" As Micah stalked forward, bodies scrambled out of the way.

Someone said, "Holy crap. Somebody do something."

"Call Mac and Nick," Micah heard Aric order, his voice urgent.

His wolf didn't care.

Jax stared at him, setting down his Ping-Pong paddle slowly. "I guess I do. What's this about?"

"Jacee." Her name emerged as a rough snarl.

"From the bar?" Jax's brows drew together, and he eyed Micah warily. "We had a thing for a while, but—"

"She's my mate."

The stunned expression on Jax's face, the knowledge that he was in deep trouble, was priceless. But Micah didn't have time to enjoy it before he lost control of his wolf and shifted completely, launching himself at the other man. Jax had barely started to shift into his wolf form by the time Micah leapt across the Ping-Pong table, and they hit the floor hard in a tangle of limbs.

Clothing was shredded and fur flew. His wolf was fully in control now. He demanded blood from the one who'd dared to defile his mate. The one who was supposed to be his Pack brother, his friend.

Traitor.

They rolled, barking and snarling, crashing into furniture. The brown wolf went for the gray's throat, but the gray was fast, twisting out of the way. Micah's enemy made only defensive moves, but no attempt to harm him in return. This angered him even more, beyond reason.

Doubling his effort, he tried to pin the gray wolf and managed to sink his teeth into one muscled shoulder. The taste of blood spurred him on as the gray cried out—

And then a sharp pain stung his right hip.

The brown wolf yelped, releasing his prey. Whirled and saw the dart sticking out of his flank. Right away, cold spread out from the spot with bony fingers, crawled through his muscles. They contracted and he began to shake, struggling to remain upright, but it was no use. Hitting the floor, he whimpered in fear, paralyzed.

Footsteps hurried all around him, people speaking in hushed tones.

"Where's Mac?"

"On her way with a team."

"Micah, it's okay," Rowan whispered near his face. She was crouched next to him, stroking his hair.

When had he shifted back to human form?

"Wh-what happened?" he croaked.

"You don't remember?"

"No."

"It's okay," she crooned. He heard the tears in her voice. "Just rest, bro."

"D-don't feel good."

"I know. It's that damn drug, honey. They're going to get rid of it, I promise."

What had he done? Mac would lock him up now, keep him from his mate.

"No."

His eyelids were so heavy. He couldn't keep them open, so he let them drift shut. Tried to listen to the whispered conversation around him.

"Do you have to lock him up? His wolf was upset, and he lost it. Hell, I might've done the same if I found out one of you had been with Kira before we met."

That's right. He'd attacked Jax. And the man was actually worried. Not angry.

"There's more going on than you know." Mac's voice, kind but firm. "Let us take care of him."

"But—"

"Look, he's got a nosebleed," Aric said. "What's up with that?"

"He'll be all right."

Someone cleaned him up. Then hands lifted him carefully onto a stretcher, secured him. Noah's quiet reassurances soothed him as they started rolling him away.

Would he be all right? He wasn't so sure. All he knew was they were taking him somewhere to be shut away from his mate. Perhaps they'd never let him out.

His wolf's mournful howl followed him into unsettling dreams.

Nick surveyed the damage to the recreation room with a heavy heart. The last time he'd been this afraid for one of his team was when he'd met Kalen Black.

More than just Micah's body had been damaged by Gene Bowman and his evil crew—his spirit had taken a near-lethal blow. What had been left behind was a twisted mess of a man and his wolf. But not broken. Despite Bowman's horrible experiments, the bad reaction to the myst, and Micah's trouble getting his head straight, that was one glimmer of light that remained—they had pushed Micah to the very limit of his endurance and sanity, but they had *not* managed to break him.

The other was Jacee. A wolf would swim an ocean for his mate. Battle an army without a single weapon, save what nature gave him. Micah finding her couldn't have come at a better time, and she just might be his saving grace.

If Mac could just get that damn drug out of Micah's system, get his head clear, the man might have a fighting chance.

But there was more trouble coming. The past wasn't finished with the wolf, not by a long shot. Micah had to get himself together, or his enemy, when he finally chose to strike, would win. Nick had tried to impress that upon the younger wolf, and he could only hope his words had taken root.

Because he'd interfered in the matter all he possibly could. He'd warned Micah of the coming danger, and that was all he could do. He'd promised himself long ago to never tamper with free will again.

And Nick was nothing if not a man of his word.

Get strong, Micah. Death is coming for you.
For both of you.

Six

When Micah awoke, he was restrained.

Flat on his back, on a hospital bed, in a stark white room, he stared at the ceiling and tried to shake the muzzy fog from his brain. They'd sedated him. After what he'd done, he couldn't blame them.

Despair threatened to overwhelm him. Not even two days had passed since his promise to keep himself in check, and he'd failed. How much of his loss of control could really be blamed on the myst? How much of it was simply the fact that he was ruined beyond redemption, deep in his soul?

He tried to move his arms again, but his wrists were securely fastened to the rails of his bed, as were his ankles. Though he knew Mac and her team wouldn't hurt him, unreasonable fear churned in his guts. Both he and his wolf hated being tied down, left vulnerable. They hated being alone, too. Wanted their mate.

But Micah didn't want her to see him like this. Never.

As the sedation wore off a little more, he realized he was nauseated. Anxious, too. Twitchy. He felt like he was going to crawl right out of his skin, and wished he had one or two of his pills to take away the terrible sensation. He knew then what was happening.

Withdrawal. They were detoxing him, the hard way.

"Oh, fuck." Sweat broke out on his face, his chest. The nausea in his gut worsened by the minute and he prayed he didn't get sick on himself, stuck like this.

He was concentrating on breathing without throwing up when the door opened. Mac hurried in, flanked by his sister, Aric, and Nick.

"Good, you're awake," Mac said by way of greeting. She was as serious as he'd ever seen her. So, for that matter, were the others in the room. Rowan even looked like she'd been crying, but surely that was the lighting. The group came to stand around Micah's bed as the doctor continued.

"How are you feeling?"

"Sick. Like I'm going to vomit. My head is starting to pound."

Mac laid a hand on his knee. "That's to be expected during withdrawal. But I'm afraid you're going to feel a whole lot worse before you get better."

Dread made his heart pound. "Well, I don't know how I'm supposed to throw up in this position, Doc. I'll choke."

"We'll unfasten one of your wrists so you can lean over to the side. Once you're detoxed you won't be restrained at all. But that's not really what I'm talking about." Mac paused, as if thinking over what she had to tell him. "Your blood work came back from the lab, and we've isolated the anomaly."

"You have? That's good, right?"

"It's good that we've learned what's going on in your system besides your reaction to the myst, yes. But, Micah, it's the anomaly itself that's going to present the greater problem in getting you healthy." Taking a seat beside his bed, she gripped his hand.

On his other side, Rowan did the same, as Aric and Nick came to stand at the foot of the bed. *Shit, this must be bad.* Everyone in the room was looking at him as if their dog had just been hit by a car.

"Micah, you have leukemia," Mac said softly.

That statement split the quiet in the room like a knife. There was no sound except the tick of the clock on the wall and his own breathing. He couldn't make sense of the words. Words that should no longer have any meaning in his world. Confusion buzzed in his brain.

"But I'm not human anymore," he whispered. "That shouldn't be possible."

Rowan started crying. Even Aric appeared on the verge. Yeah, he was fucked.

"It shouldn't," the doc agreed. "But something that was done to you in Bowman's lab screwed with your biology. My best educated guess is he tried some cross-splicing you with several other subjects. Your immunities were weakened, and a door was left open for illness."

"That's why I haven't been feeling well?"

"I'm afraid so. I believe the myst is responsible for your temper, nosebleeds, and migraines, while the leukemia is making you tired and causing you to lose your appetite."

"How far along is it?"

"Advanced. If you were human, you'd already be dead. Your shifter half is fighting it every step of the way, but the tests show it's not stopping."

"All right." Micah swallowed hard. "What's the plan? And I hope to hell you have one."

"I do. First, you detox as scheduled. We have no time to waste because we need to move on to fighting your illness."

"How do we do that? Chemo?"

"No. If your shifter half can't defeat it, then human methods certainly aren't going to work. We need stronger reinforcements, and that's where we thank whatever higher power there is in the universe that you've met your mate. We've also got our vampire allies we can call on now. I'm sure Calla will send for their doctor if we need him."

"She will," Nick confirmed. "Just say the word and she'll fetch Vicktor."

Micah fixed on the first part of that. "Jacee? She can help?"

"I believe so," Mac said. "If she'll consent, and I don't see why she wouldn't, we'll use her healthier blood to clean yours."

"If that doesn't work?"

"We'll call for the vampire doctor and use one of their clan's donors."

"And then, if that doesn't do the trick, either?"

"We won't give up. We'll keep looking for a solution."

Meaning they'd be out of options. Micah looked at Nick. "Did you know about this?"

"I didn't. I swear I never saw this coming, or I would've told you. I don't consider it tampering to tell someone they have a serious illness so they can get treatment. I would *never* let that go."

Micah believed him. The commander appeared miserable over it. Micah nodded and addressed Mac again. "So, detox and mate's blood. Bada-bing, good as new."

The doc smiled a little. "Let's keep that attitude. Okay, I'll be back later to check on you. Noah's going to take care of you, and your family will take turns staying here."

"I'll go find Jacee and bring her here," Nick said.

A jolt of panic shot through him. "No, not *here*. I don't want her to see me like this."

Rowan shook her head. "Micah, she's your mate. Not only will she want to be by your side—she has every right to be."

"No. If any of you even think of letting her see me in this condition, I'll find a way to leave. I mean it."

From the glances the group exchanged, they were more than a little frustrated with him. But his first instinct was to protect his mate from unpleasantness, and that's what he'd do.

"So, who gets to babysit me first?"

"I'm staying," Rowan insisted.

Nick and Aric promised to be back later as well, and left. Rowan talked to him for a while, chatting about nonsense while he mostly listened. Then he drifted sleepily for a while before going under. He wasn't sure how long he was out, but when he woke up, his head was splitting and his body was on fire. Pain. Every muscle burned. His stomach lurched, and he knew he was going to be sick.

Finding that his left hand was free, he rolled to his right side and leaned over the bed. Instantly his sister was there with a wastebasket, holding it with one hand and his hair with the other while he emptied what little was in his stomach. She talked to him quietly as he moaned.

"It's going to be okay. Shh, you're all right."

When he was done, Noah helped him swish out his mouth, then took the bucket away. Micah slumped back on the pillows, exhausted. His body wouldn't let him rest, though. His head and limbs still hurt, and he felt hot.

"How long?" he managed.

"What, since Mac was here and told you what was happening?"

"Yes."

"A couple of hours. Nick went to look for Jacee." She

stroked his hair, and it felt nice. "I still think you should let her stay with you."

"No."

She didn't push any more at the moment, but he knew she wouldn't give up. Then he couldn't think because a new wave of pain and sickness rocked him, this time accompanied by the shakes. Whatever his sister said, he didn't hear.

The darkness took him again.

Jacee checked her phone for the sixth or seventh time that afternoon. Weird that Micah hadn't sent any more cute texts, though she figured he was busy.

She told herself she was being stupid. The man was a black ops shifter with an important job. He didn't always have time to indulge them, even if they were missing each other. If the bar was busier today, maybe she wouldn't be aching for him so much. She could put their lovemaking out of her head for five minutes and not anticipate when they could be together again.

Yeah, right.

With a bored sigh, she wiped down the bar, then started polishing glasses and putting them away. A couple of regulars sitting at stools on one end asked for beers, but nothing kept her occupied for long.

When the door opened and Nick walked in, she was surprised to see him at the Grizzly in the middle of the afternoon. Unlike when he usually visited the establishment these days, he wasn't wearing a smile, either. His purposeful walk, back straight, eyes locked on her, expression dead serious, gave her a chill.

"Commander Westfall," she said in greeting. "What's your poison today?"

"It's Nick, please."

"Okay, Nick. What'll it be?"

"I can't stay today, Jacee, and neither can you," he said in a low voice, leaning on the counter. "I need you to come back to the compound with me."

She stared at him, dread welling in her throat. She wasn't stupid—if Nick was here asking that, and not Micah, that could only mean one thing. "What's wrong with Micah? What's happened?"

"Not here. Go tell Jack you have a family emergency and you might be gone at least two weeks."

"Two weeks! I'll lose my job."

"You won't. I'll make sure of it."

Her mind reeled. "Okay. Except Jack knows I don't *have* a family."

"You do now. We're your family," he said firmly. "Tell Jack your fiancé is sick and in the hospital. That's pretty much the truth."

"No." She swayed, her vision blurring, and he steadied her. "I just found him, Nick. Nothing can happen to him now."

"Go, and hurry. We still need to go by your place to pack a couple of bags."

Hurrying, she did as she was told. Jack wasn't happy at first, but when he saw how truly upset she was, he relented and told her not to worry. He'd call in a substitute bartender until she returned. Thanking him, she jogged out to meet Nick.

Together, they got into a black Escalade, and he pulled out of the parking lot. She gave him directions to her house, and in no time, they had arrived. He still hadn't given her details, but she concentrated on getting her things together. It was more important she get on the road first, details later.

After packing her clothes and toiletries, she lifted a large duffel bag onto her shoulder and went out to the living room, where Nick waited. He took the bag from her, and she didn't protest.

"You have someone to take care of your garden out back? I was looking out the window, and it's quite nice."

"Thanks. Yes, I'll call my next-door neighbor. She'll take care of it until I can get back here."

"Good. Ready?"

"Yeah."

Nick stowed her bag in the back of the Escalade, and then they were on their way. Finally, he asked, "Has Micah told you about his kidnapping and the months he spent in captivity?"

"He did, and it must've been horrible." She studied the man carefully. "Is that what's causing him problems now?"

"Pretty much, yes."

"I've noticed he seems tired, and when we went to dinner, he didn't eat with the hearty appetite of a man his size with the physical nature of his job. At least in my opinion."

"You're right, and that was a good observation. First of all, when Micah was rescued, he was severely traumatized and had gaps in his memory. He couldn't recall a thing about his time in the lab. Then he started having nightmares and eventually realized they were memories."

"So, it's all coming back."

"Yes. Our doctors put him on a drug called myst to help him cope during therapy, while he healed. It's an antidepressant aimed at shifters. But we recently learned that Micah's body hasn't taken the drug very well. We're pretty sure it's responsible for his mood swings, and it's giving him nosebleeds and headaches."

"So they'll just wean him off, right? That's why he's in the hospital, to let it clear his system?"

"Yes, but there was a complication," Nick replied. "The myst wasn't responsible for making him tired or for his loss of appetite. Dr. Grant had some tests run, and those came back this morning."

Jacee frowned. "He's a shifter. What on earth could be making him so sick that he can't heal on his own?"

The commander didn't answer until he'd driven all the way to the compound and through the tall security gates. He waited until he'd driven down the long road to the facility and parked outside a brand-new-looking building that had the name SANCTUARY etched into the stonework above the grand entrance. The he shut off the ignition and turned to face her.

Reaching over, he put his hand on her shoulder. "Jacee, Micah has leukemia."

"I— What? What did you say?" She blinked at Nick, shook her head. "No. That's not possible."

"I'm afraid it is," he said sadly. "Whatever that bastard did to him in the lab left him vulnerable. It's highly possible that had he never been turned into a shifter, he would've gotten the disease long before now."

"He has cancer. In his blood." Not Micah. This could not happen to her mate. "I won't accept this. What can I do to help him?"

Nick smiled a little. "I figured you'd say that, which is why you're here. Mac is going to try transfusing some of your blood into Micah's, in doses. We're hoping the healing power of your blood as his mate will cleanse the cancer from his. If that doesn't work, my mate, Calla, will call on her clan's doctor to come and use vampire blood."

The weight of what Nick was telling Jacee sank in, and she covered her face with her hands. Her mate was dying. And if this didn't work . . .

For a few minutes she hung her head and let the tears fall. The commander rubbed her shoulder, offering what comfort he could. Distantly, she was aware of the passenger's door opening and someone stepping in to put an arm around her.

"Jacee? Honey, he's going to be all right."

Lifting her face, she saw Micah's sister, Rowan. For some reason that made the tears fall faster, and she hugged the other woman tight as she tried to get her terror under control.

"This shouldn't be happening to him," Jacee rasped.

Rowan eased back and dashed away tears as well. "You already care for him."

"I do. He's important to me, and he doesn't deserve this shit."

"Then let's get in there and make sure he gets well, huh?"

Jacee got out of the SUV and was aware of Nick getting her bag from the back as she walked inside with Rowan. For a hospital, the facility was beautiful, and she said so.

"Oh, it's much more than a hospital. It's a rehabilitation center for injured shifters or other paranormal beings who are having difficulty integrating into our world. Some are sick, but some need mental care as well."

"It's incredible."

"Sure beats the old hospital and the jail cells in the main building—that's for sure," the other woman remarked. "Kira had a fit when she first saw them and the poor beings that were locked up inside. One of her rescues, Sariel, is a Fae prince who helps run Sanctuary now. You'll meet him—well, all of them—sooner or later."

Jacee tried to assimilate all of that, especially the Fae prince whom Micah had already told her some about. But her brain kept coming back to one thing. "Kira works here? She's Jax's mate, right?"

Rowan cut her a sharp look. "Is that going to be a

problem? 'Cause I'll tell you, we've got enough of them on our plate without you and Kira getting into a fight in the middle of the compound."

"I've got no issue with either of them, and I'm sure Jax couldn't care less about me as anything except maybe a friend. Eventually. Kira, I'm not so sure about. Everyone else probably thinks I'm just the slut who slept with one of their Pack bros."

"Slut?" Rowan half laughed.

"Yeah, a slut. You know, a woman with the morals of a man."

This time Rowan laughed outright. "That's a good one."

"I read that somewhere. Been waiting to use it."

"Well, for what it's worth, I don't think that about you."

"Thanks."

"Besides, none of the men has room to talk. Did you know that before most of them mated, they used to take regular trips to Vegas to hook up and get their rocks off?" Rowan said as they got into the elevator.

Nick, Jacee noted, looked uncomfortable with the turn in the conversation. "Really?"

"Yep. Every one of these guys has seen more pussy than a judge at the Supreme Cat Show. Any one of them gives you shit, you remember that."

Jacee snickered and decided she liked this woman. Maybe they would end up being friends. As they reached the third floor, however, she sobered and was attacked by nerves. They stepped out of the elevator, and she turned to her companions.

"What do I do now?"

"Mac has a room set aside for you to stay in—" Nick began.

"Wait a second. I'm staying with Micah, right? Why

do I need my own room?" Rowan and Nick exchanged a glance and worry filled her. "What?"

Nick clarified the situation. "Micah doesn't want you seeing him suffer while he's going through withdrawal, so Mac is putting you in your own room."

"Um, not only no, but *fuck no*!" Jacee yelled. Her coyote was already growling at the idea of being separated from her mate.

"You'll be close by just in case—"

"With all due respect, Commander, what part of *Fuck that stupid idea* didn't anyone understand? I'm staying with my mate, and I want to see him *now*!" Looking around, she raised her voice on that last part for the benefit of anyone listening. And there were a few people gathering. Especially the blond cutie Noah, who came running to smooth things over.

"Hey, okay! Calm down, sweetie. Deep breaths." He kept talking, patting her on the back. Clearly, he'd dealt with a pissed shifter or two in his career. "There we go. Well! I think Jacee has made her feelings quite clear on the matter, and this is now an issue for the two mates to work out. Wouldn't you agree, Dr. Grant?"

Mac hurried over to the group, and it was obvious she'd heard the commotion. "I think it's best for Jacee to stay with him, no matter how stubborn he's trying to be. He's going to need her, and he'll be glad she's there once he sees her."

"But he said he'd leave," Rowan fretted.

"He's too weak to follow through," Mac said. "There's no way he's going anywhere."

"That settles it. I'm staying with him." Jacee's voice was firm.

"There's a sofa under the window you can sleep on. Noah will bring you a blanket and a pillow. He's in room three-o-five." Mac pointed. "I'll be along later to explain what's happening, but I'll give you some time alone with him first."

Jacee wasn't alone right away. Nick followed and set her bag in the room. Rowan came along for moral support and to check on her brother. But the second Jacee stepped inside, her eyes were only for her mate.

Micah was sleeping fitfully, his dark lashes resting like lace against pale cheeks. His hair was damp, stuck to his face, and fanned on his pillow. His chest rose and fell with harsh breaths, as though he couldn't quite breathe comfortably. One of his wrists was cuffed to the bed rail, and the sight of it hit her in the gut. Scanning his body, she felt down his legs, lifted the sheet, and saw that his ankles were secured, too.

"Why is he chained like an animal?" Jacee fumed.

"Because of the withdrawal," Nick answered. "They were afraid he'd hurt himself or one of the nurses."

"He's too sick to hurt anyone! I want them off."

"Me, too, but we'll have to see what Mac says."

Those fucking cuffs were coming off if Jacee had to saw them off herself. Pulling up a chair, she sat beside Micah and laid a hand on his arm. She had to touch him, if only like this. He looked far too vulnerable, such a far cry from the wolf who'd run in the forest and made love to her. If only she'd known he was so ill.

What could she have done? Nothing but be there for him. But she was here now, so that would have to count for something.

Nick and Rowan left for a while, and Jacee just watched Micah sleep. After a couple of hours, she turned the television on low and caught the news. As usual, it was all bad. She turned to a channel that played reruns of classic sitcoms and left it there.

About three hours after her arrival, Micah began to

stir. He moaned, the sound miserable, as though he was in pain.

"Micah? Sweetheart, it's me. Jacee."

Her voice penetrated the fog, and his eyes cracked open. At first he seemed to have some trouble focusing, but eventually he found her face. Relief warred with shame in his eyes.

"Jacee," he whispered, "I told them not to let you see me like this."

"We're mates. Did you really believe they could keep me from your side?"

He tried to smile. "Guess not."

"When you told me there were things I didn't know, I didn't dream you were sick." Resting her arm on the bed, she stroked his silky hair. He turned his head into her touch.

"Too much?"

"No. Never."

"I didn't know about the leukemia. Until today."

"I know." Her throat threatened to close up with grief.

"Sorry you're stuck with this. With me." His lashes did a slow blink. He was already getting tired.

"Stop that. Do you hear me? I'm right where I want to be."

"Jacee?"

"Yes, sweetie?"

"Tell somebody to get Ryon."

"He's the blond Pack team member, right?"

"Yeah. Ryon Hunter. He's a Telepath and Channeler. Talks to dead people."

That was disturbing on many levels. "Is there a particular reason you need to see him, or just to visit?"

"He's my friend, but there's a reason. Something he needs to tell me."

"Okay. I'll have someone get him for you."

"Thanks."

"Rest for now."

Micah was out almost immediately. Mac came by shortly after and began checking his vitals and, to Jacee's immense relief, released his wrist and ankles.

Jacee gestured to her mate. "Why is he going downhill so fast? He seemed fine a couple of days ago."

"The myst has weakened his body, and now the withdrawal from it is seriously draining him. That's allowed the cancer to move in and step up the attack at an alarming rate."

"When will we start giving him my blood?"

The doc noted his temperature and faced Jacee. "Right away. I was going to wait until the detox was complete, but I don't think he has that much time, quite honestly." Her voice lowered in sympathy. "Hang in there. Noah will be by soon to get things started."

"All right. By the way, Micah wants to see Ryon as soon as possible."

"I'll call Ryon and let him know."

"Thanks." Mac left her alone with Micah again.

I don't think he has that much time.

Jacee was more frightened than she'd been since her family had been murdered. If she lost Micah, too, her life was over. She'd give up, and that would be fine by her. Losing her true Bondmate would be the final blow she'd never survive.

A short time later, there was a knock on the door, and a good-looking blond man walked into the room. Others might disagree, but she thought he sort of looked like that *Fast and Furious* actor, the late Paul Walker.

"Ryon?" she said.

"That's me," he said with an honest smile. "Good to see you outside the bar, Jacee."

"You, too, though I wish it wasn't under these circumstances."

Ryon looked toward the bed and his smile vanished. "Me, too."

"Do you know why he wants to see you?"

"Yeah. If he doesn't mind you staying, I'll tell you all about it, too."

"I don't mind," Micah said quietly. "She stays."

"Hey, bro." Walking over, Ryon gave his friend a brotherly hug. "Cancer? What the fuck, man?"

"I know, right? Bowman fucked me over good."

"He did, but Mac's going to get you well. Count on that." Taking a seat on the other side of the bed, Ryon said, "I suppose you want to know about the spirit who's hanging around you."

"Got it in one. It had slipped my mind, but when faced with my mortality? Yeah, I thought of it and kind of wondered if the spirit was important to me. If it had a message or something."

"Well, I can ask her if you want because she's sitting right beside Jacee."

Jacee jumped and whipped her head to look at the spot Ryon indicated, but there was nothing present but air. "Um, one of us is crazy and it's not me."

"Her?" Micah asked, curious.

"Yep. Your ghost is a woman. Older Hispanic lady, close to sixty years old. Attractive. She's wearing a pretty pink dress with little white flowers, says it was her favorite though she hardly ever had a place to wear it since she cleaned houses for a living. Where the hell was she supposed to go and dress up? But she loved it, and was buried in it, along with the cameo brooch she has on that belonged to her grandmother."

Micah's face paled even more, if that was possible. Staring at the spot, he croaked, "Mama?"

"She says yes," Ryon confirmed, "and that you're still the most special boy in the world, and she loves you with all her heart."

"She always said that. I love you, too, Mama." Micah cleared his throat.

"But she's got a message. She came because she sensed you're in trouble, in more ways than one. She knows you're sick and said that you're to fight and not give up. You will beat this thing. Got that?"

"Yes, ma'am."

Jacee wiped away a tear.

"She also feels an evil presence near you. She says, listen to Nick, and more important, to your own inner voice. There's a man who would do you and your mate harm, and to best him you must be at full strength again. You must fight."

"I will, I promise. Who is he?"

"He's someone from your not-so-distant past. He's a monster, but he's good at concealing himself. He'll attack when your guard is down, when you least expect it."

"His name?"

"She doesn't know it. But if you and your Pack dig deep enough, his name is there, as well as his motivation."

"Thank you, Mama. I love you."

"She says you're welcome, but she'd do anything for her children. One day you'll understand. She loves you, and she says to be happy with your mate. She'll see you again one day," Ryon said quietly. He paused. "She's gone, buddy."

"That was incredible," Jacee breathed. "I'm seriously creeped out. You're sure that was really your mother?"

"I'm sure. There's no way Ryon could've known what we buried her in or about my grandmother's brooch."

"Unless Rowan had mentioned it?"

"I swear she never did," Ryon said. "I'm the real thing. It's hard even for paranormal creatures to believe in my gift because it's something most of them can't see or touch. I don't mind most of the time."

"I believe you. It's just the strangest gift I think I've ever witnessed."

Ryon snorted. "No, watch Kalen use his necromancing skills to raise a corpse from the dead and have a conversation with it. Now *that's* weird."

Jacee shuddered. "I'll pass. Thanks."

Ryon stood to take his leave and clapped Micah gently on the shoulder. "I'll be back soon. You take care and kick this thing so we can go have a beer to celebrate." He smiled at Jacee. "And to celebrate your new mate, too."

"You know it," Micah said.

Ryon took his leave, and Jacee was alone with her mate again. Micah slumped back into the pillows, totally exhausted. "Jacee?"

"Hmm?"

"I'm glad you're here, even though I was a dumbass about it at first."

Leaning over, she kissed him on the lips. "I'm glad I'm here, too. And I'm going to make sure you live to be a dumbass for a long time to come."

He fell asleep with a small smile on his lips.

Seven

The monster raged and paced back and forth in his brother's room.

"Why is he so sick? Why have they admitted him? He can't die by any hand other than mine," he hissed.

From the bed, his companion winced. "I don't know. But isn't it enough that he's suffering? That he might die all on his own?"

"Of course it's not. That would never be enough." He paced some more and then stopped by the bed. "I thought leaving the mutilated woman near where he'd been running and screwing with his new bitch was an excellent warning. Apparently it was too subtle. I'll have to step up my game."

"Please, brother, don't harm anyone else, not on his account. No one is going to believe he'd do such a thing, anyway."

He paused. "I'll consider it. Perhaps I should just go straight to the source, eh? You keep your ears open and your mouth shut. You know what happens when I get angry, and if you tell anyone about me, I'll get *very* angry. Let me know if you hear what's going on."

"I will," the younger man said reluctantly. His eyes were dull. Tired.

That was Micah Chase's fault, too.

Dammit to hell! The monster left, but no one paid him any attention. Not in this form. But in the other . . .

Oh, in the other, they'd run screaming in terror. As Micah and his new, sweet mate would do.

Just before he ripped them both into tiny pieces.

Micah was burning in hell.

Every breath was like sucking in flames, and his entire body felt like he'd been beaten with hammers. How much was from the detox and how much was due to his other illness he didn't know. Only that he was ready for whatever treatment they wanted to try.

Either that or he could just die.

Now he understood why people welcomed the end when their time came. How did humans do this for months or years? Ironically, they were stronger than he was. One day and he was over this.

"Where's Noah?" Micah whispered. Next to him, Jacee stirred and stroked his face, his hair. It was the only pleasurable sensation among the terrible ones gripping him.

"He'll be here soon. They just drew my first round of blood."

He frowned. "You already went?"

"Yes, and came back. You've been really out of it."

"Sorry."

"Don't you dare apologize," she murmured, leaning over to kiss his cheek.

She smelled so good, his wolf whimpered in appreciation. How he wished he was well enough to claim her as his own.

"I was so stupid," he said.

"How so?"

"Should've claimed you when I had the chance."

"Hey, you *will*, and I'll return the favor just as soon as you're better! Don't think for one second you're getting out of it."

He smiled, or tried to. A wave of pain swept him from his head to his feet, and he groaned. If any mating was going to happen, Noah had better hurry with that blood and they'd all better hope it worked.

No sooner had that thought entered his mind than the door opened. The sound of footsteps hurried in, and he finally cracked his eyes open to see the blurry form of the nurse rushing around, readying an IV bag full of crimson liquid. He hung it on a metal pole, then rolled the pole close to the bed. After attaching the tube to it, he prepared to insert the needle part into the port in Micah's hand.

"Okay, Micah," Noah began. "I'm going to start the IV with Jacee's blood mixed in it, and the solution will feed into your body over the next few hours. You should start to feel better pretty fast, with all her fantastic shifter antibodies giving you that boost you need to heal."

"Sounds great. Stop talking and do it."

The nurse gave Micah a sympathetic pat on the arm and then got to work. Tilting his head down, Micah watched the needle push into the port. Then Noah fiddled with some sort of dial on the tubing, and the red liquid started down the line and into the port. It felt cold going into his vein, but nothing much different—

And then he gasped, heaving in a great gulp of air. His eyes went wide as every cell in his body came alive. It was as though each individual one had been lit by a beam of brilliant sunshine.

"Micah? Are you all right?" Noah asked. Quickly, the nurse began checking his vitals.

"Honey?" Jacee was peering at her mate worriedly, gripping his hand.

"Yes, it's fine," he managed. "It feels like I got pumped with pure adrenaline. Like I'm lit from the inside out."

"Good." Noah appeared pleased. "That's what we're going for. Don't go running around the block, though, okay? I'll be back in a bit."

The nurse walked out, and Micah gazed up at his mate. Her face wasn't so blurry anymore, and he could focus without his head feeling as though it was going to burst open.

He glanced at the IV. "That's some good stuff."

"There's more where that came from." Her stomach growled, and she blushed.

"When's the last time you ate?" Her silence was answer enough. "You can't take care of me if you let yourself get weak, too. Get over to the compound and have something to eat, please?"

She didn't want to leave him, he could tell, but she hadn't been away from his side much, and being famished got the best of her. "All right, but I won't be gone long."

Kissing him soundly, she headed out the door. He missed her presence immediately, but was comforted by knowing she'd be back soon. He just wished his new mate didn't have to deal with the "sickness" part of "in sickness and in health" quite this early in their relationship.

Hopefully the treatment would work.

If it didn't— No. He wouldn't think like that. Already tired, he closed his eyes and gave in to sleep.

But this time he literally breathed a little easier than before.

Micah seemed better. Weren't his eyes clearer? And he hadn't seemed in as much pain as before.

Jacee was so lost in thought, she didn't even see the man who'd rounded the corner in front of her until it was too late to avoid the collision. She hit his chest with a muffled *oof* and instantly stepped back, face flaming.

"I'm so sorry! I wasn't watching where I was going."

Looking up, she met the man's smiling face, and her skin crawled. It wasn't that he was ugly at all, but something about him seemed off. Like his clear eyes were looking *through* her instead of *at* her, and his smile appeared pasted on. Wooden.

He was tall, on the thin side, and although his face was that of a younger man, his hair was sparse and gray. Definitely odd. His teeth were a bit yellowed and his breath wasn't very fresh. The rest of him didn't smell very pleasant, either—sort of like milk that had gotten left out too long in the sun.

"It's all right, Miss . . . ?" He let the question hang, expecting an introduction.

Cursing inwardly, she decided there wasn't a way to get around it without things getting awkward, so she capitulated. To a point. "Jacee." He *wasn't* getting her last name.

"I'm Parker. Nice to *run into* you." He laughed at his own lame joke. "Perhaps we'll do it again some time."

"Maybe so. Take care." Giving him a fake smile, she moved around him and continued on her way without looking back.

She could swear she sensed his eyes on her, though, and she didn't breathe easy until the elevator doors closed and the lift started downward. Jeez, what a creep! He must have been visiting somebody at Sanctuary, though she couldn't imagine his presence would make anyone feel better. If she saw him lurking over her bed, she'd go into cardiac arrest.

Putting him out of her mind, she made her way to the main building. Nick had given her an access code for the direct corridor, and she got in with no problem. Finding the dining room was another matter, and she got lost a few times before finally meeting up with Aric after she'd turned down the fourth or fifth hallway.

"Hey, pretty lady, you lost?"

"As a flea in a sandstorm. Can you direct me to the dining room? I'm starving."

The redhead laughed. "This is a big place, ain't it? That's where I'm going. You can grab a bite with me and Rowan."

"Sounds good."

Jacee studied Aric slyly on the way to their destination. The man was snarky and funny as hell, and she liked him a lot. He had a strong personality, too. It was easy to see why Rowan had fallen for him. Each of the guys she'd met had his own special appeal, but Aric was one of her favorites, maybe because of his fun, rebellious attitude.

This side of him really came to the forefront around his Pack brothers. The minute they walked into the dining room, he was calling out to his friends, "Hey, you ugly fuckers! Did your greedy asses save me any food?"

"Fuck you, asshole!"

A round of good-natured insults ensued, and Jacee found herself laughing for the first time in many tension-filled hours. Maybe the show was for her benefit, but she didn't care. It warmed her to them even more.

Aric led her to a table where Rowan sat with a blue-haired, blue-winged creature so freaking beautiful, he could only be the Fae prince she'd heard about. More than a little nervous, she took a seat and smiled at her companions.

"How's my baby bro?" Rowan asked, looking worn-out.

"Better. Noah put in the IV with my blood tonight, and he said it was like pure adrenaline. He's resting pretty well right now, so he made me come grab some food."

"That's good." Rowan looked relieved.

"Yes, it is." Jacee looked at the Fae, who was watching her curiously. "Hello. I'm Jacee Buchanan, Micah's mate. Well, soon-to-be."

The creature smiled, showing off a set of gorgeous white teeth. "I'm Sariel, renegade Fae. Wonderful to meet you."

Jacee reached over to shake his hand, but he turned hers over and kissed the back of it instead. "A renegade and a gentleman at the same time. How does that work?"

"Quite well, I'm told." His golden eyes sparkled with humor.

Conversation at the table turned to general chat, and she listened while studying the Fae prince. He appeared young, maybe in his twenties, but his eyes were fathomless. She got the distinct impression he was much older than he looked.

Sariel turned from Rowan to grin at her. "Have you dissected me yet?"

Her face flushed. "Sorry. I've just never met a faery before."

"I felt the same when I was first cast from my realm and landed in Ireland quite unceremoniously. What would you like to know?"

"How old are you?" she blurted.

That made him laugh, and crinkled the corners of those amazing eyes. "Got a guess?"

"A few hundred? Five, maybe?"

That made the others around them chuckle, and Sariel shook his head. "A tad higher."

"A thousand?"

"A bit more. I'm eleven thousand years old." He paused thoughtfully. "Give or take a century."

"Holy shit! And I thought shifters were long-lived!"

For a second, Sariel's smile was sad. "Eternity isn't all it's cracked up to be, as they say. Anyway, let's eat."

Jacee dug into her spaghetti, but noticed Sariel's plate held salad and fruit. He picked at it more than he ate, but no one commented, so she guessed this was normal behavior for him. The food was delicious, placed family-style in the middle of the table, everyone serving themselves. The setup and the talk all around her created a homey atmosphere she liked and had missed for a long time.

She should've known the peaceful interlude would be interrupted. After all, she was bound to face the music sooner or later. Jax's voice sounded from the entrance to the dining room, and a woman laughed at something he said. Reluctantly, Jacee turned her head to look over her shoulder.

Jax spotted her at the same time, and whatever he'd been saying died on his lips. This caused his female companion to find the source of his dismay, and Jacee was soon being stared at like a bug in their soup. Awesome.

Not only that, but the other Pack brothers noticed the three of them facing off, and all eyes were suddenly on the unfolding drama. Talk around them died a painful death. So, Jacee did the only thing she could think of.

Getting out of her seat, she crossed the room and merely nodded and said pleasantly, "Jax, good to see you again."

"You, too," he managed.

Awkward. Then she gave Kira her most sincere smile

and said, "You must be Kira. I've heard so much about you, especially how you're responsible for starting Sanctuary."

If the other woman had been expecting hostility or open warfare, she was apparently surprised. "Oh. Yes, well, it was a team effort. I enjoy my work there."

"It shows. The facility is wonderful, and so is the staff. If it wasn't for Sanctuary and qualified staff like Mac and Noah, Micah would be in real trouble right now." Her voice wavered as she went on. "My mate means the world to me, so thank you for starting that place and making sure sick shifters and others like him have a place to heal."

At that, a great deal of the cool, aloof demeanor about Kira vanished. Her expression warmed, and she took one of Jacee's hands in hers. "I'm glad he and the others have somewhere to go, too. The doctors and nurses there are top-notch, and if anyone can get him well, they can."

"We're all pulling for him," Jax added softly. "Micah and I started out in the Navy SEALs together, and we've been through a lot of shit. He deserves to be happy."

"He's my friend, too," Kira said.

"I intend to make sure he's happy and stays that way," Jacee assured them. "He's special to me as well."

Everyone who'd been expecting a blowup went back to their meals with shrugs, and the tension popped like a balloon. Jacee doubted the three of them would be bosom buddies too quickly, but at least they wouldn't kill one another.

"I'm glad you're mated and happy." Jacee gestured to them both. "You make a great couple."

Jax grinned. "Thanks." Kira echoed his sentiment.

Returning to her table, Jacee was met with the amused smirks of her companions. "What?"

Sariel tossed down his napkin. "Well, how disappointing! I was hoping for blood and guts. Where's a good cat fight when you need one?"

"Dog fight," Rowan corrected.

"Whatever."

Aric chuckled, and Jacee sensed some inside joke in the exchange. But they didn't explain, so she finished her dinner quickly, wanting to get back to Micah. When she was done, she wiped her mouth and stood.

"I want to get back, but thanks for the chat and the break. I needed that."

"Want me to take over for tonight?" Rowan offered.

Aric nodded. "Or I can. You could go get some real sleep."

"I couldn't sleep if I was away from him, not knowing what's going on. But thanks anyway, guys."

Rowan stood and hugged her. "If you change your mind, give us a call."

"Will do."

Back in Micah's room, Jacee settled onto the sofa close by. It was past nine o'clock, and he was sleeping soundly. Was the rasp in his chest better? His lungs sounded more clear. He certainly seemed to be resting much better, not moaning or tossing as he'd done before.

The bag of crimson fluid was more than halfway empty, and it would be a few hours before Noah returned with a fresh one. She watched her mate until she couldn't keep her eyes open anymore.

Then she joined him in slumber.

Three days.

Three boring days of being poked, prodded, and tested. Micah was going out of his mind, but in the best way.

He was feeling *fantastic*.

And now that his body was rallying, his wolf was

revved up and ready to claim his mate. Every single time she walked into his room, it was all he could do to refrain from grabbing her, tossing her onto his bed, and having his way with her, regardless of who might come walking in to get an eyeful.

It might be worth getting thrown out. Maybe it would speed along his discharge papers? Nah, Mac would kill him after all and save the disease the trouble.

Next to him, Jacee laid her magazine in her lap and cocked her head at him with a bemused expression. "What are you smiling about over there?"

"Fucking you right here on this bed with your round ass turned up and me pounding into it like there's no tomorrow."

"Micah!" Her mouth fell open, and she smacked him on the arm with her magazine. "You horny wolf."

"You asked!"

"I guess you *are* feeling better. Wonder when Mac's going to have those last test results?"

"Anytime, I hope. I'm ready to get the hell out of here."

"Where do you want to go when you're released?"

"Go? What do you mean?"

Hesitating, she studied her lap for a second before meeting his eyes again. "We're mates, or will be. Are we going to live together? Or separately? I'm not sure what you want."

"Oh! God, I feel so stupid." He reached out for her hand and enfolded it in his. "I want to live wherever makes you happy, baby. Nick likes for the team to live on the compound, but your house is only a short drive into town, so he might make an exception if you want us to stay there, at least for now."

"You think so?"

She looked so hopeful, he resolved to speak with Nick the second Mac let him go. "I'm pretty sure. I'll see if I can work something out with him."

Jacee's megawatt smile was payment enough for even entertaining the idea of giving up life here with his brothers. This woman was quickly becoming his everything, his feelings growing stronger as she selflessly cared for him through his illness each day. She could easily have left him to the hospital's care and only mated with him when he got well, nothing more. But she was a kind person, with lots of love to give.

Could she really *love* him? Could he be that lucky?

"All right, who's ready to leave?" Mac burst into the room, waving a sheaf of papers and grinning from ear to ear.

Micah blinked. "I'm free?"

"Free and clear! Your test results show no sign of leukemia, thanks to several rounds of your mate's blood."

Jacee launched herself at him, and he crushed her to his chest. Then he gave her a slow, sweet kiss, which promised much more, later. Mac gave them a moment, and finally they pulled apart.

Micah cleared his throat. "What are the chances of recurrence?"

"I'll be honest—I just don't know. My guess is it's gone for good, but I want you back every six months for a checkup for the first two years. After that, every year for five years. Past the seven-year mark, I'll feel better saying you're totally clear."

"I don't know how to thank you."

"No need. Good old shifter biology got you out of this mess, I think, and mating will keep you out. Go home and create that bond, and I'm pretty sure nature will take care of the rest."

"Well, thanks, anyway. I haven't felt this good in over a year, Mac."

"How are the cravings for myst?"

Aware of Jacee's gaze, Micah thought about that. Honesty was best. "The cravings are still there, but I think I can handle them. I don't want any more drugs in my body."

"I think that's for the best. We'll continue our counseling as your memories return, and I believe you'll do well with just that now."

"Works for me."

"All right. Go, take it easy for a few days. You're off work for two more weeks, so no demon fights until then." Mac winked, and looked at Jacee. "Take care of him."

"I plan on it, if he'll let me."

"Do I look like a fool?" Micah asked.

Mac signed his release papers and left. Jacee handed him a pile of folded clothes, which he accepted gratefully. It would be nice to get out of the breezy hospital gown and into his jeans and T-shirt. He dressed efficiently, amazed at the energy coursing through him. If that was from a few pints of his mate's blood, being bonded to her was *really* going to make him feel like a new man. And wolf.

On their way out, he grabbed Jacee's duffel and draped the strap over one shoulder. In the hallway by the nurses' station, he shook Noah's hand and thanked him. Then he put his arm around Jacee and enjoyed the way she fit against him as they made their way to the main building.

"I'll show you to my quarters. You can hang there if you want while I go talk to Nick."

"I'd rather go with you, if it's all the same," she said. "Where we're going to stay affects me, too."

Immediately he could've kicked himself. "Of course,

you're right. I didn't mean to leave you out of any decisions, I just thought . . ." There wasn't any way to finish that sentence that wouldn't land him in hot water, so he didn't. "Anyway, let's see if he's in his office."

The compound was busy when they arrived. Many well-wishers stopped to talk and see how Micah was doing, so getting to Nick's office took longer than they'd expected. When they finally got there, Micah knocked.

"Come in." Nick looked up and greeted them warmly. "Well, it's good to see you two out of that place. Have a seat and tell me what I can do for you."

"You don't know already?" Micah asked.

Nick rolled his eyes, taking the ribbing in stride, and looked at Jacee. "See what I put up with? They love to play 'mock the Seer,' as if I haven't heard those jokes a million times."

Jacee giggled. Then she said, "We're here to talk to you about Micah staying with me, at my house in town. At least while we get bonded and figure out what we want to do."

"I see." Folding his arms in front of him on the desk, Nick considered that and studied Micah. "As far as work goes, that's fine because Mac has you on leave. The issue of whoever is after you is another matter."

"I know. I've thought of that." Micah ran a hand down his face. "What if we get Kalen to ward her house?"

"That works only as long as you're inside it. What about when you're driving back and forth or out running in wolf form?"

"Nick, I do those things anyway. He's going to make a move sooner or later, and if I'm guarded like Fort Knox, it's only going to put off the inevitable."

"True." The commander fell silent for a few moments, then nodded. "Okay. You have my permission to live off-base for the next two weeks. But I don't like that Jacee's house is so far outside our perimeter. And yes, even twenty minutes is too far in our line of work. I'm going to have to come up with an alternate solution if you two insist on your own place."

"Fair enough," Micah said, his enthusiasm bubbling forth. "Thanks, boss."

"Don't make me regret this."

Pulling Jacee out of the office, Micah waited until they were down the hall before he pushed her against the wall and kissed her senseless. "I feel like a teenager again," he breathed. "We're almost out of here."

"Let's go get some of your stuff." Excitement shone in her face.

Holding her hand, he led her to his quarters and punched his access code, letting them inside. He had never been more aware of how sad and stark his space was than at that moment, with his mate at his side and newfound happiness welling in his chest.

"This is . . . tidy."

"It's worse than my hospital room," he admitted. "It could use a woman's touch. Or anyone's touch but mine, since I have the decorating will and know-how of a brick."

"Well, let's say it's got potential." Amusement danced in her eyes.

"Some of the other guys have their apartments fixed up really cool." He shrugged. "I never cared much."

Because he'd been depressed and sick for months since his return. But he was slowly putting that part of his life behind him. With any luck, that was over for good.

Setting her duffel on his bed, he fished in his bedroom closet for his black one. Finding it, he tossed it on the bed and made quick work of filling it with jeans, T-shirts, and sweats. He folded a couple of nicer shirts, too, thinking of the steak house in town. Last were his underwear and toiletries, and he was good to go.

Hitching both bags on his shoulder, he turned to her. "Ready."

On the way out, he made sure to stop by Aric and Rowan's quarters to tell them where he would be. God help him if he left without telling his sister good-bye. She got all sniffly and tearful, not like her one bit. But she and Aric had been through hell worrying about him, so he gave her a pass.

Outside, he led Jacee to the hangar and into the area where their personal vehicles were parked. She was suitably impressed by all the SUVs and aircraft.

"Holy crap! Hueys? And a private plane? Jeez, how many Escalades do you have?"

"Several. All of those belong to the Pack."

"Who paid for all this stuff? The government?"

"Something like that."

"You know you're going to have to tell me that story," she insisted. "How you guys became the Pack."

"I will. Let's get to your place and relax first, huh?" He unlocked the doors and helped her in. Then he tossed their bags in the back, went around, and climbed in. Once he was headed down the road to the gate, he asked, "Are you hungry?"

"Yes. But not for food."

The look she gave him nearly made him stomp the gas pedal through the floorboard. Every ounce of his newly purified blood arrowed south, and his cock stiffened in his jeans. The twenty-minute drive to her part of town had never seemed so long, but he drove carefully. The last thing he needed was to get pulled over by Deveraux or one of his deputies. Being harassed by the sheriff once in a month was plenty. Or make that once in a lifetime.

Finally he parked in front of her house and retrieved their bags. As they started up the walk, he had a pang of momentary sadness as he looked at the place. She'd worked so hard to make it pretty and homey, but Nick would never allow them to live here. Not if Micah wanted to remain on the team. He wasn't sure what solution the boss would come up with, but living in town wasn't going to be an option.

Jacee let them in and gestured down a hallway. "My bedroom is down there. There're two. It's the one on the right."

"That's the only one we're going to need." Lips curving up, he started that way, aware of her following him.

Her scent teased his nose, arousal heightening the potency. In the bedroom he dumped the bags on the floor near the bed and turned, pulling Jacee into his arms. He couldn't wait one second longer to have her again. To feel her naked skin against his, to bury his cock in her depths and feel her clenching around him.

He took her mouth hungrily, licking into her sweet heat. Exploring, his tongue dueling with hers. She moaned, arching into him, running her palms under his shirt to skim his back. Delicate fingers mapped his scars, cruelly made what seemed so long ago.

But she made everything right. When he was in her arms, there was no reason to doubt or fear. No reason to be anything but happy that he'd found her among the millions of people in the country, and she accepted all of him. Even the scars he carried on the *inside*.

Especially those. Because of Jacee, he could heal. Was nearly there.

"Let's take this to the bed," he whispered, "because I'm going to make love to you all afternoon. And I'm going to claim you as my mate, if you'll have me."

"Oh, *yes*. Please."

She attacked his mouth again, and they fell backward together onto the mattress, tearing at each other's clothes. That was all the encouragement he needed.

It was time to claim his mate, and his future.

Eight

Micah hadn't felt so alive in years.

Not since he'd awakened in a military base hospital in a godforsaken hellhole and learned he'd become part beast. He'd been fighting ever since to reclaim some former semblance of himself. Some small measure of peace.

With his Pack brothers, he'd found belonging, acceptance.

With Jacee . . . he'd found the other half of his soul.

Driven by an urgency he'd never felt before, he covered her body with his, buried his nose in her neck. His wolf almost came unglued as her sweet scent enveloped him, and only the greatest effort kept the animal side of him below the surface of his skin. Nibbling below her jaw, he tasted the essence of her, savoring it on his tongue. That played havoc on taking his time, however, and he practically devoured her on his journey south.

From the encouraging noises she was making, she didn't mind one bit. He laved both breasts, worshipping them with the attention they fully deserved before moving on to her stomach and belly button. She gave a little giggle as he explored her inny, but gasped seconds later as he parted her sex and found his prize.

His wolf might be mostly contained, but he was a wicked boy and not above cheating. Micah allowed his tongue to shift into preternatural length and put it to good use. His mate squirmed and moaned, apparently finding this pleasing as well, bolstering his confidence. He might be damaged, but her response proved he was made for her, and she for him. No other couple fit together like true mates.

First he licked her slit, then teased the tiny nub of her clit until she was crying out and pulling his hair. Giving a throaty laugh, he crawled back up her body and propped himself over her, resting on his elbows, kissing her soundly.

Reaching between them, he guided himself into her, his eyes never leaving hers. Then he slid home and was rewarded with sheer bliss as her heat surrounded his cock, hugging him deliciously.

"How's this, baby?" he whispered. "Is this what you want, what you need?"

"Yes."

"Tell me."

"Fuck me. Claim me. Make me yours," she rasped.

"Anything you want, mate. Whenever and however you want me."

Giving them what they both desired, he began to pump his hips, driving into her hard and fast. She met his lovemaking with equal passion, giving as good as she got. He'd never been with anyone who matched him so perfectly, and it wasn't just because the fates had decreed she was his mate. She touched more than his wolf, but the man as well.

All too quickly, their passion began to spiral out of

control. Before he reached the point of no return, he gathered her into his arms and sat up, bringing her with him to sit in his lap. She needed no prompting to ride him, bouncing on his lap while clutching his shoulders. The intimate position, the grind of her body against his, sent them both to the edge—and over.

Micah couldn't hold back. His balls drew up and his release exploded, shooting his seed deep inside her. Primal instinct took over, his fangs bursting forth. When Jacee tilted her head to the side in silent invitation, he was lost.

The instant he sank his fangs into the soft flesh at the curve of her neck and shoulder, it was as though a bomb had been detonated in the center of him. As Jacee cried out, pleasure exploded in golden light, then saturated his every cell in a brilliant, sparkling shower that was so pure it almost hurt. Then the golden dust came together, solidifying into a thread that sought his mate. Searched.

"Bite me," he said hoarsely, tilting his head.

She didn't hesitate. When she sank her fangs home, a second quake rocked them both. Whimpering, she held the bite for a few seconds as their orgasms shook them again. At that moment, his thread reached out again and found hers, and they melded together, snapped into place. An impenetrable bond that would not be broken now, except by death.

"Oh, my God." He nuzzled her hair, trying to calm his racing heart.

"Right?"

"That was incredible."

Carefully he eased them apart, slipping out of her, then pulled her down with him and held her close.

"We're really Bondmates now." Jacee snuggled into his side with a contented sigh.

"Yeah. But you know what? Even if I'd been human, my heart would've known you anywhere."

"That's just about the most wonderful thing anyone's ever said to me." A telltale sniffle reached his ears.

"You'd better get used to it. I plan to say plenty more."

They remained entwined for a while, in complete contentment. Listening to the sounds of the wind in the trees from outside, birds, the occasional car, his mind drifted. He wondered how his life might've been different if he'd stayed home like his mother had wanted. If he'd never left LA, had found a decent job there, maybe followed Rowan into law enforcement. How his mother would've been spared what was to come. But he was so happy now, he wouldn't change a thing, so what did that make him? As always, a lump of guilt knotted in his throat.

"Hey," Jacee said softly. Moving, she propped herself up to peer down at him. "What's with the guilt I'm picking up from you, mate?"

"Uh-oh. You can read my mind now?" Micah eyed her with a half-smile.

"I don't think it works that way literally. But we should be able to speak telepathically now, and I believe we can sense each other's feelings, too. Yours got serious just now, sort of guilty. What gives?"

"My mother," he said quietly. "She died thinking I'd been killed overseas. I was just wondering how my life would've been different if I'd stayed at home in Los Angeles like she wanted, maybe joined the LAPD like my sister. She wouldn't have had to live through that. But then I wouldn't have found the other half of my soul. I would've been missing something all my life and never been able to put my finger on what."

"I see." Her expression was understanding. "It's natural for us to question the choices we've made, though. What we could have done differently. I'm a firm believer now that life turns out the way it's supposed to, but I didn't always buy that."

"Me, either. But I'm coming around. I joined the SEALs, and there's no changing what happened after that. And then it was just easier in some ways to let Mom believe I was dead, and have closure, than to face what I'd become. Better for her and Rowan."

"The thing is, I don't think your mom ever really gave up, not if her spirit's visit to you in the hospital was any indication. Your sister certainly never bought that you were dead, from what I gather."

"No. She never gave up searching for me, and that led her here, to Wyoming."

"How did she find you?"

"She has a friend who's an FBI agent, and he has contacts. Someone pried open the lid on our compound and let him tip her off. If Nick knows who's responsible for spilling the information, he hasn't told us."

"That kind of leak could be dangerous."

"And then some. Can you imagine what would happen if the world found out paranormal creatures are real? I mean, there are people who believe in the paranormal, like spirits and demons and stuff, claim to know it exists. But the general population has no clue what's actually lurking in the dark."

Jacee shuddered. "It would be mass chaos. The higher-ups in the government know, but they'd deny it. I'm picturing blanket persecution and another civil rights movement the likes of which we've never seen."

"Jesus, let's hope it never comes to all of that."

"Yes, let's." She paused, studying him, her chin resting on his chest. He enjoyed her being draped on top of him like a blanket. "So how did you become a wolf shifter? If it's too painful to talk about, I understand."

"No, sweetheart, it's fine," he reassured her, brushing a lock of dark hair from her face. "There's nothing I can't tell you. As horrible as that day was, I was lucky. Many of our buddies didn't make it out of there alive. . . ."

Afghanistan, seven years ago . . .

"Jesus Christ, I'm rank," Raven bitched, scratching at his crotch. "When I finally get to change this underwear, it'll probably walk off."

Micah grinned at his friend's grumpiness. For a tough SEAL, nobody loved being clean more than Raven DeLuca. How he'd survived Hell Week was anybody's guess. "With assistance from the crabs you caught from that woman in the last village."

"Shut up, needledick. She did *not* give me crabs."

Micah laughed, and Aric and a few of the guys chuckled along with him. They kept walking, and Micah continued the conversation. Nobody was paying any attention to them, everyone else lost in his own thoughts.

"Hey, Raven?"

"Yeah?"

"You ever think of settling down with one woman?"

His friend shot him an amused stare. "What the hell for?"

"Right. Unrepentant man whore. Totally forgot, my bad."

"What's wrong with that?" Raven seemed genuinely puzzled.

"Nothing." Micah just got lonely sometimes. Like maybe there was something more out here in the world that he hadn't discovered yet. He'd thought perhaps joining the military would help him find whatever he was looking for, but so far he'd come up empty. He wasn't about to say that to Raven, who'd probably make a joke out of his confession.

Instead he changed the subject. "Do you ever think maybe there's something more out there?"

"Like what?"

"You know, *stuff*. Out there, in the universe," Micah said, waving an arm at the sky in general. "UFOs, ghosts, shit like that."

His friend shot him a bemused look. "You're a weirdo—you know that?"

"So, you're a nonbeliever?"

They walked a few paces before Raven answered, "Dunno. Ever since ancient times, people have written about paranormal sightings, contact, what have you. So who's to say? Makes for some interesting TV when there's nothing else on the History Channel, anyways."

Micah smiled, shaking his head. Raven was one of the most straightforward guys he knew, not prone to speculating about such things. That was a typical answer from him. "True."

"What do you think?" his friend asked, curious.

"I say, *we are not alone*," he mimicked in his best *Twilight Zone* voice.

"Well, *you'll* never be alone. You've got those little voices in your head to keep you company." His friend smirked and walked ahead.

At least Micah had succeeded in getting Raven's mind off his hot, itchy underwear. They were all in the same boat, and nobody wanted to know. The men continued through the thick undergrowth, using the barrels of their weapons to push aside limbs and foliage. Damned if he would complain, but Raven was right. It was so fucking hot, they could literally fry an egg on the hood of one of the trucks if they had to.

If they had an egg. Or anything at all resembling fresh food and not something freeze-dried from an MRE.

"Hold up," Jax whispered, coming to a halt. Tensing, he studied the mountain forest around them, frowning. Somewhere hidden in the greenery, a footstep crunched to their left. Another to their right. And one from behind.

Micah went cold and looked at Raven. "Don't like this," he whispered, his voice barely audible. "This area is supposed to be clear. We've got miles to go before we reach our target."

Just then the forest went silent as a tomb. Never, ever a good sign. Micah's eyes met Raven's, then Aric's. The men tensed, ready for anything. Or so they thought.

Thud, thud, thud.

The ground trembled and the leaves shook. When a deep-throated roar split the air, Micah's heart almost stopped. Beside him Aric jumped, pointing the muzzle of his M16 into the trees, a bead of sweat dripping off his nose.

"Shit," Micah whispered. "What the fuck is that?"

Staring in horrified shock, he knew that if there were more of this creature, they might not live to tell anyone what they'd encountered. The thing that broke through the foliage to their left stood erect on two legs and was more than seven feet tall. Covered with a thick mat of grayish brown fur, it had a long torso, two arms, muscular shoulders, and a head sporting two upright ears and a long, snarling muzzle full of sharp teeth.

"A fucking werewolf?" Micah whispered. Nobody heard him.

Because right at that moment, their buddy Jones

started screaming, pumping bullets into the beast's chest. And everything went completely FUBAR—Fucked Up Beyond All Recognition.

The creature staggered backward and then rallied quickly, rushing Jones. With a swipe of a paw the size of a dinner plate, the big bastard ripped out Jones's throat, then tossed him aside like a twig.

Then it turned and pounced on Raven, biting into the vee of his neck and shoulder as the man screamed. Micah started to rush toward his friend, but more of the beasts emerged from the forest, and he was forced to turn and open fire. Again, the bullets seemed to have little to no effect at all. In fact, it appeared the creatures' wounds were healing before his eyes almost as fast as they were shot full of holes.

"Oh, my God," he moaned, spinning around, eyes wild. Guns weren't going to do the trick. Quickly, he threw down his M16 and slid the long knife from its sheath on his calf.

Hand-to-hand combat with a werewolf. Who was almost eight feet tall and could heal instantly.

This was not going to go well.

Nearby, Aric dropped into a crouch and palmed a grenade as their friends fell all around them after waging a battle they couldn't win. The one who'd killed Jones shook Raven like a rag doll, released him, and ran toward Aric.

Micah's friend let the grenade fly. It landed at the target's feet and exploded, sending the damn thing to hell. But it wasn't enough. Not nearly.

Micah faced his own battle, squaring off with one of the big bastards. Then it grinned, peeling back blackened lips to reveal long, uneven yellow teeth, and he fought down a shiver. *Okay. Hand-to-hand combat. He's got a throat and a heart, so go for those. You can do this.*

As if reading Micah's thoughts, the creature roared and rushed him. Ducking low, Micah made his charge, evading the lethal sweep of the sharp claws as they sailed over his head. The wolf-man grunted as Micah hit its torso, and let out a screech of rage when he plunged the blade into its chest and thrust upward. Quickly, he yanked out the knife as they tumbled to the ground together; then he leapt on the beast's chest. Its eyes were wide with very human knowledge of his intent in the split second it took Micah to slit the monster's throat.

Breathing hard, Micah watched the light fade from the werewolf's gaze and knew that moment of humanity he'd glimpsed would haunt him for a long time. What *were* they? But there was no more time to think about it.

Another one jumped on him from the side with a roar, knocking him off its fallen companion. Off balance, Micah landed on the arm holding the knife and desperately tried to roll, change positions. Get the knife free, his body in fighting position. But a strong set of jaws clamped down on one thigh, and he screamed, twisting. Agony tore through muscle and bone, and he beat on the creature's head to no avail.

The beast released him, but only to pounce again, going for Micah's throat. Instead, Micah shoved his forearm into the wolf's jaws, getting it snapped like a twig for his trouble. A hoarse cry escaped his lips, and the creature struck out once more, clamping down on his shoulder, fangs sinking deep and shaking him like a dog with a bone. With the last of his strength, Micah plunged the blade into the creature's neck.

Howling, it staggered backward and fell, clutching at its wound. Glaring at Micah, it started toward him, clearly intending to finish him, but didn't make it. The wolf fell facedown and didn't move, blood seeping out onto the ground.

Panting, Micah lifted his head, ignoring the pain enveloping him; then he wished he hadn't. His shoulder and chest were a mangled mess, as was his right leg, the bloodied femur sticking through his cammo pants. His broken arm felt like it was hanging by a thread inside his jacket.

Dying. He was dying, and he couldn't help his buddies. The knowledge was more agonizing than his wounds.

Through a red haze, he saw Jax fall, then Ryon, Nix, and so many others. All of them, one by one. Except Aric, who was still putting up a good fight.

Unsheathing his knife, Aric spun to face the beast coming up on his flank. "Come on, bitch. Let's dance."

"Get him," Micah whispered through bloodied lips. But his friend couldn't hear.

Aric rushed in and leapt, burying the blade to the handle in the creature's throat. As it fell, Aric whirled and thrust out a hand, and as Micah watched in amazement, a column of flame shot out from Aric's palm and engulfed the wolf-man. Screeching, the beast dropped to the ground, writhing as it burned.

"Take that, cocksucker!"

Micah blinked. *What the ever-loving fuck?*

Then, moving slowly, Aric palmed another grenade. "Come on, you ugly fucker. Come to Papa."

The creature ran at Aric and took him to the ground, and he pulled the grenade's pin. When the wolf stuck its nose in Aric's face, its mouth open, his friend rammed his fist down the beast's throat, pushing his arm as far as it would go. Immediately, the thing gagged and jerked back reflexively, clawing at his shoulder and arm to dislodge him. Aric scrambled backward, moving fast.

The grenade detonated, spraying fur, blood, and entrails everywhere. *God.* Aric lay still, and Micah prayed the man wasn't dead.

It came to him then that the sounds of battle had

ceased after the grenade. Now there were only the moans of the wounded and dying. He tried again to move, but his limbs felt as though they were encased in cement. His lungs felt wet, and he knew he was drowning in his own blood. It was just a matter of time.

"Mom," he choked. Tears rolled down his temples, into his hair. "I'm sorry. So sorry."

His mother hadn't wanted him to join the military. Now she'd mourn her only son. And it was all his fault.

"Hey," a voice said from above him. A palm rested on his hair. "Easy does it."

Blinking, Micah tried to focus. "Who?"

"It's me, Zan. I'm a Healer, and I'm going to help you, okay? Just stay calm."

"Say what now?" Narrowing his eyes, Micah peered up at his friend. Zan's dark hair and serious but gentle blue eyes became clear.

"I'm a Healer," Zan repeated, lips quirking some. But there was sadness in the small smile, and no little pain. "Surprise, huh? We all have our secrets."

"Who's going to heal you?" Zan's shoulder had been plenty mangled by those bastards.

"Don't worry about that right now. Let's take care of *you*."

A Healer? The guy must be out of his mind with grief and shock. It was understandable. With his good hand, Micah gripped his friend's arm. "Zan. Tell my mom and my sister I love them," he whispered. "Please."

"Shh," Zan soothed, placing a hand on Micah's mangled chest. His blue eyes were filled with pain. "Just hang on. You'll make it, trust me. You'll see your mom and sister again. I promise."

"Tell them."

"I promise, but it won't be necessary. Tell them yourself."

A brilliant blue light enveloped Micah, and warmth seeped through his battered body, to every limb. Pain and shock took their toll and finally carried him away.

Zan had been only half right that horrible day. Micah had survived.

But he never saw his mother again.

Micah finished his story and his heart clenched to see tears in his mate's pretty eyes. "Hey, I didn't mean to make you sad," he said softly, kissing her lips. "It's all in the past, no changing what happened."

"I know. I just can't imagine how terrible that day was, all those lives lost." She cupped the scarred side of his face. "It's a miracle your group of friends survived."

He gave a bitter laugh. "Not so miraculous, baby. We found out not long ago that the whole encounter was set up by our own government—or a couple of warped individuals, anyway. Our group—Jax, Ryon, Nix, Zan, Aric, Raven, and me—we were put in the path of the werewolves on purpose. They knew we had Psy gifts and were aiming to turn us—the ones strong enough to survive."

Jacee gasped. "God, that's awful!"

"Yeah. No telling how many of our buddies who were killed possessed gifts, too. All those lives, wasted because of greed. A couple of top government officials were under Malik's control, and the Unseelie made sure the rest happened like he wanted afterward."

"The testing in the labs to create super soldiers?"

"Right."

They lay quietly together, and he could tell she was waiting for him to say more. What more was there to say? He didn't want that period in his life to touch her any more than it already had.

I can feel you fretting. You can tell me anything, she whispered in his mind.

Sitting up slightly, he gaped at her. "Whoa. Was that *you*?"

Yep, that's me! Mates really can speak telepathically. She beamed down at him.

"I know the other mates can do it, but— Wow. That's so cool."

"Try it."

Um, hi? He felt kind of stupid, unsure it had even worked. Until she giggled and hugged him hard.

That's great! Want to go for a run? We can try it out some more in our animal forms.

Sure. We can try other things in our animal forms, too. He waggled his brows suggestively.

She laughed. "I don't know about that. Sort of kinky, don't you think?"

"Why? It would still be us. Just furry." He paused, regarding her in amusement. "You're a natural-born shifter. You've never done it, well, au naturel?"

She shrugged. "Most of my Pack did, and it was considered no big deal. I was just never with anyone who suggested it."

"Hmm."

"What?"

"Nothing."

"Are you going to pout?"

"I'm not pouting. You haven't said no yet."

Shaking her head, she slid off him and extended her hand to pull him up. "Come on. We have to get dressed so we can drive to your Pack lands for our run. It'll be safer there."

"Agreed."

Though he wasn't keen on giving up their warm nest with Jacee in his arms, a run with her did sound fun. So he forced his lazy butt out of bed and got dressed, more than a little regretful that his mate was covering up her gorgeous skin with clothing. It would soon be removed again, however, so he cheered right up.

In minutes, the two were racing down the road in his coupe, leaving their troubles behind if only for a while. He didn't want anything to ruin this afternoon, especially following their mating. Today should be a day of joy, not worry over the shadows that still loomed overhead.

Still, for a few moments, the dark craving for myst stole through him, beckoning to him to get lost in its oblivion. The drug might have been gone from his system but not the addiction, and he was terrified it would never abate.

Not now, he told himself. *Worry about it later.*

Taking his hand, Jacee studied him in concern. "Worry about what?"

Crap. "Did I think that out loud?"

"Um, yeah. That was totally unguarded. Not that I want you hiding your problems from me," she hurried to add. "Like I said before, you can tell me anything."

"I'm not hiding anything, baby," he assured her. Then he sighed. "It's that damn shit I was on. I refuse to put any more of it in my body, but that hasn't stopped the craving. It just sucks, that's all."

"Oh, honey. Can't Mac give you something for the cravings, temporarily? That's what they do with humans when they need it."

"I don't know if it would work. And honestly, I don't know if I want to trade one bad drug for another."

"Okay." But she didn't sound convinced. "I'll support you, whatever you want or need."

"Thanks. That means more than you know."

In minutes, he was turning down the road to the compound and accessing the gate. Once they were under way again, he took them in a different direction from before to take their run. An idea began to form, and he shoved all unpleasant thoughts from his mind. Excitement began to grow as he finally parked on the shoulder and shut off the ignition.

"Ready?" he asked.

"When you are." They got out and walked a ways into the woods before she asked, "How far are we from the compound right now?"

"Not far. Only about three-fourths of a mile, that way." He pointed past where he'd left the car.

As they'd done before, they hiked into the brush and undressed, leaving their clothing folded neatly on a fallen log. Micah took a few moments to leer at his naked woman, then shifted effortlessly into his wolf, dropping to all fours. Soon his little coyote was beside him, as eager as he was to get going.

He started them off, taking the lead. *I've got a place I want to show you.*

Okay. Where?

You'll see. It's not far from here, maybe another half a mile.

I can sense your excitement.

Oh, yeah? Just wait. If he had been in human form, he wouldn't have been able to hide his smile.

Soon, he came to a break in the trees. The clearing was dappled in late-afternoon sunlight, surrounded by majestic trees and bordered at the far side by a pretty stream. Slowing to a walk, he crossed to the center of the meadow and sat on his haunches. Beside him, she nuzzled his face, gave him a lick, then did the same, sitting next to him.

What do you think of this place? he inquired.

It's beautiful. But then, most areas around here are.

True. He paused. *Could you see us making a life here?*

At that, she changed back to human form in an instant and sat gaping at him. "You mean, *here*? On this spot?"

Shifting back as well, he smiled, taking one of her hands in his. "Yes. What do you think?"

"What about the first place where we ran that night?"

"It's gorgeous there, too, but this area is closer to the compound. I think Nick would be more likely to approve us building a home here. He has to think of the team, of course, and how fast we can come together if we get a call."

She thought about that, appearing to grow excited as well. "And since it's only about a mile and a half away from the compound, you can be there in less than five minutes."

"Yep."

"What if he gives his okay and it causes the other mated couples to want their own private residences, too? He might decide that's too many of the Pack off the main grounds." A bit of worry clouded her optimism.

"I thought of that, but I honestly don't think it's going to be a problem. Most of them truly like living there. I do, too. It's just . . . I don't know. Ever since I was rescued and brought back here, I've felt smothered. I have a deep-seated need for space, or I think I'll go nuts, and I know Nick gets that."

Happiness and hope entered her eyes again, and she smiled. "Then I think we should ask him and see what he says."

"Really?" He clutched her hand tight and pulled her into his lap.

"Definitely." She wound her arms around his neck, pressed a lingering kiss to his lips. "Though if we're going to live out here, we need to get an SUV of some kind or that Mercedes of yours is going to take a beating."

"Whatever you say."

"You know what I've noticed?"

"No," he said. "What?"

"You're not self-conscious when you smile anymore."

He felt his face heat some. "That's because you make me feel good from the inside out. I told you, when I feel ugly it's not so much about my scars. It's how I got them. How corroded those bastards made me feel, down in my soul."

"I know, honey," she said softly. "But that's changing. You're healing."

"I am, mostly thanks to you."

"I'm so sorry they hurt you. I wish I could kill them all for what they did to you and the other victims."

"My vicious coyote," he teased, trying to lighten the mood again.

"I'm serious."

"I know."

"How did they—"

"No," he interrupted, knowing what she was going to ask. "There's no need for you to hear all the gory details. They liked to hurt me, and they made me hurt others for their project. I was never forced to harm anyone sexually, but I wasn't given that same consideration where the guards were concerned. That's all I'm ever going to say on *that* matter because it's in the past."

"Is it?" She searched his gaze.

"Yes."

He meant it. How he had been abused had never been as important to him as having been made to put others through suffering. *That* was the real root of his issues. She must've felt his honesty, because she let the subject drop. Instead, she cupped his face and kissed him fiercely, straddling him and wriggling on his lap. His cock responded with enthusiasm, hardening to press into the cleft of her butt cheeks. Her movements caused shivers of excitement in his groin and the base of his spine, spreading to every cell.

Palming her breasts, he nibbled her neck, inhaling her heady scent. Inside, his wolf growled but Micah kept a tight hold on him. Barely. Both man and beast desperately wanted her wrapped around his cock. The latter was demanding things his way and unhappy about being blocked.

Her arousal sweetened the air. Through their bond, he felt her coyote respond to her mate. They were both clawing to be set free, but their human sides retained control. They ate at each other's mouths hungrily as she guided his cock to her opening, then lowered herself onto his length. He hissed in pleasure when she began to ride him, bucking against him, moving faster until he was nearly mindless.

Their bodies slapped together fiercely, their moans becoming part of the song of the forest. They belonged here, among the trees, birds, and other creatures, simply another mated pair doing what came naturally, but much more.

They were bonding their hearts as well.

He could feel it and wondered whether she could, too.

Yes.

His thoughts were so transparent. But her answer touched someplace deep inside him, a barren landscape that had been lonely for far too long. She brought color and light into his dark gray world and awakened him. Gave him hope.

Their pace quickened until they couldn't hold back any longer. Going over the edge, they shattered together, holding tightly to each other until they were spent and breathing hard. After they recovered some, he gently lowered them to the soft ground and gathered her close while they let the afternoon wane.

And later, if he finally convinced her coyote to let his wolf have his way as well?

There was nobody but the birds and squirrels to bear witness.

Nine

The two weeks following their mating were, without a doubt, the happiest time of Jacee's life.

The one blight on her sunshine was having no family to share it with. Staring out the window at the early morning, hands wrapped around a mug of hot coffee, a shaft of longing pierced her at the thought of being able to sit with her mother and sister, chatting about Micah, mating, falling in love. Boys in general. Maybe her sister would have found someone special by now, too.

They used to tell each other everything. Fight like cats and dogs, then make up and whisper long into the night, well after their parents had ordered them to go to sleep. They'd told ghost stories, gossiped about the other girls and boys in the pack, talked about their dreams for the future. There was nothing quite like the bond with a sister.

All of that wiped out by one vicious act. By misplaced hatred and cruelty.

"What did they do to you, sis? Did you even get a burial?"

No sense in going down that road, again. It only led to more heartbreak. Quickly, she busied herself in the kitchen, getting out some eggs and putting on a package of bacon to fry. Micah could eat a lot, and he'd be hungry after last night's activities. She smiled a little at the memories, each day and night better than the last. The man made love as if he planned on making up for every lonely second from before they'd met.

That was great by her, since she was doing the same.

A few minutes later, Micah strolled in sleepily, scratching his bare chest. "Christ, what smells so damn good in here? Bacon? You're a goddess!"

"I know." She giggled as he wrapped her in a hug from behind and nuzzled her neck. "Careful, don't get popped with hot grease."

"It would be worth it just to stay right here forever." He ground his half-hard cock into the small of her back, cuddling for a few. He didn't try to take things further, apparently enjoying the snuggle. "Want me to man the eggs?"

"Sure, if you don't mind." Her mate had proven himself to be handy in the kitchen.

"I've got this. I make a mean egg. You like scrambled or fried?"

"Either way."

Stepping away, he took over. He went to the fridge, rummaged around, and came out with some onions, green and red peppers, and cheese. "Any objections?"

"Are you scrambling eggs or creating a masterpiece?" she teased.

"Both."

Grinning, Micah set to work chopping the veggies while melting butter in the skillet she already had out. Once they were diced, he tossed the onions and peppers in the butter and began to sauté them, and the delicious aroma made her stomach rumble. After those were tender, he added several eggs and folded them in to the mix.

"Oh, that looks and smells wonderful," Jacee said, sniffing.

"It's easy. Why have plain eggs when they taste so good spruced up a bit?" He shrugged but she could tell he was pleased by the compliment.

They worked companionably. Before she knew it, they had a feast that could feed perhaps three or four shifters instead of two. They loaded the table with the eggs, bacon, and toast, and sat down to enjoy. Micah shoveled his food with enthusiasm, and the mound disappeared so fast one thing was certain—she would have to buy food in bulk to keep the man full.

"What?" he asked, finally setting down his fork.

"I don't think I've ever seen someone enjoy their meals quite as much as you have these past couple of weeks. It's such a positive change from before."

Before, when he'd been sick. She was so damn lucky to still have him around and healthy.

His cheeks flushed some. "I'd forgotten what it was like to feel good and be hungry. Everything tastes so awesome, I'm going to be a fat wolf with a gut before you know it."

She laughed. "No, you're not. Shifter metabolism is way too high for that. But I'd love you even if you were."

"I believe you." He looked at her sort of funny and went still. Then he blinked slowly. "You'd still love me? You . . . *love* me?"

Shoot, that had slipped out way sooner than she'd meant for it to. Scooting her chair close, she wound her arms around his neck. Kissed his lips. Then she looked into his stunned face and said, "I'm falling hard for you. It can't be that big of a surprise."

"No, it's just . . ." Just as her heart was starting to sink, he beamed at her. "I'm falling for you, too, my pretty coyote. God knows what you see in me, but for my sake, I'm glad you're blind as a bat."

"Ha, you're so funny." She kissed him again, thoroughly, tracing the scars on his cheek with her fingers. "Want me to show you just how well I really see?"

"Yes," he breathed.

She did exactly that, which meant a long, leisurely lovemaking session in bed. First, she kissed and caressed the length of his body from his face to his chest, down his stomach, then skipped his groin to knead his calves and love each foot. Who knew the feet could be an erogenous zone? At least they were for Micah.

Then, once she had him writhing, she took pity and sucked his cock, licking and stroking until he nearly came before even getting inside her. But he was having none of that, and gently disengaged, laid her back on the pillows, and slid inside her welcoming heat as though he'd been doing it for years.

They found their release together, clinging, and then drifted for a while, ignoring the rest of the world. Eventually, however, moving couldn't be put off any longer.

"Shower?" She nuzzled his chest.

His arms tightened around her. "Sounds great. Would be even more fun if I didn't have to go anywhere."

"Duty calls." It wasn't a question.

Their two weeks were nearly at an end, along with the lazy idyll they'd enjoyed. He had to get back to the compound and the Pack, and in truth she knew a big part of him was eager to go. His brothers had been on a couple of missions without Micah, and she'd seen how staying behind had almost killed him. In truth, she had to get back to work, too, though she was much less eager.

"I don't want to leave you," he said ruefully. "This time together, lazing around with you and making love, has been heaven."

"But you're not a lazy kind of guy. It's okay. I get it," she reassured him, "I understand your need to get back to work."

He shook his head, then kissed her lips. "I'm a lucky man, in so many ways."

"But?" She'd heard a strange note in his voice.

"Nothing. Except I've still got to find out who's got a grudge against me. It's been way too quiet these past two weeks—"

At that precise moment, his cell phone started buzzing on the nightstand. Rolling to his side, he picked it up, stared at the display, and groaned. "It's Nick. I *knew* better than to say that out loud."

As he answered the call, Jacee got up and walked to the bathroom to start the shower and give him a little privacy. The noise of the water drowned his words, but it couldn't hide the urgency and anxiety behind them. That ramped up her own worry, and she fretted until he finally joined her, giving her a quick hug.

"Is everything all right?"

"Not really." He stepped back and gave a heavy sigh. "Two campers were attacked last night, a father and his nineteen-year-old son. The father is dead, the son barely hanging on."

"Oh, no." Her heart went out to them. "Do they have a suspect?"

"No. Like the woman from a couple of weeks ago, they were attacked by something or someone with either sharp claws or a weapon like a knife. Nick said the sheriff is betting on the first, though, because they were both really messed up."

"That's terrible." She shook her head. "Nick hasn't seen the victims?"

"No. The Pack is on the way to the scene, and I'm supposed to meet them there. Jax is going to try to get a reading off the man's body while it's fresh. With the previous victim he didn't get the chance, so hopefully we'll learn something."

Jacee shivered. "I don't envy Jax. Seeing grisly past events is one talent I'm glad I don't possess."

"Me, too. Though it's not all bad, the stuff he sees. It's just unfortunate for him that when something terrible has happened is when we need his help to figure out who's done it and why."

She couldn't imagine being burdened with visions of the past *or* future, as Nick was. Sometimes ignorance really was bliss.

They stepped into the shower together, and though they managed some soapy fun and a few laughs, Micah was a bit pressed for time. She knew he hated that, knew he would rather have stayed and played, but it couldn't be helped. Once they were out of the shower, they dried off and dressed quickly, which was a shame. But she told herself he'd be home soon, back in her arms.

"I'll be back as soon as I can," he said, pulling her close. Then he kissed her thoroughly, leaving her senses reeling, drenched in his amazing scent.

"Hurry home."

"I will." He shot her a lopsided grin and was out the door, heading down the sidewalk to his motorcycle.

As it started up and roared away, she couldn't help the chill that settled around her heart. Their time together had been too peaceful. Too perfect. And in her life, that typically meant the other shoe was getting ready to drop on her head.

Shaking off the dread, she went to search for something clean to wear to work.

Jacee's little house got smaller and smaller in the distance, and Micah hated every second of leaving. Through sheer force of will, he focused his mind on the task ahead.

And struggled to ignore the ever-present craving in his veins. The need for the numbing effects of myst that had been suppressed by the calming effect of his mate came creeping back in like a thief to steal away his carefully constructed peace. His sanity.

His mate had no idea he was barely holding it together. He'd been so careful to shield his emotions—the fear and the disappointment that he hadn't yet defeated this thing—because he didn't want her to worry. Nor did she have any idea about the bottle of pills stashed in the leather saddlebag on his bike, the ones he was supposed to have thrown out. They had enough hanging over their heads right now. She didn't need one more thing to stress over.

Winding his way down the roads through national-park land, he was struck by how close this murder scene was to their compound. Like the other. Another taunt? Something else was niggling at the back of his mind, and by the time he rolled up and parked next to the sheriff's vehicles and Pack SUVs, he'd managed to put his finger on what it was.

Shutting off the ignition, he set off toward the activity taking place just out of sight among the shelter of the trees. As he approached, he spotted Nick, Jax, and John right away. They were talking with Sheriff Deveraux, and Micah's gut tightened at the sight of the man. Jesse wasn't a bad guy. No, he was a good lawman but gruff. Short on friendliness.

Who cared, though, as long as he got the job done and was on the Pack's side?

"Sheriff," Micah said in greeting, walking into their circle. Jesse nodded, face grim. Then Micah looked at his team, and they didn't appear any happier. Jax in particular eyed him warily, and guilt speared Micah's chest. He still hadn't cleared the air with Jax after going berserk on the man, and he couldn't blame him for thinking Micah was a serious head case.

Jesse nodded, held out his hand. "Chase." They shook, and the sheriff got down to business. "Now that you're here, we can show you the scene, get your take on what's going on, and wrap things up here."

Dread slid over Micah. "You were waiting on me, in particular?"

"Afraid so."

"Okay, that's downright alarming." He glanced around at the serious faces.

"It should be."

"Am I in trouble?"

"Should you be?"

Typical damn cop answer. "Not that I'm aware of. I don't know anything about what happened to these poor men out here any more than the woman from the other day."

Jesse ran a hand through his hair. "Well, that's where someone begs to differ. A lot of times we know more than we realize, deep down."

Dig deeper. The person after him was someone from his not-so-distant past. Wasn't that his mother's warning?

Taking a deep breath, he said, "All right. Show me what you've got."

The sheriff started off, and Micah followed, catching some shared glances between his teammates. Apparently they'd already seen whatever awaited him, but didn't care to enlighten him before they got there. He tried not to let that bother him, but it was a fight.

As they approached the area, Micah could see a couple of deputies standing around. The pair looked up at the group's approach and moved off to the side. At first, all Micah saw was . . . gore. And lots of it.

As a SEAL, he'd seen bodies torn apart by bombs or gunfire. Such was the way of war, horrible though it might be. So the dead man before him on the ground was nothing he hadn't seen before—except his death was completely out of place. He was dressed for camping in jeans, a flannel shirt, and well-worn boots. He'd been a fairly fit man for his age, which Micah guessed to be in his forties.

No, the man shouldn't have been dead on the forest floor, glazed eyes wide and horrified, mere feet from the cheerful remnants of his campfire and the hot dog picnic he'd obviously shared with his son, who was now fighting for his life.

The man had been slashed and torn to pieces, with chunks of flesh missing from his limbs and torso. From his chest. Wide swaths of flesh and muscle simply cut away cleanly, but by something . . .

Micah squatted and peered at the body. "A knife didn't do this. The furrows are too large."

"No," Nick spoke up. "You're right. The wounds weren't caused by a knife."

"Animal," Micah guessed, looking up. He met Jax's eyes. "Or a paranormal creature. Did you do a reading?"

"Right before you got here. The man didn't see what attacked them because it came from behind him—and from above."

That gave Micah pause. "Above?"

"Yeah. The weapons were big claws, like talons."

Standing, Micah let that sink in. "So, what type of creature are we talking about here? A demon? A vampire? They can shift into another form."

"The lack of feeding suggests it's not a vampire," Nick said. "Besides, I don't know a rogue who'd pass up a good meal."

There was a morbid thought. "True. A large bird, then? A dragon shifter? Hell, do we even have those for real? Or something else."

Nick stared at the unfortunate man. "I wish I knew. I'm getting nothing right now."

"I still don't get what this attack has to do with me."

"This." From his inside jacket pocket, Jesse retrieved a plastic Baggie. Inside the Baggie was a small square of cream-colored paper. Without removing the note, he handed the Baggie over to Micah, who read the writing through the clear plastic easily enough.

SS-509: I am what YOU made me. They may have created me, but you trained me. This blood is on your hands.

"Oh, my God." Micah thrust the bag into Jesse's hands and leaned against a tree, panting for breath. He was going to be sick.

The sheriff's voice was quiet. "Nick said you could shed some light on the meaning."

It took Micah a long moment to find his voice. He hadn't wanted to talk about this again, ever. Especially not to anyone besides his Pack brothers.

"What a fucking nightmare." Micah closed his eyes. There were shuffling sounds, but the others gave him time. Finally, he opened his eyes again and faced the music. "I'm SS-509. Lab subject 509 in the Super Soldier project, to be turned into a weapon of destruction answerable to a new, corrupt government—had things gone the way Malik and Bowman intended."

"Jesus Christ," Jesse muttered. "I don't suppose anyone wants to start at the beginning of *that* story?"

Nick gave a humorless laugh. "Over a few beers sometime."

"What this means is, the killer blames me for what happened when we were prisoners," Micah explained, staring down at the poor, hapless victim. Guilt had bile rising in his throat. "He's someone I tortured into madness on Bowman's orders. Now he's burning for revenge, and is crazy as hell. This is my fucking fault."

"No," Jax said firmly, stepping up to him. "It's not. Whatever you did, you didn't have a choice. Besides, *you* were tortured within an inch of your life, same as the others, and you didn't turn into a killer. This isn't on you. Whoever is doing this, he snapped."

"He blames *me*. In his mind, I'm responsible."

"Which means he's twisted and wrong." Jax clamped a hand on Micah's shoulder. "He's tipped his hand, bro. He's narrowed down our search considerably, and we'll ID him now. It's only a matter of time."

"But how many people will have to die before we find him?"

That, they didn't have an answer for.

"The note isn't the only warning," Micah told them. "The proximity of the murders to the compound is another one, I think. Both killings took place just outside the perimeter that Kalen has warded against intruders."

"I don't believe that's a coincidence, either," Nick agreed. "He's leaving them on your doorstep, so to speak."

"The sick fuck." Micah turned to Jesse. "Is anyone watching the kid who survived?"

The sheriff nodded. "I've got a deputy on his hospital door. The doctor will give us the okay to interview him once he's stable and awake."

"I sent Zan ahead to sneak in and speed along his healing. And he needs one of my Pack men to guard him," Nick insisted. "No offense, Jesse, but your deputies are human. They're not prepared to fight a crazed shifter who has God knows what abnormalities making him even more dangerous than he should be."

The man sighed, looking annoyed. But he relented. "Shit. Fine. I'll let my man know to expect a replacement from one of your team."

"Thanks. I think that's the safest thing." Nick paused. "My gut says our insane shifter won't come after the kid, that he's already moved on, but we can't be too careful."

Micah said, "We need to find out what he remembers of the shifter, see if we can get a description. Then have Kalen wipe his memory and replace it with a bear attack or something."

The others agreed. If humans at large were to learn about the paranormal world— Well, that didn't bear thinking about. The Pack had had some near-misses in recent months where the public was concerned.

"I'll stand watch on the kid's door," John volunteered.

"Good." Nick approved. "In the meantime, Micah and I will go over the list of all the shifters rescued from the facility where he and Aric were found. Hopefully we'll get a lead."

"Were all of those victims taken to Sanctuary?" Jax asked him.

"Initially, yes. Some have been released, and some are still being treated. We have records on all of them to keep track, even the ones who've left us to return to their families and such. They'll be monitored for stability for some years to come."

Micah frowned. "Well, apparently someone has slipped the leash, so to speak."

"It seems so. Let's go see if we can have any luck with that list." Nick turned to Jesse. "Unless you need us here any longer?"

"Nope. In fact, if your whole bunch packed your bags and moved out of the state, that would suit me just fine."

Nick smirked. "Take that up with the U.S. Government, my friend."

"Might as well shit into the wind."

"Nice image."

"Truth."

Jesus. Maybe those two were long-lost brothers and didn't know it. Wouldn't that be a kick in the nuts?

The group broke up, and Micah headed back to his bike without looking at the man's torn body again. He was already craving oblivion, what with the picture of the poor bastard burned into his brain.

Straddling his Harley, he sat for a few minutes and watched as the sheriff and his deputies finished and the medical examiner arrived to remove the body. He wondered whether the ME was fully in the loop, like Jesse, or if the man found himself speculating on just what really went on in the Shoshone when the moon came out.

A few yards away, Nick answered a call on his cell. After a few seconds, he hung up and spoke briefly with the sheriff before bidding him good-bye. Then he walked over to Micah. "Want to go with me and Kalen to question the boy in the hospital?"

Not really. Who wanted to see a defenseless teenager hurt and grieving? But the commander expected his presence, and they might learn something. "Sure."

"Good. Let's drop off your motorcycle, and we'll pick up Kalen. The sheriff will meet us there. When we're done there, we'll go back and work on that list."

Fucking awesome. "All right."

Micah would rather have fought hordes of goblins and Sluagh than revisit any part of his past, for any reason. But it was determined to bite him in the ass again and again, so he had no choice. In seconds he was following Nick's SUV to the compound. The drive was short, and Kalen was waiting. Jax offered to get started on the list until Micah and Nick could return, and the commander gave the task over with relief.

Micah still hadn't been able to have a word with Jax alone, and that ate at him.

Soon they were on their way, Nick driving and Micah riding shotgun. Kalen was sprawled in the backseat, staring out the window and tapping one booted foot to the classic rock on the radio. John, who was riding along to take up guarding the teen, leaned against the opposite door, lost in thought.

Micah turned halfway around in his seat to address Kalen. "How do you wipe someone's mind?"

Kalen shrugged. "The best way I can explain it is, I reach in with my magic, go searching for what I need. I find the right memory and use my power to erase it just like an eraser does writing on a chalkboard. Then I insert the memory I need them to have."

"That's some pretty freaky shit."

Nick snorted. "That's not the freakiest shit he can do, by far."

"I know, and I haven't even seen half of it."

Kalen just smiled and shook his head. For a half-Fae and powerful Sorcerer, Micah mused, the man was humble as hell. He could probably destroy most of the world in less than a day with the right motivation, but he didn't let his abilities go to his head. The Sorcerer could open a serious can of whoop-ass if he needed to, and had, but only when necessary.

At the hospital, Nick parked in the visitor's lot, and they went inside, riding the elevator to the fifth floor. The appearance of four dangerous-looking guys striding through the hallways caused no little curiosity—and some concern—and twice they were politely asked if they could be "helped" to find their destination.

Outside the teen's room, John relieved the deputy, who appeared quite grateful to be let go. The big former agent was only slightly less impenetrable than Fort Knox, so Micah figured the kid was in good hands.

They left John to it, and quietly filed into the room. Jesse must've gone straight to the hospital, as he was already in the room waiting for them. On the bed was a young man who hadn't quite grown into his long limbs. He was a good-looking kid, sable hair falling into scared, grief-stricken, red-rimmed blue eyes. All told, he was in much better shape than he should've been, thanks to Zan's covert visit. The young man's gaze lit on each of them, but he kept looking at the sheriff as if for an explanation.

Jesse began the introductions, his voice more gentle than Micah had ever heard it. "Guys, this is Tristan Cade. Tristan, this is Nick, Kalen, and Micah," he said, pointing to each of them. "These men are consultants to the sheriff's department. They—"

"I don't care what they are as long as they catch that fucking thing that killed my dad," the kid said, his voice breaking. His eyes filled with tears.

Micah's heart wrenched with sympathy. *Shit.*

"Did you see what it was?" Nick asked softly. "Was it a bear?"

Tristan blinked at him and gave a watery laugh that bordered on hysterical. "A *bear*? Are you being serious right now? Right, because it takes a sheriff plus four men who obviously aren't law enforcement to come and question me about a goddamn bear."

Clearly, he wasn't buying their bullshit.

"No," Tristan went on, his voice shaking with emotion. "It had w-wings, and it swooped down from the sky. It w-was f-fucking *huge*. It looked like something out of a bad movie."

Micah exchanged glances with Nick. Then he asked, "What else can you remember about the creature?"

For a few moments, the kid shivered with remembered horror, clutching the covers. Taking a deep breath, he bravely pushed on. "I swear those wings were fifteen feet or more from tip to tip. When it l-landed on me, I remember looking up, way up, into its ugly face, and thinking it must be seven or eight feet tall."

"What about its face?" Micah prodded. "What did it look like?"

"Brown feathers. Dirty, muddy brown all over, and dull. Like it wasn't healthy. Big yellow beak, strong talons. The head was sort of wrong, though."

"How so?" Kalen asked.

"It was misshapen. Almost as if someone hit it in the head with something and the skull got flattened. The eyes were kind of off, too. Crooked."

Micah's brows furrowed. How would someone hide such a deformity when in human form? Unless it was only present in the shift, which would be strange.

Hell, everything about their world was strange.

Nick stepped closer to the bed. "Do you remember noticing anything before the creature attacked? Did it do anything unusual, make any noises?"

Micah knew what he was getting at. The commander wanted to know if the shifter had spoken to the boy or his dad. Made threats. But the kid shook his head.

"No. One minute we were finishing our hot dogs, and the next, this thing was attacking me. My dad tackled it and shoved it off me, and it turned on him instead,"

Tristan whispered. A tear rolled down his cheek. His lids drooped.

The kid was exhausted and traumatized. Any second they were going to get kicked out by the doctor or nurses. It was clear Tristan had told them all he could, so Nick nodded to Kalen. As the Sorcerer stepped forward, Nick said, "Take away his recollection only of the attack itself, not the rest."

Kalen's eyes widened, not just at the order, but at the commander speaking so openly in front of the kid. "You sure? He'll know about the creature"—he lowered his voice—"and may figure out things about *us*. Maybe not right away, but eventually."

Nick's gaze was far away—a vision. "It's important that he knows. Now and to his future. This day will shape the man he's to become, and he must know that what we are is also his destiny."

Tristan looked confused, a little frightened, as Kalen laid a palm on top of his head. But one whispered word from the Sorcerer and the young man's lashes drifted downward. He fell deeply and instantly asleep, allowing Kalen to do his work of removing the sight of his father's murder from his mind.

As promised, Tristan would remember all else, but the terrible act itself would forever remain blank.

Finished, Kalen withdrew his hand and gazed down at the boy with sadness. "I hope Kai never has to endure what this young man did today. I'd do anything to spare my son from carrying a burden like that."

It was a sobering thought. Shifters, and even the most powerful of Sorcerers, could be killed. They lived with that reality every single day.

Filing out as quietly as they'd arrived, they left John to guard Tristan. Nick promised to send relief in shifts, to keep the men fresh and alert. According to Jesse, once

Tristan was released, he would probably go live with an aunt who was on her way to care for him. Somehow, he'd be fine.

On the drive back to the compound, Micah kept going over in his head what type of shifter they were looking for—a huge, ugly, crazy-ass bird of some kind, capable of ripping people to shreds.

They had a witness, a description, and a list from which to start narrowing down the bastard's identity.

How hard could that be?

Ten

Tyler stared at his brother, sickness rising in his throat. "No more innocents. You promised."

"No, I didn't. You made a request, and I said I'd consider it."

A request. So casual, like Tyler had asked for a steak and gotten a hamburger instead. When had his brother become this hateful creature? This heartless thing with a black soul, incapable of caring for anyone, except maybe Tyler? He doubted even that, at times.

"Two wrongs don't make a right," Tyler said.

The other man chuckled. "Ever the peacemaker, aren't you? It was the same when we were in that horrible place, taking all the abuse they dished out. Bound to their whims with no choice."

"I think you just like making others suffer," Tyler accused. "Bowman and his damn experiments only brought out the ugliness that was already lurking underneath the surface, as they were meant to do. You reveled in being taught to kill, as much as you like to blame him and Chase for what you are."

"What I am," Parker mused. Stepping closer to the bed, he laid a hand on Tyler's leg, the cold clamminess of it seeping through the covers. "What *I* am? You lie here day after day, and you say nothing about me to anyone. And do you know why? Because you're loyal to me. What does that make *you*?"

His stomach turned. "You're my brother, but I'm nothing like you."

"Aren't you?" Parker laughed softly. "Blood is thicker than water, and I saved you. Remember that."

No, the Alpha Pack had saved Tyler. But he wisely kept his mouth shut.

"I'll see you later." With a flutter of his coat, his brother was gone, passing the nurse who was on his way into the room.

Tyler tried not to tremble as Noah started checking his vitals. Tried to appear normal.

He was so afraid. Had no idea where to turn. The threat had been there, unspoken. But a threat all the same.

Brother or not, Parker would kill him for saying a word about his existence.

"Hey, did I hear you say that guy is your brother?" Noah asked, cutting Tyler a curious look as he checked his temperature. "I thought you told me he was a friend of yours."

He fumbled for a way to cover his blunder. "Yes, but he's *like* a brother. We call each other that, you know?"

"Hmm. Yeah, I guess I do." Noah busied himself, but didn't remark on Tyler's visitor again.

Once the nurse was gone, Tyler slumped in his bed and agonized over what to do. If he warned someone, even anonymously, Parker would know it as him. *Would the Pack be able to keep me safe?*

He wasn't sure. That troubling thought chased him into an uneasy sleep.

*   *   *

"Hey, Jacee?"

She looked up from wiping the bar as Jack approached. "Yeah, boss?"

"It's dead today, so go on home if you want. I've got Tracy coming in to cover the evening shift."

"You sure?"

"Yep, take off before I change my mind."

She grinned. "Thanks."

Collecting her purse, she clocked out and left. She'd barely put in seven hours today, but it always felt longer when they weren't busy. The time tended to drag unless the place was hopping with business.

Though she knew it was probably too early, she was hoping to see Micah's motorcycle in the driveway when she got home. No such luck, though. She was more than a little bummed, but her mate had a job to do, same as she did. The bills didn't stop coming just because you'd found your other half.

Climbing out of the car, she walked up to the porch, up the steps, and let herself in the front door. For a moment, she stood in the tiny foyer and daydreamed about the kind of house she and Micah might build. It didn't have to be huge but definitely bigger. With a circular driveway in front. Maybe it would even lead around to a side garage and a more private entrance. Studying her small living room, she decided something more open and spacious would be nice. They could have friends over, barbecue, laze around, and not be sitting on top of one another.

Which meant a deck out back, too. Maybe a pool. It would be a constant battle to skim the leaves out of the water, but—

Wait. As she scanned the living room, the daydream vanished, and her senses suddenly came to life. Something was off. What, exactly, she couldn't say. The back of her neck prickled as she inched farther into the house, scenting the air.

She smelled nothing unusual. Just traces of Micah's scent, of their breakfast. The general, sort-of-musty old scent of the house itself. At first glance no items appeared to be moved or taken. So what was that itch between her shoulder blades? She told herself she was being ridiculous. And yet . . .

Moving slowly, silently, she did a closer inspection. Since she'd recently dusted, there was no way to tell if the pictures, lamps, and such had been moved, so she walked on to the kitchen. They'd left it clean, dishes washed, and the space was undisturbed. For no reason in particular, she opened the fridge.

Yeah, part of her had half expected to find a dead cat with a note pinned to its carcass or something. She was that creeped out. But nothing. Her arm was in motion, closing the door, when she spotted it.

A plastic container of leftovers wasn't on the same shelf where she'd left it. She was sure of it. Reaching out, she grabbed the container and set it on the counter. Then she lifted the lid and peered at the chicken-and-rice casserole. It was only from the night before, but it smelled weird. Not like it was too old to eat, but a different sort of weird. Chemical. Her coyote couldn't identify it, but it made her want to hurl.

Frowning, she replaced the lid but didn't put the container back in the refrigerator. A quick scan of the other contents revealed nothing else strange, but she decided she'd toss all the perishables if the casserole had in fact been tampered with. Micah would know how to find out.

Leaving the container, she crept through the rest of the silent house. The place *felt* empty. Couldn't be too careful, though. Her shifter senses reached out to every part of the house, every corner of every room. Exceptional hearing and smell told her she was alone, and yet someone had been here.

Why couldn't she pick up a clear scent on the intruder?

Her bedroom was last, and when she entered . . .

Destruction. Complete, utter devastation.

"Oh, my God," she gasped. Her hand went to her chest, her heart pounding underneath her breastbone.

The sheets and quilt had been ripped from the bed and were piled in ribbons on the floor. Literally sliced with either claws or a knife. The mattress had fared no better, cut in long, ragged gashes. The anger of the person who'd done this was horribly evident in the personal nature of the attack, and it permeated the very air she breathed.

Unable to take her eyes off the scene, she yanked her cell phone from her jeans pocket. Hands shaking so badly she almost dropped the device, she managed to punch in Micah's number. After three rings, however, it went to voice mail.

"Dammit," she moaned, ending the call. Should she wait for him to come home? Try again?

Somewhere, a creak sounded in the house. Almost like a footstep on the old boards near the back of the house, perhaps outside. On the porch. Her pulse leapt and she tried Micah's phone again, but her mate wasn't answering.

"Fuck this." As soon as voice mail picked up, she left a message, voice wobbling, trying not to cry. She was already moving toward the kitchen. "I'm driving to the compound. Someone broke into the house while I was at work. Whoever it was tore up our bed, Micah! I'm getting the hell out of here. See you soon. Call me."

Scooping up the container of possibly contaminated

food, her purse and keys, she jogged out the door, barely pausing to lock it behind her. She definitely wasn't staying long enough to pack an overnight bag for them both. They'd worry about a change of clothes later.

In seconds she was on the road, glancing in the rearview mirror, trying to calm her racing heart.

She could've sworn she felt malevolent eyes watching her as she raced away.

Micah rubbed his tired eyes and again scanned the list that he, Nick, and Jax had been over several times.

"We don't have much," Jax remarked, tossing down his section of the list in frustration. Then he stroked his goatee thoughtfully. "The shifters who healed and have been released from Sanctuary are doing remarkably well, according to our sources. All of them are accounted for."

"And the worst cases are still inside, under our care." Micah sighed. "Some are getting close to release, but none of them is fit enough to cause the damage we saw earlier today."

Nick nodded. "Agreed."

Picking up a paper from the center of the conference table, Micah looked over the names of the deceased again. "These people who didn't make it out alive—do we have verification on every single one?"

"That's the problem," Nick said. "In a few cases, we only know what other shifters told us, that some of the captives disappeared and were presumed dead, although we didn't find their bodies. They may have been disposed of long before we made the rescue. We'll never know for sure, but we have to assume they're dead."

Micah's jaw clenched as he studied the names.

"What's wrong?" Jax asked.

"There are names in all three of these groups belonging to shifters Bowman made me torture. Any of them would have motivation."

"But not opportunity." Jax frowned.

Nick handed him a highlighter. "Mark the names in question. We'll see what turns up."

"I never knew *all* their names and can't remember many of them," Micah clarified. "But Bowman liked to tell me because it made them more real in my eyes. Made it even worse, what I was about to do to them. He wanted to desensitize me to my human side and theirs, over time."

"Sick fucker," Jax spat. "Wish I could kill him all over again."

Bowman had gotten what he deserved when Jax ripped him apart—or so the team had said after that particular mission, in which they'd rescued Nix from the last-known lab. Micah had wanted so badly to accompany his Pack brothers, but hadn't been well enough back then.

Micah highlighted the names he could remember, and he was ashamed at how many there were. Not that the number made a difference—one or twenty, his role was equally terrible. Once he was finished, Nick and Jax scanned the names.

Nick tapped the sheet listing the rescues recovering in Sanctuary. "There are four shifters in particular that I know came in here in really bad shape. Much more so than the others. I think we should interview them first."

Micah thought about that and winced. "You're right. But is it a good idea for me to be there? They suffered at my hands, and my face is going to be the last one they want to see."

"Which is exactly why we need for them to see you," Nick said grimly. "I'll check with Mac and Melina, of course, but I believe that seeing you whole and healthy, being productive, will be good for them. Give them hope."

"I feel like I should apologize for my part in their suffering."

"Then do that if it helps you. It might help them, too. And if there's someone among them who knows anything about these attacks, or is connected in some way, their reaction to you might be telling. Either way, I'd appreciate your take on each one."

"*Someone's* connected," Jax put in. "Whoever wrote the note and left it with Mr. Cade's body knew your lab-subject number. Only a prisoner or one of Bowman's cronies could've known that."

Nick gathered the lists. "All right. Sit tight while I go get the okay from the doctors to question these patients."

That might take a few minutes. The docs were fiercely protective of their charges, as they were all aware. After Nick walked out of the conference room, Micah studied the polished surface of the big table. The silence was suddenly a living, breathing entity, weighing down air in the room. He struggled for the perfect words, but there weren't any.

So he settled for the ones that were eating at his soul. "I'm sorry for how I reacted to hearing about you and Jacee," he said quietly, meeting his friend's gaze. He found no censure there, only understanding. "I was out of control. I hope you'll forgive me."

"There was nothing to forgive. You were already on edge from all the shit your body was going through."

"But I—"

"Forget it, Micah. I mean that. You're my brother, and nothing is going to change that." Jax smiled to show he really did mean his words.

Relief flooded him, and the breath whooshed from his

lungs. "You don't know how I've been beating myself up about that day."

"I have some idea. It's past history, okay? I think maybe our mates might even become friends one day."

"Yeah?"

"Yeah," Jax said. "They seemed to get along fine when you were recovering. Translation: they didn't rip each other's faces off."

They both laughed, the tension broken, and Micah clapped his friend's shoulder. "They might not do lunch and shopping anytime soon, but they'll make it."

"True that."

Jax's phone buzzed and he checked a text. "Nick says come on over to Sanctuary. Mac and Melina said we can interview the patients on the list as long as they're not sleeping. If we upset anyone, we have to leave."

Micah rolled his eyes. "And what are the odds of us *not* upsetting anyone with our presence at any given moment?"

"About the same as our chances of winning the lottery."

Together they strolled over to the new building, where Nick was waiting on the fifth floor. Dr. Melina Mallory was standing next to him, her expression as composed and serious as ever. She wasn't the same woman Micah remembered from before the ambush that had killed her mate, Terry, decimated the Alpha Pack, and landed Micah and Nix in captivity.

She'd let her dark hair grow out some, though, and it almost reached her collar now. The tresses feathered around her face, softening her sharp elfin features. Her eyes were a bit warmer these days as well, her overall appearance the more approachable friend he remembered.

"I mean it, Nick," she was saying sharply. "You guys

say or do anything to set back any of my patients' progress, I'll have your balls for breakfast. *All* of you."

Well, her appearance was softer — her attitude, not so much.

Nick grinned, unruffled. "My balls are spoken for, Doc. So are theirs."

"Then you'd best not endanger them, or your mates will be awfully lonely in the days to come." With that, she gathered a chart and marched off.

Jax stare after her. "That is the most miserable woman I've ever known."

"She's a tough cookie," Micah agreed.

"Girlfriend just needs to get *laid*," Noah piped up from the nurses' station. At Nick's arched brow, he flushed. "*Anyhoo*, gotta run."

Micah chuckled as the guy hurried off. "Nix is gonna have his hands full with that one."

"And then some." Jax snorted. "Once he finally pulls his head out of his ass."

"All right, let's get this done," Nick said, shaking his head.

The first patient, a cougar shifter named Boris, was hostile. He was not one of the captives Micah had been forced to torture, but he had suffered terribly, and he wanted no part of them or their questioning. Only when Nick told him about the two murders of innocent people did he relent. Softening the slightest bit, Boris told them everything he recalled about the shifters with whom he had been locked up.

There really wasn't anything they didn't already know. The names Boris gave them were on their lists, no surprises. They left the interview disappointed.

The next two shifters were wolves, and they were shy. Afraid. The trauma they'd been through had rendered them nearly incapable of speaking, and any apology for

Micah's part in their misery were neither wanted nor appreciated. At least for the time being. One actually started screaming when he saw Micah and had to be sedated by Noah. They left quickly, before Melina could get word and kick them out, and went on to the fourth survivor.

"This one's name is Tyler Anderson," Jax read from the paper. "Eagle shifter."

"One of mine, too." Micah felt sick. "He was one of the most vulnerable, and Bowman knew it. The bastard brought him to me many times. Him and his brother."

"His brother?" Nick's gaze bored into him.

"Yeah, Parker. He's on the names of the deceased. I don't know how he died, though. Bowman stopped bringing him around, and I never knew what happened to him."

Nick seemed to consider that for a moment, then nodded. "All right. Let's see if we can get a read on this one."

Just then, Micah's cell phone buzzed in his pocket. He couldn't answer it right then and made a mental note to check it after they were done visiting Tyler.

When they walked in, the young, slight, brown-haired man on the bed was drowsing. The second he noticed them, however, he jolted awake, eyes widening in fear. Especially when he spotted Micah.

"You," he whispered. His face turned paper white, and his green eyes were luminous. "Why are you here?"

Micah took a deep breath. "First, I want to say how sorry I am for what happened in that hellhole we were held captive in. For the terrible things I was forced to do. And I was forced, Tyler."

The other man's voice was almost inaudible. "I know."

"I hated every second of that place, and I loathed Gene Bowman. As a member of the Alpha Pack, my job is to protect people, not hurt them."

"I believe you."

Tyler was taking this better than Micah had hoped.

"Perhaps someday you can forgive me. I know it's a lot to ask, but—"

"Of course. We were both victims, Micah." Tyler's eyes were sad as he studied him. "I don't blame you."

"Thanks. That's more than I deserve."

The eagle glanced at Jax and Nick. "Somehow I don't think it takes three of you to come tell me you're sorry. What's the rest of this visit about?"

Nick spoke up. "We're here because someone is killing innocent people in the area. Campers. The killer has ties to Chase here and to his time in captivity with Bowman."

If possible, Tyler paled even more. He swallowed hard as he addressed Micah. "That's t-terrible. But how would I know anything about that?"

Micah sighed. "The killer left me a note with his last victim. He addressed me by the number I was assigned in the lab, and only someone who was actually inside with us would know that information. Can you think of anything at all that might help us identify who this killer is before more innocent people die?"

Jax spoke softly. "The killer has a grudge against Micah. And while a lot of shifters from that time period might feel he's getting what's coming to him—which is *wrong* and not fair—he's newly mated. She *is* innocent, and should something happen to her, and someone had information that could've saved her, that's on their head, too."

"I—I wish I could help you. I haven't done anything but stare at these four walls and try to get better, you know? I really hope you catch him. I mean that."

There was an interesting note to Tyler's voice at the end. A certain fierceness to his tone, a sincerity. Micah glanced at his two companions, and judging from their expressions, they'd noticed, too.

"Yeah," Nick said. "Well, we'll leave you to rest. If you think of anything important, day or night, call any of us. That's my card with my cell phone on the front. Jax's and Micah's cell phone numbers are on the back." Taking a card from his pocket, he handed it to the eagle shifter.

"Thanks. I will."

They filed out, Micah taking one last look at the shifter on the bed. Tyler was staring at the card Nick had handed him with a torn expression on his face. Then he took the card and stuffed it inside his pillowcase—hidden.

Once they were safely down the hallway, Micah said, "He knows something. He hid the card you gave him inside his pillowcase."

"Hid it from who? That's the question." Nick gazed thoughtfully in the direction of the room. "We'll need a list of visitors to Sanctuary."

"I'll get Noah on it," Jax said, and jogged off in the direction of the nurses' station.

Curiosity finally got the better of Micah. As he and Nick followed Jax, he pulled out his cell phone and saw he had a missed call from Jacee. Smiling, he played her message.

His smile quickly died.

"I'm driving to the compound. Someone broke into the house while I was at work. Whoever it was tore up our bed, Micah! I'm getting the hell out of here. See you soon. Call me."

"Oh, fuck!" he yelled, and ran for the elevator.

"What's wrong?" Nick shouted after him.

Jax took off, and Micah wasn't sure if he'd even gotten the chance to talk to Noah. At the moment he didn't care. He punched the elevator button several times, but that was too slow. Whirling, he bolted for the stairs.

"What the fuck's going on?" Jax grabbed his arm before he hit the door to the stairwell.

"I got a call from Jacee right before we went into Tyler's room." Micah was panting. Panicking. "She— Someone broke into her house while she was at work today. She got home and it was a mess. Whoever it was tore up the bed."

"Shit." Jax's worried eyes bored into his. "Is she okay?"

"I—I think so. She said she was driving here."

"Call her. *Now*."

"Okay. God, why didn't I think of that?"

"Because you're in panic mode. Call."

Leaning against the wall, Micah made the call. He was in agony waiting for her to answer as his phone rang. And rang. "She's not picking up. What if . . ."

He was going to pass out. Right the fuck out, in front of them.

"Micah!" Nick shouted in his face, grabbing his shoulders. Micah blinked at him. "She's driving. She's not going to answer while she's scared and driving, all right? Calm down. Let's go downstairs to the driveway and meet her. She should be here any minute."

"You're right." He took several deep breaths, and the spots in front of his face began to clear up. "Let's go."

The thundering of his heart wouldn't stop as he jogged down the stairs, his friends right behind him. At the bottom, he exited the stairwell and jogged through the lobby and out the doors. Outside, he crossed the lawn and ran partway down the drive, then stopped, waiting, listening.

"Where is she?"

"She'll be here," Jax soothed.

At last, he heard a car's engine. Coming up the long road to the compound at a good clip. When her car rounded the last turn and he spotted her behind the wheel, he could've keeled over in relief, after all. She screeched to a halt, threw the car in park, shut off the ignition, and was out, running to meet him.

The look on his mate's beautiful face, he'd never forget. Pure fear.

Micah met Jacee halfway, held out his arms. She barreled into him, nearly taking him off his feet, and he wrapped her up tight. Held her and kissed her hair, whispered comforting words as best he knew how. She was shaking from head to toe as she hugged him close, like she'd never let go.

"I was so scared," she said, her voice breaking. "He was there. At first I thought I was imagining it, but then I saw the bedroom. He tore it to pieces!"

Oh, God. That could have been his mate. If she'd been home when the monster came, or if he'd waited for her.

"Shh, I'm here, baby. I've got you."

"I feel so violated."

"That's exactly what he intended. We're going to catch that son of a bitch," Micah promised. "He's had a fucking busy day, since he's already tipped his hand once today."

Leaning back some, she looked up into his face. "Really? What happened?"

He told her about the attack on the Cades, father and son. And the note blaming Micah left with Mr. Cade. About referencing Micah's lab number.

"So it's someone who knows you." Her eyes were wide, more afraid than before, if possible. "This monster is killing and threatening you directly."

"Yeah." There was more. But now wasn't the time to tell her about Nick's horrible vision. Not with an audience. "Like I said, we're going to get him."

"Damn right." She gestured toward the car. "I brought something that might help."

"What's that?"

"I think he tampered with some food in the fridge. Maybe your lab folks could run some tests on it?"

Nick walked up then and nodded. "They can, and if

it's been contaminated on purpose, they'll be able to pinpoint the source, most likely."

Jacee walked to the car, leaned in, and retrieved a plastic container. Then she brought it to Nick. "What should I do with it?"

"I'll take it up to them. No worries. After I drop this off, Micah, Jax, and I are going to drive back to your place and pack what you need for the foreseeable future."

Jacee's shoulders drooped. She looked so forlorn, Micah pulled her against him again.

"You're pulling rank, huh?" she asked.

"You bet. Until this twisted monster is caught, we're closing ranks around you two."

Micah hated it, for both of them, but he couldn't blame the commander. He had to protect his people, and he couldn't do that if they were miles away.

Micah turned to his mate. "Sweetheart, why don't you go to my quarters and rest while we take care of the packing? You worked all day and then had a scare. Some sleep will do you good."

"No. I don't want to be alone, even though I'm not really alone in the compound," she insisted. "I want to be with you. We can rest together, when we get back."

"If you're sure . . ."

"I am. Besides, there's stuff a girl needs and she doesn't want guys pawing through it." She gave them a wan smile.

Jax rolled his eyes. "God forbid we should have to touch the girly stuff."

Micah laughed in spite of the situation. It was good to see her bonding with his team. Even Jax. Who woulda thought it?

Nick took the food to the lab, and then they were on their way in two of the Pack SUVs. The better to get more of their things. Dammit, he couldn't wait until the killer was caught and they could concentrate on their relationship. To talk to Nick about building on that patch of land and look at house plans.

He wanted so much to believe he had a future with his mate.

First, he had to lay the past to rest.

Eleven

Jacee had never been so tired. Strung out. Stressed to the max.

A long day at work, followed by being terrorized in her own home. Then a heart-pounding drive, glancing in her rearview mirror with paranoia dogging every mile, topped off by packing her things and moving the most important of them to Micah's apartment at the compound.

Not on her list of Top Ten Most Fun Days Ever.

She was a wreck. Which was why, in hindsight, she lost her head when she found the bottle of myst hidden in Micah's things.

Exhausted, she, Micah, and their friends trooped into the dining room for a much-needed hot meal and to rest their tired bodies.

She liked these people. They were warm and welcoming, and they knew when to give a person space.

The meal went down fast, without her pausing to really savor it. But it filled the hungry spot, and she was satisfied. Her nerves were no less frazzled, though, and her mate took notice.

"Why don't we turn in, sweetheart? You look ready to fall over."

She shot Micah a grateful smile. "That would be nice. Thanks. This is one day that definitely needs to end ASAP."

He took her hand, and she let him pull her up. They said their good-byes and headed to his quarters—now theirs for a few weeks or months, at least. Once they were back inside, he pulled her to him, held her close. They stayed that way for several long moments while she just breathed his wonderful scent. Listened to his heartbeat.

Never had she felt so safe. Not for years, anyway.

"Get ready for bed, baby. Before you fall over." Kissing the top of her head, he moved away.

She felt the loss of his warmth immediately, but planned to get in some serious snuggling as soon as possible. "Okay."

Micah disappeared down the hallway into the master bedroom, and she heard the bathroom door shut. Following him, she went into the bedroom and, her hands on her hips, stood surveying the boxes full of their belongings everyone had hastily thrown together. Which one contained her toothbrush and face wash was anybody's guess, so she dug in.

A quick look in the first box revealed jeans and T-shirts, plus a few other tops. The second, pajamas, panties, and bras. The third—success. Her makeup case was there, and inside would be the items she needed to get ready for bed. As she lifted her makeup case out, however, something caught her eye.

In the bottom of the box was a small black case. It appeared to be a man's bag, something Micah might carry his toiletries in, but she'd never seen this one before. Placing her bag on the floor, she reached down, then paused, glancing guiltily toward the bathroom door. Inside, the toilet flushed, and water in the sink started running. She wasn't a snoopy person and didn't want to be that kind of mate.

Of course, she was being stupid. Everything in these boxes was their stuff, so why shouldn't she look? There was no harm in satisfying her curiosity.

Snatching the bag, she unzipped the top and pried it open, peering inside. Normal items, as she'd thought. A couple of disposable razors and a mini tube of shaving cream. A toothbrush, travel toothpaste. Dental floss. A tiny bottle of cologne. Not much different from the contents of her own bag.

Except for the small brown prescription bottle almost buried at the bottom.

Hand trembling slightly, she held it up. Read the label. Even then, she couldn't wrap her brain around what she was seeing. "Myst?"

That couldn't be right. Her mate had suffered through a hellish detox, and he was clean. He knew to stay far away from this shit, had let her believe he was doing fine. And yet here was proof right in her hand that he wasn't fine. At all.

"Hey, if you find the body wash, I want to . . ." Shirtless, jeans unsnapped, Micah stopped just outside the bathroom door. The cheerful expression on his face crumbled to dust, and he froze, eyes wide.

"What the fuck is this?" Even as Jacee spoke those five words, she knew she'd started the conversation on the wrong track. But this was the final straw in an already craptastic day, and she was *done*.

"Jacee, it's not what it looks like," he said hoarsely, taking a couple of steps forward.

"It's not? You mean you didn't hide these pills? You didn't swear you were going to stay away from them and then do the exact opposite? You didn't lie to me? To Mac and your team?"

"Baby, please—"

"Tell me the truth!"

"Okay! Yes, I lied!" He buried his fingers in his dark hair, his chest heaving. "But it was a lie of *omission*."

"And that makes it right?"

"Of course not. But, baby, I didn't take any, I swear." His voice was pleading for understanding. "I wanted to, so badly. Just to help me cope, just one or two."

She flinched. "I thought these past two weeks have been as wonderful for you as they've been for me. Why would you need the pills?"

"They have been! But that's not what addiction is about. It's the craving that's driving me crazy. That's what I'm having trouble coping with, don't you see?"

"No. How could I? Because you didn't confide in me. You *lied* to me."

With hurried motions, he yanked his shirt back on. "I'm sorry. I wish I hadn't kept them."

She pushed to her feet. "But you did, and you didn't tell me. Didn't trust me to help you."

"I do! I just wanted to handle it on my own," he tried to explain. "Is that so wrong?"

"Are you kidding?" She stared at him, incredulous, and her voice rose as she went on. "Now I know I have a mate who'll keep things from me as it suits him. If I can't trust you, what do we have?"

The heartbreak on his face had her regretting her harsh words the instant they left her mouth. But she couldn't take them back. Not fast enough to stop him from grabbing his jacket and motorcycle keys.

"Micah, wait."

He shook off her hand and bolted, ignoring her pleas. She jogged after him, but he was fast, slamming the apartment door behind him. For a few seconds she considered going after him, but there was no catching him. Not when he was so upset. Besides, there was also no need to air their argument in front of other Pack members, which would surely happen if she caught up to him.

No, best to wait until he returned.

Please, come back, she said through their mental link. *Let's talk it out. I'm so sorry.*

Nothing. He'd already shut her out, then.

Disheartened, she walked into the bedroom and sat on the edge of the bed. Over and over, she replayed the incident, and the knot in her stomach grew. She'd mishandled things from the start. If she hadn't been so tired and strung out from today—

No. That was no excuse for how she'd treated her mate. Instead of acting like an accusing bitch, she should've shown him understanding and support. He'd been through hell these past few weeks. Months, to tell the truth. How he was doing so well was a miracle.

Yes, he had lied by omission. But it was totally understandable that he might hang on to a few pills and have trouble resisting the terrible craving. Mac had warned it wouldn't be easy for him to stay off of them.

Micah told her he had resisted taking them, and she believed him. He'd been strong enough not to give in.

And she'd upset him so badly, making him believe she had no faith in him.

"What have I done?"

Saddened, disappointed in herself, she hung her head, barely noticing the tears streaming down her cheeks.

Christ, what a day.

Nick was wrapping things up in his office, getting ready to join Calla in their quarters, when the vision hit.

The argument between Jacee and Micah had changed

somewhat. It wasn't quite as vicious as his previous visions, because Micah *hadn't* used drugs again. He'd taken that much of Nick's and Mac's warnings to heart, and it was a damn good thing.

But the result was nearly the same. Nick knew instantly part of the vision had already taken place. The argument. Micah leaving, but not from Jacee's house like before.

Cranking the bike, Micah sped away from the compound. From the loss tearing out his insides. He ran from his ruined life, the destruction of his hopes and dreams. With the Pack, with his mate.

He'd tried, so hard. But his mate didn't trust him. God, he was in agony.

And so he didn't see the shifter with the huge wings swoop down from the sky, talons extended, intent clear.

As always, Nick couldn't scream. Couldn't warn Micah of the danger.

The creature hit Micah from the side, hard, knocking him from the speeding motorcycle. Micah went airborne, flying through the air for awful seconds—until he slammed headfirst into a tree. Falling to the ground in a crumpled heap, head at an unnatural angle, he stared into the sky. Struggled to breathe.

And then stopped, brown eyes fixing on a point he could no longer see.

Micah had left, but the attack hadn't taken place yet. Nick knew it. He had only minutes to warn the man.

"It's not going to happen like that. Not if I can help it."

Snatching his cell phone, he called Micah. On the fourth ring, voice mail picked up, and he left a message. "Micah, the vision I told you about! This is it! Turn back! And for God's sake, keep your eyes on the skies!"

Hanging up, he sent a text.

Turn back, and keep your eyes on the skies! My vision of you, it's now, tonight. Call me.

After he hit send, he got moving, sounding the alarm. The Pack was ready in less than five minutes, and they assembled at the SUVs. They didn't question him when he explained his vision, their faith in his ability as a Seer and a leader was that unshakable.

"What the fuck are we waiting for?" Aric growled. "Let's go get my stupid brother-in-law before he gets his ass killed."

They climbed in the vehicles and took off.

Nick just prayed they weren't too late.

Speeding along the dark road, Micah's brain was in turmoil.

"If I can't trust you, what do we have?"

I've tried so hard. But my mate doesn't trust me and I've ruined everything. God, this is agony.

He had no idea where he was going. Or when he'd go back. Maybe he wouldn't return at all, would just keep riding on to California or the East Coast. Anywhere but here, where he was nothing but a failure.

As soon as he had the thought, he knew he wouldn't actually follow through. His wolf snarled inside at the idea of leaving his mate for good, of giving up. The man wasn't ready to give up either, hurt or not. He just needed to get out, clear his head.

In his pocket, his phone buzzed. Ignoring it, he kept riding, uncaring of the darkness, wanting only to be part of it for a while. To disappear. But the device buzzed again, this time shorter, signaling a ping of voice mail. Not even a minute later, the buzz of a text. Someone was determined to reach him.

Careful to keep one hand steady on the bike, he slowed

his speed a bit, dug the phone from his pocket and punched the button at the bottom to light up the screen. He couldn't maneuver the device enough while driving to actually unlock it and listen to his voice mail, but he could see the text was from Nick. He could only read the first part, but what he saw sent a chill of foreboding down his spine.

Turn back, and keep your eyes on the skies!

That was all the warning he got.

Twisting in his seat, he tilted his head up to scan the night sky—and saw the shadow of a great, winged creature framed against the stars.

"Fuck!"

The beast dove for him, and he turned to face the road, bending low over his bike and hitting the gas. The action was too little, too late, and he braced himself. The impact hit his back and shoulder with the force of a speeding train, taking his breath away and unseating him.

But somehow, instead of flipping over the handlebars, he managed to shift his weight to fall to the side, laying his bike down. He hit the ground hard, lost his grip on the bike and his phone, and skidded across the pavement, off the opposite side of the road, and headed for a stand of trees. There was nothing he could do but thank God he'd worn a helmet.

And then his flight came to a gradual halt as he rolled to a stop on his back—right next to a tree. It was a miracle he'd missed it. But he needed at least one more to survive this.

Because the monster, shrieking in triumph, was closing in fast, talons extended. Ready to deal out an early death. The figure loomed larger the closer it got to the ground. And God, the thing was fucking huge! Just before it struck, Micah rolled to the side, grunting in pain.

The creature struck the ground instead of his body, and trumpeted in outrage. Sweat popped out on Micah's brow as he tried to drag himself to put the tree between him and his attacker, but several broken bones and torn ligaments slowed his progress. White-hot knives tore through his thigh, and he was dragged backward.

His fingers scrabbled in the grass and dirt as he desperately tried to find something to hold on to. Or a limb to jab at the monster. No, he needed to shift. To fight in his wolf form. But the precious seconds he needed to complete the shift were lost to him as the creature sank its talons into the vulnerable flesh of his torso, tearing at him.

Screaming, Micah grabbed frantically at the tough hide of the monster's talons. Tried to pry them lose. He might as well have tried to break free of bands of solid iron, big and strong as they were. Writhing, Micah gazed up at his captor in horror.

The monster was everything Tristan Cade had described. Even worse. Whoever this thing was in human form was nowhere in evidence now. What once had been a majestic bird of some sort was mutated and twisted almost beyond recognition. The feathers, though brown and muddy, might once have belonged to a golden eagle. The resemblance to that beautiful bird ended there.

The creature screeched, hatred in its red eyes, and struck. Agony ripped through Micah's shoulder, and he screamed again. And again as it struck his chest, then his stomach, its jagged beak tearing. Rending flesh.

The monster was taking him apart. Piece by piece. Making him suffer as Micah had once made him suffer.

Perhaps he deserved this, after all.

As the creature's claws sank deeper, he thought he

heard a familiar noise. Then he turned his head and saw the sweep of headlights coming on fast. Several vehicles.

Nick. The Pack. It had to be, out here in the middle of nowhere, so close to the compound. He could've wept, if he'd had the strength. *Hurry*.

The monster, however, wasn't so pleased. With an angry cry, it launched into the air—without letting go of its prey. Micah's broken body was lifted into the sky, a piece of meat to be devoured by the one who'd carry out his vengeance.

"Oh, God . . ."

Head dangling, he watched the ground fall away. Saw the vehicles skid to a halt, his brothers pouring from inside. Weapons were drawn, and a series of *pop, pop, pop*'s ensued. The creature dipped, but then continued to rise.

Far below, a man with red hair raised his hands and took aim. *Aric*.

When the column of flame spiraled upward, Micah closed his eyes. He knew the instant the fire hit the creature. It screeched, its talons opening in reflex, ripping from Micah's body.

And he fell.

Jacee. Please believe in me. Love you.

Wind whipping through his hair, the darkness enveloped him, and he welcomed it.

The scene that greeted Nick and his men was like something out of a horror movie. And not something he'd be able to erase from his brain as long as he lived.

Aric was at the wheel of the lead Escalade, Nick riding shotgun. Everyone was tense, anxious. Then the vehicle rounded the bend, and they spotted the trail of wreckage from the bike. And off to the opposite side, by a stand of trees, a monster of a creature, wings expanded to their full width, its prey pinned underneath enormous talons. The beast was striking Micah again and again, determined to tear him apart.

"Motherfucker!" Aric yelled. He gunned the SUV, and it leapt forward, closing the distance.

The beast was finally alerted to their presence and took to the sky, but it didn't turn Micah loose. Nick could only watch as the younger man dangled limp in the monster's grasp, and pray he wasn't already dead.

Aric brought the Escalade to a stop, and they jumped out, weapons blasting. The bird faltered but didn't stop, and Aric raised his hands.

"Don't hit Micah!" Nick shouted.

"I won't!"

Fire shot from Aric's hands and whirled into the sky, seeking its target. Higher and higher until the flames blasted the creature, and it let out a terrible shriek—and dropped its prey. Micah fell, tumbling toward the ground at dizzying speed.

"Kalen," Nick yelled.

But the Sorcerer was already on the job, sending out a spell to stop Micah's plunge and bring him toward where they were parked. As Micah floated toward him, Nick's heart sank. The young wolf was a torn, bloodied mess, clothing hanging from his body in ribbons and wide gashes visible in his flesh.

Finally Kalen lowered him gently into their waiting hands, and they eased his battered body into the back of the lead SUV, where someone had already put down the seats and covered them with blankets. Zan waited there to keep him stable during the drive back to the compound.

"Goddammit, look at him," Aric whispered, his face a mask of rage. "And that fucker got away."

"We'll get him." Nick gripped his shoulder. "In the meantime, we need to get Micah back. Let's hurry."

Nick climbed into the back with Zan, and they were on their way. Micah's eyes were closed, and his breath rattled in his lungs, the sound wet as he struggled. "Hang on, Micah. You've been through too much to give up now. You're a survivor—remember that."

"I'm not going to let him die," Zan said, his jaw set determinedly. Placing both hands on his patient's chest, he began to work.

The blue glow enveloped Zan's hands and then spread to Micah's upper extremities. Then on to the rest of his body. The entire ride, Zan never let up, nor did he speak.

As they pulled up to Sanctuary, Nick noted that Micah seemed to be breathing a little easier. The blood flow had slowed as well. The back doors were yanked open, and Zan slumped backward, clearly worn-out. "I did all I can," he said hoarsely. "He's a fucking disaster inside. The monster's talons got some major organs."

"You did good," Nick assured him.

Mac nodded as she and Noah prepared to get their patient onto a gurney. "You did, my friend. We'll take it from here."

Nick and Aric helped load Micah onto the stretcher; then Mac and Noah took off with their charge. "I've never felt so useless."

From beside Nick, Aric's voice was quiet. "You did what you could. God, what am I going to say to Rowan?"

Just then, Rowan came jogging around the corner and across the drive toward to where they stood near the emergency entrance. Selene, Zan's mate, was with her.

"Dad!" Selene called to Nick. "What happened?"

"Micah was attacked," he said to the women. Their faces reflected their shock and worry. "By that creature who's after him."

"Is my brother going to be okay?" Rowan clutched at her mate. "Tell me the truth."

"He's in good hands, baby."

That wasn't an answer, and they knew it. But it was the best they had. As the women held on to their mates, Nick dug out his cell phone and placed the one call he dreaded the most.

"Hello?" Jacee answered.

Shouted orders reached his ears.

He was flying. No, bumping along, moving fast. Feet running beside him.

Everything hurt. Breathing was agony. Cracking open his eyes, he was nearly blinded by white light and too much movement. But as his vision cleared a bit, he saw walls and doorways rushing past. At his side was someone in nurse's scrubs with SpongeBob characters all over them.

Noah. "Hey, you're back. Stay with us, okay?"

"I'll try," Micah said. Or thought he did. He turned his head to try to look where they were headed, and that was when he saw her in the hallway. Sitting calmly, oddly enough. "Jacee?"

Reaching out, he tried to take her hand as the gurney rolled past, and her surprise struck him as odd. He couldn't see well, blood and sweat in his eyes, but . . . it had been her. Right?

No, wait. The face was too young, the hair too light. His mistake.

Then the doctors and nurses were pulling him into an operating room, or at least that was his guess. A mask went over his nose and mouth, and a sting pricked his arm. Things grew fuzzy again, and he began to float away.

"You're going to be all right," Noah said, his kind blue eyes gazing down at Micah.

If only he could believe that.

Then he knew nothing more.

Jacee. Please believe in me. I love you.

I do believe in you, and I'm so sorry. I love you, too. Micah?

He didn't answer, and she paced for a while. Should she go after him? She wouldn't know where to look, though, besides the Grizzly, and he hadn't had time to get there yet.

When she saw Nick's number on the caller ID about a half an hour later, she wasn't too worried, initially. Micah hadn't been gone all that long, and she figured the commander was trying to reach his team member for some reason. Micah wouldn't be able to answer while riding.

"Hello?"

"It's Nick. I need you to stay calm," he began.

Immediately, her heart kicked in her chest. "What's wrong?"

"We've got Micah over at Sanctuary. He's been attacked."

Shoving the phone in her front pocket, Jacee ran, not waiting to hear the rest. In the wake of her panic, exhaustion fled. Her feet flew as she raced down the corridors, finally coming to the connecting passage between the main building and Sanctuary. Quickly, fingers shaking, she punched in the code, hitting the wrong buttons the first time and cursing; then she let herself in and took off again.

Nick was waiting for her at the lobby level, and one glance at the sorrowful expression on his face sent her heart plummeting to her toes. Rushing up to him, she grabbed his shirt—and realized it was covered in drying blood. Shaking her head, refusing to accept what that meant, she met his gaze.

"I'm sorry," he began. "I didn't have time to change clothes yet."

"How is he?"

"They took him into surgery. We don't know anything yet."

"You know more than you're saying." Of that, Jacee was certain. He couldn't hide the anxiety brimming in his eyes.

"Not here. There's a private waiting room upstairs."

Her mate's condition was bad, then. Her legs barely supported her as they started off for the elevator, and Nick gently took her arm. When they reached the right floor, she was hardly aware of anything around her because she was concentrating so hard on making sure her bond with her mate was still solid.

What she found was frightening. The thread was wavering, thin and weak. That, more than anything they could say, told her just how terrible the attack had been and that Micah's life was literally on the line.

The commander led her into the private waiting room, which, as it turned out, wasn't all that private. Zan and Selene were there, along with Aric and Rowan. The Healer's shirt was covered in blood as well, and she fought not to be sick.

As soon as Micah's sister and brother-in-law spotted her, they walked straight over and enveloped her in a group hug, saying nothing for several long moments. When they let her go, Aric took her arm and guided her to a chair, where he made her sit. He took one side of her, Rowan the other. Aric spoke first.

"We're not gonna lie to you, Jacee. It's bad."

She swallowed hard, fighting back tears. "I can feel how weak our bond is. Tell me who or what did this."

"That monster who's after him waited for his chance and took it." Aric's jaw clenched with anger. "It attacked while he was out on his motorcycle, caused him to wreck. He didn't stand a chance."

Nick lowered himself into a chair across from them. "I don't understand why he'd take a risk like that, especially after I warned him about my vision, more than once."

"Vision? What vision?" Jacee gazed at the commander in dread.

"He never told you?" Nick released a heavy sigh. "I foresaw tonight's attack, but I didn't know when it would happen. I've warned Micah on more than one occasion to look out for it."

"And he never told me." She couldn't wrap her head around that.

"He was probably trying to protect you," the commander said gently. "And it wasn't my place to interfere."

"This is my fault," she whispered. "We argued, and I drove him away."

"No, you absolutely did not. He forgot my warning and went to blow off some steam, that's all. But he either got my messages or remembered just in time to change the original outcome, because he's still alive."

She blinked at Nick. "Y-you mean, he should've died?"

He gave a brief nod. "In my vision, he wrecked when the creature attacked and was killed when he hit a tree and broke his neck. Tonight, he managed to avoid the tree."

"But he could still . . . Have you seen a new outcome?" she asked anxiously.

"I'm afraid not. All we can do is wait."

As endless minutes dragged by, she hated sitting,

not knowing what was going on in surgery. At one point Rowan took her hand and Jacee squeezed it like a lifeline, concentrating on the fragile bond between herself and Micah. Exhaustion and the day took their toll, however, and she wasn't aware she'd started to doze.

Until the bond began to flicker, like a lightbulb losing power. And finally burning out.

Instantly awake, she bolted upright in her chair. "Micah?"

"What's wrong?" Rowan asked.

"Our bond," she gasped, pushing to her feet. Frantic, she clutched her chest, seeking the golden thread. But there was only a gaping void where her mate should have been. "Micah!"

Around Jacee, the others stirred. Nick stood as well, and started toward her. But before anyone could stop her, she was out of the room, searching for her mate. The only one who would ever complete her. She set her coyote's senses free, seeking him out, ignoring the staff who attempted to stop her from entering a set of double doors marked RESTRICTED AREA.

Pushing through them, she followed her mate's scent to another door halfway down the hall marked OR-3 and barged inside. The sight of a team of doctors and nurses standing over her beloved mate, administering CPR, made her blood run cold.

"No." The word emerged as a sob, and her hand went over her mouth. "Micah?"

One of the doctors raised her head and snapped, "Somebody get her out of here."

She recognized the voice as Melina's, but had eyes only for the man on the operating table. His face was obscured by the oxygen mask, his eyes closed, dark brown hair like an ink spill on the white of the sheets underneath him.

This couldn't be possible. Her mate couldn't be dead.

A howl rose from the depths of her soul, and she shifted.

And cried out her grief to the heavens.

Twelve

The coyote's howl was distant. But it still reached the quiet room where Nick waited with Micah's small family. High and mournful, it caused chill bumps to break out on Nick's arms, and dread to darken his heart.

Rowan's face was pale as she stood, trembling. "No. Nick. Tell me it's not true. Not after all he's been through. Tell me it doesn't end like this."

"I wish I could," he said miserably. "I just don't know."

She stared at Nick, then looked at Aric. "I have to go to him."

Her mate shook his head, his expression sad, but his voice firm. "No, sweetheart. The docs have their hands full right now. They'll tell us—"

"I want to see my brother! You can't keep me from him!"

She started for the door, but Aric stopped her, wrapping her in his arms. Struggling, she put up a good fight at first, but soon sagged in his arms and let him hold her. Her shoulders shook with sobs as Aric whispered comforting words they all hoped were true.

Rowan was right, Nick thought. It wasn't supposed to end like this for Micah. None of this was fair. He tried to summon a vision, but couldn't force one. They didn't work that way.

"Hold her," he said to Aric. "I'm going to see if I can find out what's going on."

Aric nodded grimly, and Nick strode out of the room.

"Jacee, we need your help!"

Distantly, she heard someone calling to her, but couldn't make sense of it through the sadness pouring from her heart and soul. Hands shook her, hard, and she stopped howling, peering with her coyote's eyes at the intruder on her grief.

"Shift back," Mac commanded. "Now. If you want to help your mate, shift. Understand?"

Mate. Help him?

That penetrated the fog, and Jacee obeyed, shifting back to human form. She was briefly tangled in her clothing, but the doctor quickly helped her straighten the garments and get to her feet.

"What can I do?" Jacee asked, her voice thick with tears. "He's gone."

"We've got a machine breathing for him, buying some time. We're going to give him some of your blood, and we've called Calla, Nick's mate. She's on her way to donate as well."

Hope sparked in Jacee's chest. "Whatever will save him. I'm ready."

"I can't promise this will work, but we're doing our best."

"I know, but it's a chance, right?"

"Yes, the best one he has."

Jacee followed Mac, shaking so violently she thought she might throw up. This couldn't fail. Could not. If Micah didn't make it, she'd have no reason to go on. No desire left.

"We're going to do two transfusions," Melina said, pulling Jacee to a chair beside Micah. "One from you and one from Calla to give him that rich, healing vampire blood. She'll be here any second, so let's start yours. Both will be direct from the source to your mate."

The faster, the better, as far as Jacee was concerned. Once she was seated, Noah stretched out her arm on a small platform attached to the chair, designed for taking blood. Then he wrapped a stretchy rubber tube around her arm above the elbow and felt for a good vein. When he was satisfied, he wasted no time sliding the needle in and starting the flow into the tubing directly to Micah's left arm.

"Blood flow from the left arm goes to the heart first," Mac explained.

Jacee just nodded, anxiously watching her mate. The machine continued to breathe for him, but there was no spark of life. Not yet. Even though there was still a black void where their bond should have been, she reached out through their mental link. If there was any chance, she had to try.

Come on, honey. I know you're tired and hurt. But you can do this. Don't leave me here without you. Please.

Melina readied the pads on her mate's chest and nodded to Noah. A shock jolted Micah's body, and the line on the heart monitor jumped a couple of times and went flat again.

Another shock. Four blips.

Calla burst into the OR, Nick on her heels. Jacee didn't know the vampire princess well, but she'd never been so glad to see anyone, ever. If her blood couldn't save Micah—

"Okay, time to switch," Noah said briskly. Working

fast, he removed the needle and tubing from Jacee, wiped the puncture, and applied a cotton ball and strip of medical tape.

Jacee moved so Calla could take her place in the chair, and Noah repeated the procedure all over again. She was amazed at how speedy he was, hands steady, completely calm, at least on the outside.

When Jacee crept to Micah's side and took one of his hands, nobody stopped her. His skin was too cool, but not cold. Not yet. Lashes like black lace fanned across his cheeks, and his hair was silky around his face and neck. He could've been sleeping—if it weren't for the bloody, partially healed gashes on his chest and stomach and the multitude of other wounds.

Come back to me, baby. You can do it.

Several blips.

That's it. Reach out to me, Micah! Can you hear me? Fight for us!

Just then, the bond flared to life, so bright and sudden the brilliance of the reconnection took her breath away. Every eye in the room turned to her, silently questioning.

"I feel our bond," she gasped. "It's there!"

And then the heart monitor began a steady beep. This time, it didn't stop.

There was a collective sigh of relief, and a few murmurs of thanks to whatever gods where listening. Jacee sagged and would've hit the floor if it hadn't been for Nick's quick reaction.

Melina turned to Jacee, her tone much kinder than before. "We're going to stabilize him, and we may have to remove his spleen and a kidney if they don't heal. Nick and Calla will go with you back to the waiting room, and we'll come talk to you as soon as we can."

"Thank you." Jacee's voice was barely a whisper. "So much."

As Nick and his mate accompanied Jacee from the room, she glanced back at Micah. *Stay strong. Keep making your way back to me. I'm not going anywhere. I love you.*

There was no answer, but she was patient. As long as he was still in the world, she could wait.

The next two hours seemed like forever, but at last the waiting room door opened. Rowan, drained from crying, was asleep on the sofa with her head in Aric's lap when Mac and Melina came into the room. Aric shook his mate awake, and when she saw the doctors, she bolted upright, rubbing her eyes.

Jacee stood, ready to face whatever they had to say. She knew her mate was alive—the bond was still humming and strengthening every minute.

"Micah's going to recover," Melina said, giving them a rare smile. "That man is one of the bravest fighters I've ever seen."

"Thank God," Rowan said. Aric took her hand. "What about the surgery?"

"We had to take his spleen and appendix. They were too damaged to heal properly, even with the vampire blood. The kidney repaired itself, however, as did the gashes and other cuts, abrasions, and broken bones."

Jacee sighed with relief. "Is he in a room? Can I stay with him?"

"They're moving him now. Shouldn't be too long. Noah will come get you, okay?"

"All right."

Nick and Calla stayed until Noah showed up and then excused themselves. "Family first," Nick said, in spite of the others' protests that they *were* family. "We'll come tomorrow, after everyone's rested."

The blond nurse took Jacee, Rowan, and Aric to Micah's room. Jacee took a seat on one side of his bed and held his hand. It was warmer, but she'd feel better when he woke up. At least he was breathing on his own now.

"You can't do this to me anymore," she ordered him. "My heart can't take it. This is it—do you understand?"

"I second that, little brother." Rowan's expression was as exhausted and relieved as Jacee felt.

They watched him for a while, talking in quiet tones, until finally Aric insisted Rowan go home with him and get some sleep.

"We need to give Jacee some time alone with her mate, too," he pointed out. That made the other woman relent, and after she gave her brother and then Jacee a kiss on the cheek, they were both gone.

As much as Jacee was coming to love them all, she was glad to finally have some privacy. The horrid hours of grief, believing she'd lost her love, caught up to her, and she wept, burying her face in her hands. She meant what she'd told him—she couldn't take this again.

How was she going to handle him going on missions and fighting all sorts of monsters? Never knowing if he'd come home alive or in a body bag? But what else was he supposed to do for a living? As far as the world was concerned, Micah Chase, U.S. Navy SEAL, was MIA and presumed dead.

She worried it in her head until she was so tired she couldn't think anymore. One thing was for sure: she could never ask him to give up his Pack brothers. This place and these people were more than just a job. They were family.

Asking him to leave here would be like ripping off one of his limbs. She couldn't do it.

After checking on him one more time, she settled herself on the sofa close to his bed. Noah had thoughtfully provided a pillow and a blanket, and she soon dropped headfirst into the sleep of the stone-dead exhausted.

But tired or not, she had the most wonderful dream. . . .

She and Micah were taking a walk through their new home: their dream cabin in the forest not far from the compound, but just far enough for privacy.

Surrounded by trees, situated on the pretty plot of land he'd shown her that day, months ago, it was perfect. With four bedrooms, three baths, a media room, a den, and a pool and hot tub out back, it would be perfect for the two of them and for when friends or family stayed.

And for when they began having kids. Seeing other mated couples at the compound starting their families had her excited about a future she never dreamed possible. Kalen and Mac had their precious son, Kai, and Nick and Calla were expecting. Jax and Kira were trying and hadn't given up.

Maybe she and Micah would be next?

Hand in hand, they discussed what kind of furniture to get, where to place it, but in truth she couldn't have cared less as long as she was with him. The man who was the other half of her heart.

"Want to see out back?" he asked, smiling.

"Yes."

Through the den, they went out the double doors and onto the large cedar deck. On the deck was the hot tub, bubbling away and looking very inviting. A few steps below was the pool, sparkling and blue in the sunlight.

"I'll bet it looks beautiful at night, too," Jacee sighed.

"I'm sure it does. Want to see?"

She cocked her head at him. "Sure, but we'll have to wait for it to get dark."

Micah grinned. "No, we don't. This is our dream, so we can make it however we want."

"Dream?" She looked around in confusion. "How do you know it's a dream? Being here with you, it feels so real."

"Maybe it is real. What's reality, anyway?"

With that, he snapped his fingers, and instantly the scene around them changed. Suddenly the cloak of night had fallen, but the pool area was gorgeous, all lit up with the water a more brilliant blue than before.

"How did you do that?" She glanced around them in awe.

"Dreamwalker, remember?" He winked.

"What?"

"That's my Psy gift. I'm pretty sure I told you."

"I—I think you did. But this . . . this is incredible!"

"And real."

She frowned. "But you said it was a dream."

"When you're mate's a Dreamwalker, it can be both. You'll see."

"I think you're one fry short of a Happy Meal."

He laughed, the sound deep and rich. "We'll see about that. Come on."

"What are we doing?"

"Christening our pool and hot tub properly. What do you think?"

"That sounds like fun!"

Taking her hand, he pulled her along, jogging toward the pool. She shrieked when she realized he intended to yank them both into the water, and she tried to get away. But he was having none of it and jumped, keeping a firm grip, and hauled them both over the edge.

As she plunged in, squealing, she suddenly felt very naked. And as she surfaced, she noted that, indeed, her clothing had vanished. "More liberties of your Dreamwalking skills?"

"Hey, why have it if you can't take advantage?"

"You look very smug."

"I'm very horny."

"And smug."

"That, too, because I know my mate's going to put out."

"Hey! Arrogant much?"

"Confident."

Micah lunged for Jacee, and she took off through the water with a shriek. She laughed as he gave chase, and she thought in that moment that she'd never been happier. If this was a dream, did they have to wake up?

Eventually, baby. But for now, let's enjoy this.

She went with it, letting him catch her. He spun her around, pulling her against his slick body and kissing her until she had no air left in her lungs. His stiff cock rubbed between her thighs, a new experience in the silky coolness of the pool.

They kissed for a while, tongues dueling, tasting. Then he walked her backward to the edge of the pool and lifted her up to sit with her legs spread.

"Mmm. A feast just for me. Lean back, baby."

She did, bracing her arms behind her. The position was decadent, him still in the water, hair slicked back, with her sitting on the rim of the pool, legs spread. He buried his face in her mound, licked, and sucked, driving her crazy with every pass of his tongue.

"Oh! Oh, God."

"Like that, sweetheart?" he murmured.

"Yes. Don't stop."

He continued as long as she could stand it. Edging her toward oblivion only to bring her back and then do it again.

His voice was a low growl. "Come all over my face. Do it."

She had no choice. He ate her, laving both her slit and

clit, and she bucked, out of control, as her orgasm shattered. Crying out, she gave him what he wanted, creaming all over his tongue, much to his satisfaction. Then he was pulling her into the water again, turning her to face the edge.

"Hang on."

Grabbing the lip, she floated some as he spread her from behind and slid his cock deep. All the way into her heat. He began to shaft her, deep and hard, and another orgasm began to build even in the wake of the first one.

Faster and faster, he pumped, and when his fangs sank into the curve of her neck where it met her shoulder, she detonated for a second time. Her walls spasmed around him, and he came with a hoarse shout, filling her with his release.

At last, he had to pull out, and she felt a sense of loss.

"I wish we didn't have to leave here," she said sadly.

"But we'll be back one day. I promise."

Jacee wound her arms around his neck and kissed him, holding on to him for a very long time.

She woke, her lips tingling and her body singing with the phantom pleasures of her mate's kiss and his lovemaking. The press of him against her. She smiled, remembering the dream, the sheer joy of playing with him.

Too bad it had just been a dream.

From the bed, Micah stirred and whispered, "I promise."

She rose on one elbow and stared at him, stunned. He'd spoken those words, but he wasn't awake. Could it be?

Her mate was a Dreamwalker. It was entirely possible they'd had a meeting of the minds, as it were.

Smiling, she let that comforting thought carry her back into sleep.

This time, she didn't dream at all.

*   *   *

Micah first became aware of the incessant beeping that he hated. Then the smells.

The one scent he was glad to pick out was that of his mate. She was the sole reason he'd struggled so hard to return to the living. To open his eyes. Otherwise he wouldn't have given two shits if he ever moved again.

Micah tried to recall what in the holy hell had happened. An argument with Jacee. About what?

Oh. Shit. She'd found the bottle of myst. They'd had words. He'd left, intending to just go blow off some steam for a while. Damn, he wasn't used to having to answer for his every fucking move, and he was trying. So hard. He hadn't even taken any of the goddamn pills, but she hadn't believed him, had she?

Maybe she had. But he remembered she kept saying Micah had lied. By omission.

Truth. No way around that. He hadn't wanted to worry her, but maybe that hadn't counted for anything. She'd felt she couldn't trust him, and the hurt had driven him away. Temporarily.

Wasn't like he'd planned to stay gone. But the creature had attacked first, blood and vengeance on its mind. It had intended to tear him to pieces, carry him away, and then finish the job. Perhaps even eat him for dinner.

God. He'd narrowly escaped that fate. The last real memory he had was of his Pack arriving, Aric shooting flames at the beast. Of falling. And then nothing.

Had he even hit the ground? Something told him he wouldn't have been alive to talk about it if he had. Kalen was probably to thank for intervening there.

After quite a bit of effort, Micah managed to open his eyes. Focusing took a few more minutes, but when he did, he saw his mate sleeping on the sofa under the window. She looked so small and vulnerable lying there, his heart broke for what she'd endured because of his stupidity.

And the monster's cruelty. He couldn't forget that. Yes, he'd tortured innocents. But he was coming to understand that his friends were right—only a soul that was truly twisted to start with would end up at this extreme, killing and maiming. Perhaps Bowman had merely made sure the outside of the creature matched the inside.

The "good doctor" had tried to accomplish the same thing with Micah. He'd tried to mold Micah into a ruthless killer, but thankfully the lessons had never taken. Micah hadn't been able to kill an innocent, no matter what punishments Bowman threatened him with. That was the truth, and he'd swear it in front of anyone.

As though sensing his stare, Jacee stirred and stretched. After a couple of minutes she opened her eyes to find him watching, and sat up fast.

"You're awake! My God, I thought I'd lost you." Tears flooded her pretty eyes, and she came to sit by his bed, taking his face in her hands.

"You didn't," he croaked. "I'm made of tougher stuff than that."

"You almost died. It took my blood and Calla's to bring you back. Don't ever do that to me again. Please." She kissed his lips tenderly.

"I'll try. How long have I been out?"

"Since last night. You were really messed up. The doctors had to remove your spleen and appendix. But everything else healed on its own. Well, with some help."

"I'm so grateful. Thank you, baby. I'll thank Nick and Calla later, too."

"They won't want your thanks, just for you to get well. How do you feel?"

He thought about that. "Like hell. But it beats the alternative."

"Yes, it does."

She got quiet, and he asked, "What's wrong?"

"I was wondering if you remember having a dream about me last night?"

He smiled. "About us, at our cabin? Making love in the pool?"

She nodded, wide-eyed. "How did you know?"

"Because it wasn't *just* a dream. We reached out to each other, and so I directed us in our dream. That's what a Dreamwalker does."

"So it happened, and yet it didn't."

"We met on almost a spiritual level. Our minds connected. I helped with the rest."

"That's just . . ."

"Weird, I know."

"But sort of cool." She stroked his hair. "You need to rest, honey. I can see how tired you are."

"I don't really want to," he grumbled.

But his healing body didn't give him a choice. As if she'd commanded it, the weight of sleep dragged him under to the stroke of her hands on his hair, his face. He knew nothing more for quite a while.

Jacee was dozing again when Mac came into the room.

"Hey," the doc said softly, "you awake?"

"Barely." Sitting up, Jacee wiped her face.

"How's our patient?" Mac glanced toward Micah, who was sleeping.

"As well as can be, considering."

Mac busied herself checking his vitals, then addressed Jacee. "He's doing pretty well. By the way, I've got the lab results back on those leftovers you brought to us last night."

"With everything that's happened, I'd almost forgotten about them! What were the results?"

"Well, your coyote's nose was correct—the food was laced with rat poison, something anyone can buy at any supply store. With your shifter biology, the stuff would've made you sick, but it wouldn't have killed either of you."

"So the crime wasn't very well thought-out," Jacee mused. "Sounds almost like an afterthought, like he had the opportunity and did it on a whim."

"Well, I'm a doctor, not a cop, so I couldn't say. But that sounds about right." The doc tucked her stethoscope back into the pocket of her coat. "Anyway, I'll let Nick and the sheriff know the results."

"Thanks. Any idea when he might be released?" Jacee glanced at Micah, who was still totally oblivious.

"If it hadn't been for Calla's blood, his healing would've taken a lot longer. As it is, perhaps a day or two. Even so, I want him to rest for a few days when he's released."

"I'll make sure he does."

One thing was starting to become clear—she was going to have to cut back on her hours at the bar. She might have to quit altogether, which would be kinder to Jack than keeping such a sporadic schedule. And bartending, though she loved talking to people, wasn't what she wanted to do forever.

What she *did* want to do, she didn't know. Go back to school? To study what?

A tiny bubble of excitement started to form, and she decided to speak with Micah about her options as soon as he was awake and coherent. One thing she did know for sure was that her mate would be supportive of whatever she chose to pursue. That was a very liberating feeling.

A short while after Mac left, Micah began to wake up. He moved around, cracked his eyes open, and groaned. "Hey," he said, his lips turning up. "You've been there the whole time?"

"Haven't left, but I'm going to shower and change, then get something to eat soon. Want me to bring you back anything?"

He thought about that. "No. Just you."

"That, I can do." Leaning over, Jacee kissed him. "Mac was here. They're going to spring you in the next day or so."

"That's fast, considering how bad that bastard tore me up," he said in amazement.

"I'll say. We have Calla and her vampire genetics to thank for that. She and Nick are going to stop by and see you soon, by the way."

"Okay."

"You sure you'll be all right while I run out for a bit?" She bit her lip.

"Stop fretting. I'll be fine. Just do what you need to, and I'll be here plotting the untimely death of a certain monster who put me here."

"All right, but I'll be back soon."

After giving him another kiss, she left. But not before looking at her mate lying in the bed and reassuring herself that he really was going to be fine. John was guarding his door as well, which added some relief to her worry. There wasn't anyone in the world who meant more to her than that battle-scarred wolf.

He was hers, and nobody was taking him away.

Back in their quarters, she puttered around, finding a bra and a pair of clean underwear. Then she laid out a fresh pair of jeans and a blue cotton top. Just as she turned to go into the bathroom, the small brown pill bottle caught her eye. It was lying rather innocently on the floor, and a sudden spurt of anger seized her chest.

Bending, she grabbed it. Carrying it to the bathroom, she opened it, poured the contents in the toilet, then flushed them. "Good fucking riddance!" Then she buried the bottle at the bottom of the trash can, where it would end up in the dump, never to be seen again.

That wouldn't end his cravings, she knew. But she'd be there to help him every step of the way.

After her shower, which felt really good, she dried her hair and put on the barest of makeup. Just enough to cover the circles under her eyes and put some color in her cheeks. Then she went to the dining room in search of food.

Lunch was in full swing, and she was instantly surrounded by Micah's Pack brothers, all demanding an update. They hadn't wanted to bombard his room all at one time, but now that he was on the mend, they promised to stop by.

Jacee sat with Aric, Rowan, Kalen, and Sariel. One thing her friends steadfastly refused to discuss was the actual attack.

"You don't want to hear a blow-by-blow account," Aric said firmly. "Trust me on that."

And that was the end of it. He did describe the creature, but that was as far as he was willing to go. Jacee shivered at the knowledge of how close to death her mate had come.

Her friends changed the subject, and she enjoyed listening to Sariel talk about the wonders of this world. She'd never thought about their plane of existence from the perspective of someone from another realm before, and it was intriguing. Well, the prince himself was fascinating.

"So, you don't have phones or anything in the Seelie realm?" Jacee asked.

"Phones? Whatever for?" He cocked his head, jewel blue hair cascading over one shoulder. His large blue wings rested against his back.

"Guess not. How do you communicate with each other?"

"Oh. If not in person, then we use mind-link. Much like mated shifters can do, but Fae can all do it from the time they're children."

"Wow, that's cool."

Sariel grinned. "Very. For the most part, though sometimes siblings can be a pain when you want privacy. Especially my brothers." At the mention of his brothers, his face fell. "I miss them."

"I'm sorry." Reaching out, Jacee touched his hand. "Do you think they'll ever come here looking for you?"

"I'm not sure, but I like to imagine they'd find a way," he said wistfully. "I look for a portal, once in a while. I was cast out of my realm through one, so I know they exist. I just don't know where."

She hated to see the Fae prince so sad. All too well, she understood what it was like to suddenly be without your family. Only his weren't dead, just out of reach. "What do you like to do for fun?"

"Hmm, I like to watch television."

She laughed. "I mean *real* fun. TV is boring."

"Not if you've never seen one before." He gave it some thought. "I like the video games, and I like to shop."

"Really? How does that work, with that hair and those wings?" She eyed the gorgeous creature, imagining the riot he'd cause in town if people got a look at him.

"I use magic to cloak my appearance when I go out. I've been at the Grizzly with the team, and I'll bet you've never even noticed me," he said, smug.

She blinked at him in surprise. "You have?"

"Yes. I don't use the same disguise every time because I don't want people to remember me."

"Makes sense. Can you do it now? Show me a disguise."

"Of course."

The air around him shimmered, and in two blinks, a rather ordinary-looking young man with short brown hair and green eyes sat in front of her. No wings. Then the air shimmered again, and he became a portly, older bald man. Then a buff, muscular black man.

"Wow! That's incredible." The others around the cafeteria were getting into the fun, calling out suggestions. Sariel did a few more before reverting back to his normal self.

He shrugged. "It allows me to move freely in your world. If I can't be myself, the ruse will do, for a short while."

That sobered her some. She couldn't imagine having to pretend to be someone else just to move freely in society without censure.

But then, there were regular people who had to do that every day.

Purely on a whim, she asked, "Would you like to go shopping with me sometime?"

He beamed with pleasure. "I would love to. There are so many things I haven't discovered, and I enjoy getting out of the compound. If your mate wouldn't mind, that is. I wouldn't want him tearing out my throat."

She seriously doubted even Micah could tackle an eleven-thousand-year-old Fae prince, but Sariel's words were endearing. "I'm sure. He's not like that."

"In that case, yes."

"How about you?" she asked Rowan. "Think you could get away from Pack duties for an afternoon for some retail therapy? We've been under plenty of stress, and shopping is the cure."

"As long as Nick approves and Sariel is with us, I think we'll be safe enough." Rowan nodded. "I'm in!"

"Great! We'll get that mate of mine home, and then it's a date."

They were all due for some fun. She couldn't wait.

Thirteen

"Admit it. You like Sariel more than you like me," Micah grumbled. "What's he got that I don't?"

Jacee paused in stirring the chili on their stove. "Hmm. Besides the pretty wings, the rock star hair, and the magic? Nothing, sweetie."

Growling, he grabbed a pillow off the sofa, threw it into the kitchen at her. And missed.

"Now, now, my grumpy wolf." Retrieving the abused cushion, she brought it back to him, plumped it, and placed it behind him. "You're just going nuts because you hate being inactive and the doctors are being cautious about clearing you."

It was true. He was going crazy, and the whole team knew it.

"I don't mean to take my foul temper out on you. But dammit, they know I'm fine!"

"You lost two major organs, superhero. Give yourself a break." She arched a brow. "And me, too."

Instantly he was contrite. "Sorry. I'll try to chill out.

You deserve a break, too. When are you going shopping with Rowan and Sariel?"

"Day after tomorrow."

He still didn't like it. But she'd sworn up and down it would be okay. Nick had cleared it since the Fae prince was powerful, and they were going in broad daylight, sticking to populated areas. Micah wanted to go, too, but knew he couldn't stay in her hip pocket at all times. That wasn't reality, and it could take weeks or months before the creature who'd attacked him was ID'd and caught.

Besides, he had something to work out. A tiny niggle in his brain, struggling to bring itself forth. It had to do with the night of his attack—but not with the creature. No, it was afterward. When he was fighting to survive.

He vaguely recalled being rushed through the hallways in Sanctuary. Bleeding, hurt. Watching, dazed, as the walls and doorways rushed past. And then—

He'd seen a woman. One who looked like Jacee. In fact, he'd thought at first it had been her, but the woman's face had been too young. He remembered reaching for her, and the surprise on her face when he said Jacee's name.

The incident had happened so fast. One second or two, and she was gone. Then he was unconscious again.

He didn't even want to voice what he was thinking. Especially not to Jacee. It was just a weird circumstance, probably nothing. He was likely wrong, and he sure wasn't going to watch his mate get crushed all over again. He'd put in a quiet inquiry to Mac when he walked over for his checkup later.

"What're you thinking so hard about?"

He blinked up at her to see her smiling at him, bemused. "Oh, nothing. Just about my appointment with Mac and how tired I am of doctors." That was true enough.

"Ah. Well, come eat and forget about that for a while."

They shared a good meal, and he ate like he hadn't been fed in weeks. His energy was returning, and he was freaking glad. Had he been human, shit, he would've been dead four times over by now.

"Thank you, baby," he said, patting his full stomach. "That was awesome. I don't want to move now."

"Got time for a nap?"

He checked his phone. "Nope. I've got to go see Mac, and then see Noah about that list of visitors he was supposed to get together. I'm not sure if Jax ever asked him about it in all the chaos."

"Okay. I guess I'll stay here and clean up, but I'll see you later?"

"Soon as I can get back."

After hurrying to the bathroom, he brushed his teeth. Then he returned to the kitchen. Wrapping her in his arms, he made sure she knew how much she'd be missed in the hour or so he'd be gone. Leaving her thoroughly kissed and mussed, he headed for Sanctuary.

On the way, he spotted Jax and stopped him. "Say, I'm going over for an appointment with Mac. Thought I'd check with Noah on that visitor's list while I was there. Did you ever talk to him about it?"

Jax's eyes widened. "Holy crap, I totally forgot to ask him. With everything that's been going on, it slipped my mind."

"No worries. I'll talk to him."

"Thanks, man."

"No prob."

Micah wandered to the new building, feeling pretty good. In the reception area to the doctors' offices, he spotted Noah. "Just the guy I wanted to talk to."

"Me? How come?"

"Can I get a list of visitors to this building over the past month? We're searching for a common link between any of the patients and me. This is by Nick's authority, of course. Check with him if you need to."

Noah waved a hand. "Sure, be glad to. The sooner you guys catch whoever is doing this to you, the better. Go on in. Mac's ready for you."

"Thanks." Giving the younger man a smile, Micah headed in for his checkup.

In the end, it went well. She poked and prodded, took his temperature, ran more blood work. Listened to his heart and lungs. But he was as fit and healthy as ever, a minor miracle, given what he'd survived.

Nick and Calla had come by the day after his attack, and Calla had waved off his thanks, as he'd known she would. But he was grateful nonetheless.

"You're cleared for duty," Mac told him once they were in her office.

"Really? That's great!"

"Just try not to get any more body parts ripped out. You don't have that many to spare."

"Ha-ha."

"Get out of my office. And try not to come back for at *least* a year. Well, until your six month checkup, anyway."

"Damn, you're getting as prickly as Melina."

"Watch it, buster."

With a wink, he walked out. In the reception area, Noah was waiting, a sheaf of papers in hand. Micah took them, glancing through each of the pages. "I appreciate it. Thanks. There aren't many names here."

"No. But I think you might find it more interesting to learn what name *should* be on there and isn't."

"Oh?" Micah's pulse sped up. This could be their break.

Noah's blue eyes danced with excitement. "The other

day, I was about to enter a patient's room, and I heard him call someone by name. The patient referred to the man as his brother when they were talking, but after the man left and I checked on the patient, I made a casual remark about it. The patient backtracked and said the guy was his friend, and he called him brother in a friendly sense, you know?"

"Yeah. But you didn't feel that's the way he meant it?"

"Right. I thought to myself, no, he definitely was calling him brother. But whatever. It wasn't a big deal, so I forgot about it. Until I checked the visitor's list."

"And?"

Noah pointed. "The brother, or whoever the man is, isn't on it."

The excitement grew, but Micah remained calm. "Okay. Who's the patient?"

"Tyler Anderson."

"I knew it," Micah hissed, resisting the urge to pump his fist in the air. "What name did you overhear him call the other guy?"

"Parker. Does that help?"

"Yes! I fucking knew it!" Grabbing Noah, he wrapped the smaller guy in a big hug.

Which, of course, was the exact moment Nix stepped out of the elevator, wearing a huge frown. "What the fuck, man? Don't you have a mate?"

Letting go of a flushed Noah, Micah grinned at his friend. "Yes, you idiot, and so do you. But that's beside the point. We've got him. I know who our monster is, and Noah's the one who had the puzzle piece all along!"

"He did?" Nix looked at Noah, who smiled shyly. "Awesome. Good work, man."

The nurse shrugged. "I was just in the right place at the right time."

"Anyway, we need to get this info to Nick and the team. I need a current description of Parker, too."

"Better yet," Noah suggested, "we can pull up the security feed. Hand out his picture."

"Great thinking. We need to know how often he's been showing up, whether there's a pattern. When the last time was he visited. Then we'll need to see Tyler, and let him know we're on to his brother. Lean on him."

"We've got to call a meeting with Nick and the team," Nix said. "Run all this past him. Maybe there's a way we can set a trap when Parker comes back to visit."

"Okay, meeting first. We'll see what Nick says."

Nix started back toward the elevator. "I'm on it. See you in the conference room." He left without looking back.

Micah couldn't help but notice how Noah's face fell once the man was gone. "Give him time, my friend."

"That's what everyone says. But I'm not sure all the time in the world will be enough." He smiled sadly. "I'll get to work on having one of the guys pull up that security footage."

"Cool."

The blond walked away, and Micah shook his head. Stupid fucking Nix. What the hell was his problem?

The other detective mission would have to wait. In a hurry, Micah pulled out his phone and called Nick. The man didn't answer, though, so he had to leave a voice mail. "Hey, it's Micah. Conference room with the team, ASAP. I've got info on our mystery creature. Not a mystery anymore."

You were right, Mom. He was someone close to me, from my not-so-distant past. Thanks for trying to help me. I love you, and I miss you so much.

He could've sworn he felt a touch on his face, and then it was gone.

Rowan and a few of the guys were in the conference room already when he arrived. Though they had questions, he opted to wait for Nick and everyone else so he could go over Noah's revelation once. The rest of the team filtered in, and they sat around, shooting the breeze for a few minutes.

Nick arrived last, looking harried. "Sorry, guys. I was on a call with Jarrod. What's up?" His steely blue gaze found Micah. "You've got a positive ID on our monster?"

"It's not one hundred percent, no. But it's as good as a smoking gun as far as I'm concerned."

"Who ID'd him?"

"Noah."

There were a few murmurs of surprise at that announcement. Even Nick blinked. "How so?"

"Noah overheard Tyler Anderson speaking with a visitor the other day, someone he referred to as his brother. He called the man by his name—Parker."

Nick whistled. "So Parker was either mistakenly placed on the list of deceased or had his brother lie for him."

"I'm betting on the latter. When Noah made casual conversation and inquired about Tyler's brother, Tyler denied he meant the visitor was literally his brother, but rather just a friend."

"So Tyler's a liar. And a nervous one at that." Nick stroked his thumb over his bottom lip in thought. "If Parker's our monster, he's evil. That means Tyler's in a horrible position, likely agonizing over what to do."

Micah agreed. "He seemed nervous when we questioned him, and now I believe his brother is why. He fears Parker's wrath. And having been on the receiving end of that wrath, I get it."

"Yeah, Tyler seems about as lethal as a Hostess Twinkie," Jax said. "So what's next?"

"Noah's getting footage of the security feed pulled, hoping to get a good current picture of Parker for us. Then I'd like to set up a trap for him. With Tyler's help."

"That's risky," Nick said, frowning. "Blood is thicker than water, as they say. If we can establish a pattern, it might be better to wait until he visits on his own."

"True, but we wouldn't have as much control over the time or place," Micah argued. "If he gets all the way inside Sanctuary before we know he's here, a lot of patients will be at risk if we try to take him."

"We need to get his ass before he goes inside the building," Aric put in.

"That means he's outside, in wide-open spaces." Rowan sighed. "Giving him more room to maneuver and fly away isn't ideal, either."

Micah sat back in his chair. "I think we need to talk to Tyler. Yes, it means tipping our hand, but he knows Parker better than anyone. If we promise to move him, keep him safe from his wretched brother, I believe he'll cooperate."

Nick gave a feral grin. "We'll have to move him anyway, once we've tipped our hand, for *our* own good as well as his."

"Good point." Micah blew out a breath. "Your call, boss. That's why you get paid the big bucks. And if your mojo would make an appearance and tell us what to do, that would be great."

"Gee, thanks." The seconds ticked by as Nick mulled over the issue. Finally he nodded. "My gut is telling me to talk to Tyler, too. He'll help us. Beyond that, I don't know. If we can set up a trap of some sort for Parker, we will. If it can be away from the compound and Sanctuary, even better."

Micah couldn't see how that would work, because they'd need Tyler to lure in Parker. He didn't say so, however. Instead, he said, "What if we lure him into one of the iron-and-silver-reinforced rehab cells?"

Nick sat forward, interested. "How would we do that?"

"We'll have Noah tell him Tyler has been moved to a new room. When he gets in there, we shut the gates."

"It's risky, but it could work."

"There won't be anyone in the bed, of course, but we'll make it look like there is. He just has to get inside the room."

"Okay. These are all a bunch of big *ifs*. Jax, let's you, me, and Micah go back and talk to Tyler. Find out if he's got a regular visitation day, or if he can get his brother here somehow." Nick checked his phone. "Got a message from Noah. We have a picture of Parker."

The conference room's laptop was hooked up to a data projector. Nick wasted no time sending the pic to his e-mail account, then downloading it to the laptop. In moments, he had a decent photo of a very creepy-looking Parker Anderson displayed for everyone to see.

The time in captivity, plus the last year or so, had not been kind to the eagle shifter. Tall and gray-skinned, hair thinning and unkempt, he appeared more like a cadaver than a man. Nick sent the picture to everyone's cell.

"Yummy," Aric muttered, lip curling. "I'm gonna make Mr. Hotness my screen saver."

Rowan snorted, and several guys chuckled.

Tension broken, the meeting adjourned for the time being. Micah walked over to the other building with Nick and Jax for a repeat visit with Tyler. This time, when they walked in, it seemed as though he'd been anticipating what was coming.

"You know," he said simply, his expression tired. Resigned. "He's going to kill me now."

Crossing his arms over his chest, Micah started off the

questioning. "What do we know, Tyler? Who's going to kill you?"

"Oh, come on. There's no need to play games anymore, is there? I've tried to tell Parker over and over that he wasn't going to be able to get away with what he's been doing, but he's crazy," the younger man whispered. "I mean, completely bat-shit Jack Nicholson in *The Shining* crazy."

"Yeah," Micah deadpanned. "I got that message."

"I'm so sorry." Tyler's face was anguished. "He's always been so good to me, but these days it's the kind of nice that scares me. That smile someone gives you right before they tear your face off. If he ever lost it around me, I don't think it would even register that I'm his brother until I was in pieces at his feet."

"We can help you," Nick said, "if you help us."

"What do you want me to do?"

"First off, if you tell him that we've talked?" Nick indicated all of them. "Deal's off. You're not our problem anymore, and you get no protection."

Tyler's face paled, and he clutched the sheets. "I won't, I swear. He's made his bed, and I can't save him."

"Okay. Next, is there a set day he comes to see you?"

"He sometimes comes on Fridays, but not every time. He didn't come last Friday, but I can find out if he's coming this Friday."

"You have his phone number?"

"Yeah, cell."

Tyler recited that for them, and they saved it. Micah knew Nick would have the number run as soon as they left here.

Jax spoke up. "Be careful when you talk to him. Don't make it sound like it's important that he show up one way or the other. But imply you're lonely or something. We want him to come this Friday."

"I'll get him here. Don't worry."

"Good," Micah said. "We'll take care of the rest. The less you know about the particulars, the better."

Nick pinned Tyler with a hard look. "All of your calls and contact will be closely monitored from here on out. Just so you realize."

"I figured as much. I won't double-cross you guys, I promise." In spite of his obvious misery, Tyler also looked a great deal relieved to have the secret out.

They took their leave and headed for the elevators. As they waited, Nick said, "I believe him."

"So do I," Micah said. "But if we're wrong, this is gonna be a hell of a clusterfuck."

Jax smirked. "And then some."

They parted ways, and Micah hurried back to his mate. All of that had taken much longer than he'd wanted. And he wanted his mate.

He found her in the bathroom, cleaning the tub, her tight little ass poking straight up in the air. Sneaking up behind her, he reached out and grabbed both globes in his palms.

Squealing, she straightened and whipped around, smacking him in the chest with a wet, soapy rag. It hit him with a squelch, leaving a dripping spot on his T-shirt. Her eyes widened; then she giggled. "There! See what you get for scaring me?"

"Yeah? I'll show you what you get for running around with your ass sticking up in those shorts like that."

Intent on getting some of that gorgeous skin, he grabbed the waistband of her shorts and pulled the material apart. The zipper ripped and the button popped off and went flying, hitting somewhere with a plink.

"Micah! Those were one of my favorite pairs!"

"I'll buy you some more."

Working his fingers under the material, he slid them

down her hips, along with her panties. A little afternoon delight was in order, and his wolf couldn't have agreed more.

"But I'm all hot and sweaty," she protested. The words, however, came out pretty weak and pathetic.

He decided on a compromise. "Got it covered."

Reaching out, he turned on the shower to let the water warm up. Then he finished undressing his mate, uncovering every inch of her delicious golden body. Her proud breasts with their rosy-tipped nipples begged to be tasted, so he did exactly that, laving one, then the other. He sucked them next, and she arched into him, digging her fingers into his hair.

"I like that," he murmured. "Pull my hair if you want."

She took him at his word, gripping a little harder when he reached between her legs and began to play with her clit. He rubbed the tiny bud, getting her good and worked up, until she moaned and writhed against him. Satisfied that she was ready, he quickly undressed and pulled her into the shower with him.

The spray made a nice, warm, silky curtain over them as he turned her to face the wall. He kneaded her shoulders and back, smiling at the small sounds of pleasure escaping her throat. All the way down her spine, he kept going, to her butt, and he worked the muscles there as well.

"You *do* have magic in your hands," she said in appreciation.

"That's not the only place."

"Show me."

"How about my tongue? And my cock?"

"Both, please!"

Kneeling on the stall floor, he nibbled her ass, then spread the creamy mounds. From behind, he licked her slit and laved it until she was wet, dripping for him. Gently he worked two fingers into her channel and pumped, making sure she was ready.

Then he stood and brought the head of his cock to her entrance, began to ease himself inside. She was so snug around him, just the right fit, clasping his shaft like a soft glove. Suddenly he had to concentrate not to come like an overeager teenager.

"Oh, Micah. Yes . . ."

He relished the feeling of being inside her. Couldn't believe that she belonged to him. *You're mine, and I'm yours, too.*

Yes, my mate.

I love you, sweetheart.

I love you, too, so much.

Holding her close, he thrust deep inside her, increasing the tempo. There was nothing on earth better than this closeness, this sharing and connecting with another person meant just for him. He was the luckiest bastard ever.

He drove them both to the peak, flirting with the razor's edge of release. And finally he could take it no more, and his balls drew up. The tingling started at the base of his spine, and he exploded, rocking inside her. His orgasm sent her over as well, and she cried out, tensing, reaching back, burying her fingers in his hair.

When at last they were spent, he pulled out, and they took turns soaping each other playfully, laughing. A few short months ago, he never would have believed there'd be a time when a smile would cross his lips. When laughter would warm his soul.

When a beautiful mate would capture his heart.

He'd do anything to protect what was his.

Later, they were relaxing on the sofa, Micah sprawled out with Jacee between his legs and resting against his back. Two glasses of wine were half full on the coffee table beside them, and he was cozy. Soft seventies pop was playing on the stereo.

"This is the life," he said happily.

"I wish we could stay like this forever."

"Might get cramped and hungry."

"Silly." She was quiet for a few moments before she spoke up again. "Tell me about today."

Leave it to reality to intrude. "Well, thanks to Noah, we ID'd our monster as Parker Anderson. His brother, Tyler, is one of the patients at Sanctuary."

Wiggling in his lap, she craned her neck to see him. "Really? Wow."

"Yeah. We cracked Tyler like a walnut. In truth, he was ready to break, though. Seems the pressure of having a psycho for a brother is getting to be a tad too much."

"I can imagine."

"I tortured both of them, under Bowman's orders. Yet they turned out so different."

"You know that lab twisted Parker into something evil, and you had nothing to do with that. You're just a convenient target because there's no one left."

He didn't completely agree that he'd had nothing to do with how Parker turned out, but he kept the thought to himself. "Tyler's left. And he's terrified of his brother."

"What are you guys going to do?"

Quickly, Micah outlined the plan to lure Parker to see his brother on Friday and be waiting with a trap. "It's risky, but it's all we have. We don't know where Parker's lair is at this point."

"Friday, you said?"

"Yeah. Why?"

She frowned. "Nothing. That's just when Rowan, Sariel, and I were going shopping."

"Maybe you should reschedule. I don't like the idea of you being out while we're trying to trap Parker."

"I don't know. Maybe it's a good idea if I'm *not* here. And if we all change our plans and suddenly act weird, he'll know something's up."

"Baby, I wish you'd reconsider."

He knew the instant she gave him the puppy-dog eyes he wasn't going to win this round. Dammit. "Fine. But you'll check in with me every hour the whole time you guys are gone."

"Whatever keeps my honey happy. And you have to promise to be careful trying to trap that lunatic. There's no telling what he'll do when he realizes he's been tricked."

That's what Micah was afraid of.

They lazed around for a while, but eventually the burning question on his mind wouldn't be put off any longer. "Hey, honey, I need to go talk to Nick. I'll be back before long."

"Oh. Okay."

He hated lying to her. Again. But there was no *way* he was going to get her hopes up and then be wrong about this. Giving her a quick kiss, he disentangled himself and pushed reluctantly from the sofa. Then he left before he could change his mind.

All the way to Sanctuary, he told himself he was a fool. This would turn out to be a wild-goose chase. Before he could lose his nerve, he approached Noah and lowered his voice.

"Got a question. It's private."

Nodding, the nurse led him to an alcove away from the main flow of traffic where they wouldn't be overheard. Still, Micah kept it down. "Can you tell me if you have a patient here by the name of Faith Buchanan?"

Noah blinked at him, eyes widening. And Micah's heart sped up.

"I, uh . . . I'm not supposed to give you that information." But the younger man was clearly uncomfortable.

"And by whose order would that be? Nick's? The doctors'?"

"No."

"Then who says?" Micah let Noah squirm for a few seconds before he continued. "Let me guess. The patient's? And why would that be?"

"I'm not allowed to say." His voice was quiet, his gaze sympathetic. "Confidentiality and all that."

"And what room is she in? Because I promise you, if I have to go door to door and harass every single person here until I find her, I will."

Noah stared at him, then sighed, running a hand through his blond hair. "Shit. I could get in so much trouble for this. She's in 521. And, Micah?"

"Yeah?"

"Go easy on her, okay? She's had it rough. *Really* rough. If she hasn't approached you or Jacee yet, she has her reasons."

Something unpleasant coiled in Micah's gut, and he nodded. "I will."

So, the truth was going to be more complicated than some happy reunion. Didn't that just figure? All the way to the young woman's room, he told himself it still could have been a case of mistaken identity. Some other girl by the name of Faith Buchanan. Who happened to end up in a hospital for lost and broken shifters.

Right.

Outside the correct door, he paused. Then knocked, knowing that somehow this visit was going to change his and his mate's lives.

"Come in?" Soft-spoken, posed as a tentative question.

He pushed inside the room and left the door open just a bit, hoping that would make her feel a little more comfortable in his presence.

His first good look at her confirmed exactly who he believed her to be, even without solid proof. The woman was a younger, waiflike version of Jacee, pale and far too thin. The bones stood out on her delicate face, and her hair was lighter, chestnut in color. Almost colorless eyes of blue crystal stared back at him, but not so much with fear.

With shame. Exhaustion. Longing. Curiosity. Her face was an open book of emotions, her hands clenched in her lap. She was sitting in a chair by the window, a book on the table beside her. She wore a dressing robe more suitable for someone four times her age, and it was fastened all the way to her throat.

"I wondered when you'd come, Micah Chase," she said, her voice soft and melodious. "I thought you might bring my sister."

His mouth fell open. "You've known who I am? That your sister is here and mated to me?"

Sorrow pinched her features. "Only since I saw you come in the other day, so badly injured. You reached for me and called me by my sister's name. I was so shocked, I had to learn what was going on. I asked a few questions."

"And got your answers."

"Yes."

"I'm confused," he admitted. "Do you know how much she mourns your loss? My God, she thinks you're dead!"

Faith plucked a tissue from the box on the table and dabbed at the tears that rolled from her eyes. "I believed she was, too. That's what I was told."

"By whom?"

"The Hunters who captured me, who started selling me as a prostitute."

Horror choked him, and bile threatened to force his wine to reappear. "You were barely more than a girl when you were taken. Twelve? Thirteen?"

She gazed at him sadly. "Thirteen. I haven't been young for a very, very long time, wolf."

They'd sold a child. His mate's sister. God help her. He wanted to kill them all.

"I can read your emotions in your face, and believe me, I've felt them all. The Hunters who took me are all dead, you know. I was rescued by your vampire allies several weeks ago and brought here to recover."

"And you'd been with those Hunters all those years?"

"Well, the group's members were fluid, but yes. Basically. So the ones unfortunate enough to still be around when I was liberated were killed by Prince Tarron and his coven. To hell with those evil bastards, and long live the prince."

A bit of fire, then. His lips turned up, and hers did, too. Just a fraction.

"Why didn't you come to us or send for us? Or at least your sister?" But hearing her story, he thought he understood now.

"I needed time. I'm still coming to grips with what I am. Or was. I don't know who I'm supposed to be or where I'm going. I'm ashamed, even though my head knows I did what I had to do to survive."

"You're afraid to face Jacee."

"Yes." More tears. "She has a wonderful life and a new mate. I'm a disaster. The last thing I want to do is burden her with the stain that has been my life."

Moving forward, he took the seat opposite her. He leaned toward her, but sensed she wouldn't want to be touched, so he refrained from taking her hand. He hoped his voice and expression conveyed his deepest sincerity.

"Believe me when I say nobody was more broken

than me when Jacee and I met. I was a drug addict, fighting too many demons to list, and I'm still working on both of those."

Faith's eyes widened. "Really?"

"Yes, though I wish it wasn't true. To top it off, I was very sick, and it wasn't a sure thing I was going to live. But you know what? Your sister has the biggest, most giving heart of anyone I've ever known. She *is* love personified. You can trust her, Faith."

The young woman was silent for a time, dabbing her eyes and shredding the tissue. Finally she looked up. "Give me some more time. A few more days. Then I'll either come see my sister or send for her."

"You're asking me to keep a secret from my mate." He hated that, with his whole heart.

"Please," she begged. "Just a little more time. I give you my word it won't be much longer. I want to have a plan for my life when I speak with her. I don't want to appear so . . . broken."

"She won't think that of you. Even I can see you're stronger than you realize." She waited for his verdict, and he relented. "But okay. A few days, no more. Then either you reveal yourself, or I'll drag her over here myself."

"Thank you."

"I'm glad you're here, recovering. This is going to make her so happy," he said softly. "I happen to know her deepest sorrow was losing you, and getting you back is going to be her greatest joy."

"I disagree, wolf." She smiled. "Somehow, I believe I'm looking at my sister's greatest joy."

Fourteen

Friday came, and all was in place. Micah hoped.

Tyler swore that Parker was coming to see him in the afternoon, around one o'clock. The staff at the hospital had moved Tyler to a new room on a different floor, and placed John inside it with him as a guard. Tyler's old floor as well as the unit where he was supposed to have been moved was cleared of patients, though the doors to the rooms would be closed so their emptiness wouldn't be evident.

Noah and the doctors would move around as normal.

Nick and Jax would be working the video monitors and would trigger the cell door when Parker stepped inside. Micah and the other Pack members would hide at intervals throughout the two floors, in the restrooms and in the stairwells, close by but out of sight. They couldn't risk tipping off the creature.

Before lunch, Micah told Jacee good-bye and found he was sort of relieved she wasn't going to be around now that the op was imminent. She would be in town, protected by one Pack member and one powerful Fae.

That seemed a better option than being anywhere near Parker's brand of crazy.

It was almost over. The one blight on his sunny days was *the secret*. Jacee knew he was acting funny, but she couldn't put her finger on what was going on. He could read her like a book, and he could tell she was trying to figure him out. It was really starting to make him sweat. He hoped Faith didn't wait much longer, because he couldn't stand keeping something this huge from his mate.

"We're going," Jacee told Micah, leaning in for a kiss, which he gladly gave.

"Don't forget to check in. Text me."

She rolled her eyes. "I will."

"I mean it."

"'Bye!"

She trotted out the door, and he shook his head. Women. It was so funny-strange: he'd never thought he'd share his life and space with one and deal with all the day-to-day mundane things like "Check in when you're out shopping so I'll know you're safe." But now? Yeah. Lucky bastard.

With Jacee gone, he went to meet his team. They had some time yet, but it was best to be prepared in case Parker was early. The team would get into position and wait, all day if need be. Sometimes the job could be really boring.

But he'd take boring over the last time he met up with the monster any day.

Once Nick and Jax had surveillance under control, he and the others walked over to the hospital. Noah was overseeing the transfer of the last patients, some of whom appeared confused. A couple were complaining about being inconvenienced, and Micah was glad he didn't have to work with strangers like that all day. He'd go nuts.

Once in the building, Micah, Aric, Kalen, and Ryon situated themselves in the basement-level stairwell. Keeping Parker from realizing he was actually in the basement instead of on a regular floor posed a problem, so they'd spent two days rigging the elevator to appear to be taking him to the first floor. From there, they'd put up directional signs designed to keep him away from any outside-facing walls—and thus from realizing there *wasn't* an outside on his floor.

What if, what if? Too many hazards.

Micah shut out the negative internal voices and focused on listening to Nick through his headset. This time around, that was their best way of communicating, since there were too many enclosed spaces and hiding spots to see every team member.

Every half hour that ticked by was interminably long. The worst of it was they couldn't even talk to make the time pass quicker. Shifters had notoriously awesome hearing. One scuffle at the wrong second, and the game was over. The headsets, however, were designed for their ears only, and were safe from anyone on the outside overhearing conversation coming through them.

At last, Nick's voice broke the silence.

"The target is on site. He's approaching the entrance on foot, so I'm assuming he flew in and shifted a safe distance away."

A pause. Less than a minute later, "Noah has intercepted the target and is redirecting him. The target appears visibly unhappy about the change in rooms."

Stay cool, Noah.

"Target is on his way down."

"Copy that," Micah said, palming his pistol. "We're ready." He didn't dare speak again.

A pause. "Target is off the elevator, heading your way."

Pause. "He's outside the room, looking in. Damn, he's suspicious."

Go in, you fucker. Go in!

"Target's turning back! He's on the run! Apprehend him!"

Fuck!

Micah and his teammates spilled from their hiding place and cut off Parker's escape. The man skidded to a halt in the middle of the hallway, then turned and fled back the way he'd come. At the end, he disappeared around a corner.

"Dead end," Nick called out. "You've got him cornered. But watch out! He's armed!"

Just then, Parker popped into view and fired three shots in their direction. Just behind Micah, a couple of the bullets struck flesh. Micah, Ryon, and Kalen flattened themselves against the wall, but Aric was lying on the floor, bleeding. And cursing.

"Motherfucker!" Crimson was spreading across his left shoulder and his left side, soaking his shirt.

Lunging for him, Micah dragged him off to the side and leaned him against the wall. "Aric's down," he called into the headset. "Two gunshots, shoulder and torso."

"Backup's on the way," Nick said. "Hang on."

Parker fired more shots, but they ricocheted down the hallway without striking anyone. Seemed they were at a stalemate. Until the fucker ran out of ammo.

"We've got him pinned, but—" Micah began.

Just then, Parker's hand appeared around the corner. And in his hand . . .

A grenade. Jesus Christ.

Micah yelled, "Fuck! Grenade! Hit the floor!"

They dove, and the explosion came, deafening in its power. But the grenade hadn't been lobbed at them, much to Micah's shock. As the debris and smoke cleared, he got up on his knees, looking around. The damage wasn't to their end of the hallway, but Parker's.

"Shit, did the asshole blow himself up?" Ryon asked, then coughed.

Aric snarled. "One can hope."

Kalen dusted off his leather coat. "Let's go look. Stay here and hold down the fort, Red."

"I plan on it, Goth Boy."

Cautiously, the three of them crept to the end of the hallway. Micah went around the corner first, and drew his weapon. Only to find himself staring into the sunshine. Open, empty air.

"Son of a bitch!" he yelled in frustration. "He blew a hole in the wall and escaped!"

"I'll be goddamned." Ryon gave a disgruntled sigh. "Back to square one."

Kalen kicked at a piece of Sheetrock with one booted foot. "And now we have a hell of a mess and a shitload of repairs to do. My mate's going to kick my ass."

Micah shook his head. "Let's check on Aric and get him upstairs. We need to make sure Tyler's protected at all times now, too. Parker will know he helped us."

"Clusterfuck," Kalen bitched.

Ryon snorted. "With extra clusters on top of the fuckity fuck."

"Come on, idiots." Micah hurried back to his brother-in-law, who was in pain, but more pissed off than anything. A good sign with Aric. The bleeding had slowed, but he still needed attention.

They got him upstairs, and the staff whisked him away. More than an hour went by as they dealt with the aftermath, and Micah finally remembered to check his phone. He was relieved to see that earlier he'd gotten a text from Jacee saying they were having a good time. He wasn't looking forward to Rowan's reaction when she learned Aric had gotten hurt, and decided he wasn't going to be the one to tell her.

Aric had insisted they wait until she got back. It was his ass.

He did text his mate and tell her, *Mission failed. Parker got away. Tell you more when you get back.*

She didn't reply, so he tried their mental link. *Jacee?*

Sorry. Just got done with lunch and saw your text. Why do we text when we can communicate like this, anyway?

He smiled. *I don't know. I guess it's a modern habit. And I can't always talk mentally if I'm supposed to be on a mission.*

True. So that bastard got away!

Yeah. Listen, Aric was injured. He's going to be fine, but I just wanted you to know in case Rowan wants to come back early.

You want me to tell her? No way! That's a dirty, rotten trick, trying to get me to do it.

Didn't work?

Not unless it's really serious.

Could've been, but he's okay. Really. He said he wants her to stay and have fun.

Damn. If it was me, I'd still want to know, Micah.

You're telling her.

Yep. Whatever she decides is fine.

You know, baby, personally, I'm so okay with you coming home early and holding me. I've had a bad day. He put plenty of pout into the suggestion, and heard her laugh through their link.

You are so transparent. I'll see you soon.

Love you.

Love you more.

With a relieved sigh, he shut their link. Then he pitched in and started helping with the cleanup in the basement.

*   *   *

Lunch and shopping had been fun. Rowan and Sariel had been awesome, and they were well on their way to becoming good friends.

It had been a bit strange to see Sariel in his guise as an ordinary brown-haired young man, and Jacee thought once more that it was sad he couldn't show the world his true self. Yet he clearly enjoyed himself despite having to assume a different form.

He was this joyous sponge, soaking up every bit of information, no matter how trivial. And yet at times he would say something like "My brothers would be amazed by this!" Then he'd look so sad for a few moments that she wanted to cry.

His sorrowful mood never lasted long, and he was soon chattering again about everything.

The mental conversation with Micah, however, put a damper on her mood. Her friends noticed as they were leaving the restaurant in Cody.

"What's up all of a sudden?" Rowan asked.

Jacee debated how much to tell them. The truth was always best, though, even if you thought you were doing the right thing by holding back. "Parker Anderson got away."

"What? Why didn't Aric tell me through our link?"

"Um . . ."

Rowan closed her eyes for a few seconds. Jacee knew she was trying to speak to her mate, and when Rowan opened her eyes again, she was starting to look panicked.

"He's not answering me. What's going on?"

"Micah said he was injured, but he's okay," Jacee rushed on. "He's probably getting treated right now."

Rowan paled. "Injured how? What happened?"

"He didn't say, just that Aric's fine and he said for you to have fun. That's all I know."

"Oh. Well, if he said that, it can't be too bad, right?"

"Right." But her friend still looked worried.

Sariel took Rowan's arm. "We can return if you'd like. It's not a problem. We've already had plenty of fun for one day."

"If you guys don't mind, I would like to check on him," Rowan said, worry etched on her face.

"Then by all means, let's—" Sariel gave a soft grunt and his eyes widened in surprise as he jerked backward. Two holes appeared on his shirt, and blue—not red— liquid, began to spread across his chest.

"Blue!" Rowan shouted.

Jacee lunged for him, intending to catch him. She managed to grab his shirt and stuck her hand right on one of the strange blue bloody spots. But pain exploded in the back of her head, and she stumbled and fell. She hit the ground, head spinning. Shouts reached her ears as she was picked up and bodily thrown. Her palms scraped on carpet as she landed and fell limp.

She heard Rowan yelling at their attacker.

Then she knew nothing more.

Micah wasn't too worried when Jacee missed the next check-in text. It hadn't been that long since he'd spoken to her via their mind-link, so he let it go. For a while. But when he sent her a text and she didn't answer, he grew uneasy.

Still, she'd missed one last time, and things had been fine. Really, though, he couldn't believe Rowan hadn't insisted they come home when she'd heard Aric had been injured. The man was the love of her life, and it would be unlike her to just keep shopping like it was no big deal.

That concerned him more than anything. Aric, too,

when Micah walked over to the ER and stepped behind the curtained partition to ask if he'd heard from Rowan.

Aric frowned. "No. Come to think of it, I'm kind of surprised. You told Jacee about me, you say?"

"Yeah. She was going to tell Rowan, and I figured they'd be back by now."

"Huh. Well, let's don't borrow trouble just yet."

Turned out they didn't have to borrow it. After Zan did a bit of healing on Aric's wounds, Aric was bandaged and released. As he and Micah were standing outside, inspecting the blown-up wall, trouble came roaring up the driveway in the form of the sheriff's car.

The men jogged over to greet Deveraux, others coming out of the buildings to see what was going on. It didn't take long to spot Blue lying on the backseat, bleeding from a chest wound. Micah's heart damn near stopped.

"What happened to him?"

The Fae had shifted back to his real form, and his wings were taking up the entire back of the car. He was gasping for breath, but struggling to push himself upright. Jesse got out and ran to open a back door and help him, leaning inside. Micah and Aric joined them, and Micah was aware of others crowding around the vehicle.

"Parker Anderson shot me," Blue gasped. "He just walked right up to me and pulled the trigger. Probably thought I was some regular guy and didn't realize I couldn't die that way. But I was out of commission for a few minutes, and he got away with the women. I'm so sorry. I'll take whatever punishment I deserve once we get them back safely."

"Blue, shut up," Micah growled. Fear rode him hard, but this wasn't Blue's fault. "You're not to blame for this. I shouldn't have let her go with that monster still out there."

Aric agreed. "Me, too."

"I should've protected them," Blue said, clearly ashamed. *Jacee? Baby, where are you?* No answer.

Micah shook his head, rage building. "You couldn't help what happened. But we're going to get them back. Did you see which way he went? Did he say anything?"

"No. But I believe Jacee got some of my blood on her after I was shot, when she grabbed me. If she did, we can trace her that way. Or, rather, a Sorcerer can."

From the other side of the car, Kalen nodded. "His blood is a Fae element we share, and I can track the source. If she's got some on her, we'll find her."

"Then do your thing," Micah said. "I've got a monster to kill."

Mac and Noah tried to get Blue to go to the infirmary, but he refused, waving them off and climbing out of the car under his own steam. Kalen touched the blood on his brother's shirt, spread it on his fingers, and closed his eyes. Then he began to chant a spell, his voice hypnotic. Micah had seen him work a few times, and it never failed to awe him.

A few moments later, the Sorcerer's eyes opened. "Six miles from here, in the forest. I've got her pinpointed."

Quickly, they loaded up in the SUVs. Aric refused to be left behind, and nobody blamed him. A couple of measly gunshot wounds were not enough to keep a wolf from his mate.

Blue took to the sky, following them that way. Micah knew the prince must have felt horrible. He never joined in on missions unless specifically called, claiming he was a lover, not a fighter—even though he was, ironically, probably the deadliest of them all.

It didn't take long to find the road Kalen directed them to and, a few miles beyond that, the ramshackle cabin almost obscured by undergrowth. Careful to park a good distance away, they set off on foot. Not fucking around this time, Micah had already shifted into wolf form by the Escalade, as had several others. His wolf was stronger and faster. More lethal.

That would be what counted.

He was going to tear Parker Anderson into very small pieces. There wouldn't even be enough left of him to feed the worms.

Jacee awoke to find herself bound with her hands behind her back, sitting in a corner of the main room of a filthy cabin. Thankfully, Rowan was right beside her, and a glance showed that her friend was pissed as hell at their captor. If her brown eyes could kill, the creature would have been dead.

But crazy people didn't care. Parker was one of those special kinds of insane bastards who got off on seeing others suffer for the hell of it.

At the moment, he was smiling to himself, showing yellowed teeth, singing a song with garbled lyrics that made sense to nobody but him. He was sitting at a table, puttering with some objects on top of it, arranging. Re-arranging. Picking one up, inspecting it. Putting it down and selecting another.

Jacee frowned until she realized what he was looking at—tools. Pliers, wrenches, hammers. A couple of small handsaws. Garage tools of all kinds. Suddenly she felt as though she'd been dropped into a terrible episode of *Criminal Minds*. And she wanted out. Now.

A glance at Rowan showed her friend had made the same realization, and some of her anger had bled to fear as well.

"Your mates won't think you're so pretty by the time

they get you back—if they get you back." Parker picked up a pair of pliers. "I think this one will do for a start! Who's first?"

Micah crept through the foliage to a low window, careful not to disturb so much as one leaf or twig. His Pack was equally stealthy. They listened, hard. For any sound, any movement at all.

The plan was to get a bead on the monster. Wait until he was in a different room from the women and then strike.

But when Micah heard Jacee's bloodcurdling scream, that plan went to hell.

Without a second thought, he backed up, got a running start at the window, and let his feet fly, digging into the turf. He hit full force, shattering the glass into a million shards, not even feeling the pain on his muzzle.

What he saw took the rage in his heart, blackened it, and boiled it over, like tar.

Parker was holding a pair of pliers, twisting a vulnerable piece of flesh at the curve of Jacee's exposed breast. Torturing her, as so many of the women had been tortured under Bowman's rule back then.

No. No more. This ends here, and now!

Parker's face twisted in anger at the interruption, and he shifted into his monstrous form just as Micah launched himself across the cabin. Jacee scrambled out of harm's way, and the battle was on.

The two of them collided, opposing forces with years of pent-up hatred consuming them. The huge, awful bird was a strong enemy. A deadly fighter. He countered Micah's moves, blocked his attempts to go for the neck. They crashed around the small space, tearing up furniture, cracking the walls, breaking windows.

Micah rolled, getting in a good rip on the creature's

leg with his teeth, enjoying its screech of pain. Talons sank into his back, and he cried out and rolled again, dislodging them. The tide turned when his Pack joined the battle, distracting the monster.

They tore and bit at the creature. Came at him from every angle, and soon he was strictly on the defensive, unable to get in any more good blows. For all the creature's strength and hate, he was missing two vital things—

Love and Pack.

Without those things, an enemy was doomed. Parker seemed to realize this and, too late, tried to double his efforts. It was in vain.

When the creature fended off a strike from Aric, Micah finally got his opening. He leapt onto the bird, taking it to the floor. Clamping his jaws around its neck, he ripped out the monster's throat.

And he kept tearing, ripping at the body after its eyes went cold and dead to make sure. Really fucking sure it could never hurt him or his mate again ever. At last he became aware of a soft whine and a warm body nudging him.

My mate, come back to me. He's dead, and he can't hurt us anymore.

Whirling, his wolf found his beloved coyote standing there, gazing at him with love and understanding. She yipped at him in joy, and he realized it was over. They could start their lives together, follow their dreams, with no threats hanging over them. Only good things in their future.

For his mate, even more good things than she realized.

Yes, let's go home.

They stayed in their shifted form, curled up together in the back of one of the SUVs all the way back to the compound. Everyone left them alone.

In fact, they didn't surface for a solid two days, most of that time spent making love.

Micah's cravings for myst were almost completely gone, and when the urge came, it was a mere echo now, thanks to the love and support of his mate. His life was good.

And that was just about as close to paradise as he'd ever been.

Defeat a bad guy, throw a party.

Jacee was beginning to sense that was a theme with the Pack, and that was fine by her. The mood outside was festive as some of the guys and girls played football. Sariel and Kalen argued, as usual, over who'd get to hold baby Kai, the doting uncle or the daddy, and of course Sariel won.

Kira had finally introduced Jacee to a little creature called Chup-Chup, who looked like an adorable gremlin but was prone to biting when scared of strangers, so Jacee made sure to hold out her hand so he could sniff her thoroughly, letting him decide she was a friend before scratching his ears. After that, and Jacee sneaking him a piece of hot dog, they were golden.

Some of Calla's family attended, and Jacee had to admit to her mate that she was fascinated by the vampires. Especially the extremely sexy Prince Tarron Romanoff, who was single, but not for lack of several females vying for his attention.

Micah snorted, eyeing the vampire. "What's he got that I don't have?"

She rolled her eyes. First Sariel and now the vampire prince. "Nothing, sweetie. You're my main man—you know that."

"Your *only* man."

"That's right." She made kissy faces at him, and he laughed.

Her mate lapsed into thoughtful silence, plucking at the grass. Why did Micah keep checking his phone? Finally, he said, "Can you wait right here? I've got something I have to do."

"What?" she pouted. "Right now? We're enjoying this nice day together."

"Yes, we are. But I promise I'll be right back. I have, um, sort of a surprise for you."

She brightened. "Oh! Well, in that case, carry on. We like surprises. Especially if they're chocolate."

His brown eyes sparkled with happiness. "Oh, this is better than chocolate, I assure you."

"If you say so."

Sitting on their picnic blanket under the trees, she watched him disappear into the crowd. For a time, she simply let contentment wash over her. She'd lost so much in her life, but she'd gained this new family. These people, the Pack, were wonderful. In spite of the rough start and history with Jax, they'd accepted her. They'd saved her life, in more ways than one.

"Jacee?"

She thought, at first, that the woman's voice was a figment of her imagination. That she'd conjured the ghost because of her thoughts, and somehow her sister was here to watch over her in spirit. But then she looked up.

And if she hadn't been sitting, she would've fallen. Passed out.

Jacee couldn't breathe. The young woman in front of her was a pale vision of beauty. Too thin, almost as if a strong wind would blow her away. But she was real, long chestnut hair blowing gently around her face, wearing jeans and a pink blouse.

Slowly, shaking, Jacee stood, hand going over her pounding heart. "Faith?"

The woman nodded, crystal eyes flooding with tears. She tried to smile, but her face crumpled. "I've missed you so."

And then they were in each other's arms, hugging and bawling, barely aware of the attention they were attracting. Jacee didn't care. "This is a miracle. A miracle."

"Yes."

Jacee repeated it, over and over. Cried her heart out, for all the loneliness and pain they'd suffered apart. When they managed to pull themselves together, Jacee took her sister's hand and urged her to sit on the blanket with her.

"I can't stop looking at you," she breathed, staring at Faith. "Where have you been?"

"Like I told Micah, the Hunters took me that night."

"Wait. You told Micah?"

"Don't be angry with him," her sister urged. "That night he came in so badly hurt, he saw me in Sanctuary, where I've been staying. He was so out of it, and he thought I was you."

"Oh, my God."

"Yeah, I guess it was fate, because it led him to find me and bring us back together."

"But that was days ago. Why didn't he tell me? Or why didn't you come see me?"

That hurt.

"Please, don't be upset." Faith gazed at her, earnest. "I asked him to give me a little more time. I've been through a lot, and I was afraid . . . you'd be ashamed of me."

"Never, honey," Jacee said firmly, wiping her sister's face clean of tears. "Nothing that's happened since the night we were torn from each other has been our fault. What happened when you were taken by the Hunters?"

"They told me you were dead, and then they used me. Forced me into service for them as a prostitute."

"But you were just a kid!" Jacee was horrified.

"You see why I needed time? I was rescued by Prince Tarron's men, brought here to heal. Then I learn you're here, successful and mated to a handsome wolf who's part of this really cool team, and I just felt like this broken, used-up *thing*."

"Baby, you're anything but. You're beautiful and strong. And we're going to help you heal, every step of the way."

"We?" That one word was full of hope.

"Yes, we. Will you stay?"

"At the compound, yes. But I'll ask Nick for my own room once I'm released from Sanctuary. I'm not going to intrude when you're newly mated, and that's final. And before you protest, I really don't want to hear you guys going at it, so yeah. My own place."

Jacee blushed. "Well, when you put it like that . . ."

"But I'm here, and I'm not going anywhere for the time being. That's the important thing."

"Yes, it is." They hugged again, until a shadow loomed over them.

"Did I give you enough time to recover from my surprise?"

Jacee smiled up at her wonderful mate. "I don't know if I'll ever quite recover from this one, but you're forgiven. Forever."

"Oh, I like the sound of that." He smiled at Faith. "How about we introduce you to some of our friends?"

She smiled shyly. "I'd like that."

For someone who'd spent the last few years trapped in her own special brand of hell, Faith was very good with people, and they loved her right away.

Especially a certain vampire prince, who couldn't seem to take his eyes off her.

Jacee filed that information away for another day.

She was so happy and couldn't remember when she'd ever felt so blessed. After Faith had gone back to her room at Sanctuary, and the party died down, Jacee finally stole her mate away and showed him just how happy she was.

They made love long into night.

"Micah?" she murmured later. "When we build our house, can Faith live there if she wants?"

"Yes, sweetheart." He kissed her lips. "She's family. She can stay with us, if she wants, or wherever, as long as she wants. Don't you know there's nothing I wouldn't do to make you happy?"

She did know.

And she planned to spend the rest of her life making her wolf smile, too.

Several weeks later . . .

Cold. So cold. Thirsty.
  Starving.
  Can't make it.
  Yes, you can. One more step.
  Another. Keep going.
The wolf panted, so thin his bones rattled in his body. His fur was matted, dirty. Skin covered in sores, paw pads bloody. He'd traveled for so long, but now was in such bad shape, he moved purely on instinct. On will.

As if there was a homing device in his brain, he'd know when to stop.

The driveway was almost a surprise. The endless Shoshone simply stopped and, suddenly, civilization. Lifting his head, he blinked up at the buildings. One was new? He barely had time to register that, took two steps, and collapsed.

That was it. He was done.

He'd made it, and now he wouldn't die in some un-marked grave, all alone.

Suddenly there were shouts, footsteps on the gravel. Someone bent over him, and his wolf opened one eye, but he couldn't see more than a blur. Couldn't shift to speak, to answer his brothers' rapid-fire questions.

Where did this wolf come from?

Who is he?

My God, it can't be.

His answer came only in his head, dredged from the depths of near-forgotten memory.

My name is Ari.

And I'm home.

Turn the page for an excerpt
from the first book in the Alpha Pack series,

PRIMAL LAW

Available from Signet Eclipse.

K ira Locke had thirty seconds to lift the samples and get the hell out. Every second counted.

And then, technically, she'd be a thief. A criminal. The police wouldn't know quite what to do with the items she'd stolen should she be caught, any more than she knew what to do with them if she wasn't. Her brilliant plan had included getting them out of here, not where to go afterward. Or who to give them to. Who did she dare to trust when she offered little more than some dead tissue and a couple of wild accusations? Who would believe her?

A metallic scraping noise from somewhere down the hallway caused her to jump, her hands trembling so hard she nearly dropped the precious containers. *Scratch that thirty seconds. Shit.* Quickly, she checked the lids once more to make sure the formaldehyde didn't leak out, and then slipped the small film-sized canisters into her purse.

There. Let's see what Dr. Jekyll and the ghouls are up to.

The scraping sound came again, louder this time. Closer.

The steady, heavy tread of boot heels on concrete, the systematic opening and closing of screeching metal doors announced that one of the night guards was making his rounds. Checking all of the labs and other rooms in this restricted area of her place of employment that she had no clearance to breach.

Make that *former* place of employment, if she got caught.

The footsteps came nearer, another door squealed open, and she silently cursed the bad luck that A.J. had called in sick tonight. The young guard would've covered for her, considering that he harbored the same suspicions Kira did about something being hidden in this place. Something terrible. Then again, it was probably good that her friend hadn't known what she'd planned to do tonight because now he couldn't be accused of helping her.

Heart in her throat, she considered her options—find a spot to hide and hope the guard moved on, or stroll nonchalantly from the room and try to fool him into thinking she had every right to be here. Play it cool, and then get lost.

A sinking feeling in her gut told her the second choice was out of the question, and that the cops were the least of her worries. Glancing around the lab, she zeroed in on the long worktable built on a solid base, the only object large enough to shield her from view. After switching off the light, she skirted the edge, moved to put the table between herself and the door, and crouched. Just in time.

The door swung open, the light flipping on again. The guard paused and she could picture him eyeing the area, trying to decide if anything appeared out of place. His boots scraped the floor as he moved inside a bit farther, and she huddled like a frightened rabbit in a hole, certain that any moment he'd decide to step around the table. Catch her there and call her boss, Dr. Gene Bowman. And if the pompous prick knew she was snooping, what was in her possession, and what she suspected . . .

Go away, please. Please. Her pulse hammered at the hollow of her throat and she was certain he could sense her fear. Smell it, sour and thick in the dank air.

Gradually, his steps retreated after he flipped the lights off again, and closed the door. Only when his tread faded down the corridor did she slump in relief, dragging a hand through her hair. Taking a few deep breaths, she stood, the temporary reprieve at an end. She still had to get out of the damned building unseen, though at almost midnight with nothing but a skeleton crew, the odds were slightly better.

Right. Keep telling yourself that.

Clutching her purse straps in a death grip, she eased toward the door. Turned the knob and slowly inched the weighty metal door open. A bit at a time, just enough to slip out and close it again. Her patience was rewarded with the tiniest squeak of hinges, but even that small noise sounded like a trumpet blast to her ears.

The corridor was clear. Of course it couldn't be dimly lit with lots of inky shadows to hide in, like in the movies. The tunnel-like space was as brightly lit as a football field at halftime, and if the guard came back, she was toast. At least the lack of cover meant no one could sneak up on her, either.

Walking fast, she forced herself not to break into a run. Just a few more yards and—

"Nooooo!"

She froze, heart thundering, eyes wide. "Jesus Christ," she whispered.

Straining her ears, she listened. Nothing. The faint wail of despair might've been her imagination—the product of nerves and too little sleep. For a crazy second, she felt compelled to turn around and search for the source. To find out once and for all whether the spirit that constantly begged for help at all hours of the day and night was real, or if she was out of her mind.

A door opened at the end of the corridor and a burly guard stepped into view. "Hey! What're you doing down here? I need to see some ID."

Kira turned and ran, ignoring the man's angry shout. Fast as her feet could carry her, scrambling to think of another way out, she hit the door at the far end and kept going. A service elevator loomed ahead, which she assumed was for deliveries, being located at the back of the building and away from the general staff.

And if it was for deliveries, it should open near the parking lot.

She punched the button, nearly frantic. The elevator doors slid open, but the guard wasn't far behind. Leaping inside, she hit the button marked L—*Oh, God, let it mean "Loading Zone"*—then the one to close the doors, slapping it repeatedly.

The fat guard rounded the corner, belly jiggling, face red, hand on the butt of his gun. "Stop!" He drew the weapon, kept coming, one pudgy hand reaching out to catch the doors.

Too late. He missed, ruddy mug disappearing from view, and the box lurched, started upward. According to the panel the ride was only one level, but it seemed an eternity. Right now, the guard was probably on his radio calling for backup to stop her from getting away with . . . whatever it was she had in her purse.

And if her suspicions were correct, and she was apprehended? Bye-bye Kira, never to be heard from again.

The elevator stopped, and she held her breath as the doors opened. Nothing but dark, empty space greeted her and she hurried out, scanning the large area. It did, in fact, appear to be some sort of loading area, or garage. A couple of vans emblazoned with the NewLife Technology logo sat empty on the far left. Those were pretty much the contents of the cavernous space, save for a few discarded boxes.

Across the way, there were two big bay doors wide enough for just about any kind of truck to pull through, and to the right of those, a regular door with a lit EXIT sign above it. She took off, not caring how much noise she made. She had to get the hell out of there and to her car, *now*.

She pushed outside, into the night, the heat of June in Las Vegas hitting her like a slap. The still-soaring temperature, however, was the least of her worries. As she ran around the corner of the building toward the main employee parking lot, shouts sounded from just ahead and to her right.

"Shit!"

Two guards, including the burly one, burst from a different exit, clearly intending to cut her off. Her old Camry was just a few yards ahead, and she sprinted faster, fumbling with her key chain, pressing the button to unlock it. As she yanked open the driver's door, a series of loud pops rang out, pelting the side of her car.

"Oh, God!" Jumping inside, she slammed the door, tossed her purse onto the other seat, shoved the key in the ignition, and fired it up.

She peeled out, fishtailed, then straightened the vehicle and sped toward the company's entrance. A glance in the rearview mirror revealed that a couple of men in suits had joined the guards, who were waving their arms in agitation. The men broke off from the guards and jogged toward a dark sedan parked close to the building.

Kira turned her attention to the small guardhouse at the entrance, the orange-and-white-striped arms extending across both the in and out lanes. Normally, she'd stop and swipe her badge to raise the arm, but with two goons chasing her who were probably also armed and ready to shoot first, ask questions later? She'd skip the formalities.

Flooring the accelerator, she gripped the steering wheel tight and rammed through the barrier, cringing at the awful crunch of wood and metal. She risked another look to see the arm go flying, snapped like a toothpick. The dark sedan was now in hot pursuit.

And unshakable. Whatever the sleek model was the assholes were driving, it obviously had more juice than an ancient Camry held together by wire and duct tape. She was lucky it had crashed the gate and come through in one piece, and from the sound of the gears grinding and the engine wheezing, her dubious fortune wasn't going to last much longer.

Correction: Her luck had run out weeks ago when she'd started hallucinating visions of a sexy dead guy—was that an oxymoron?—begging for help, and she'd actually listened.

Where in the hell could she go? The police station wasn't far. She knew a couple of officers, one a detective. And she'd tell them, what? That she was in possession of stolen property and being shot at? That would turn away her pursuers for now, but she'd likely be arrested, the property returned to NewLife, and she'd have nothing to prove her claims. Such as they were.

So the police were out. Which left the airport. If she could just lose these pit bulls, she'd go there, buy a ticket to anywhere. Somewhere random, get a hotel room. Then she'd call a colleague who was a doctor specializing in genetics, arrange to meet him. With someone in the medical field on her side, she might have a chance at getting somewhere with proving what the docs at NewLife were up to.

Which would have been a great plan if the Camry hadn't given up the ghost. The damned thing coughed, sputtered . . . and died.

"No!" Yanking the steering wheel, she guided the car off the side street and into a darkened parking lot. Coasting to a stop, she put the car in park and took in her surroundings.

She was one street off the Strip, behind one of the casinos and off the beaten path. And the bad guys had just screeched to a stop next to her car, on the driver's side.

Both of them emerged from the sedan, the moonlight reflecting off the guns in their hands. They exchanged a look and then approached with slow, confident strides, wearing identical expressions of malicious triumph.

The man who'd been the passenger opened her door, grabbed her by the arm, and jerked her out, slamming her back against the side of her car.

"Seems you've been snooping where you don't belong," he sneered into her face. "The underground level is restricted for a reason. Why don't you tell us what you hoped to discover down there? Or maybe you *did* find something you shouldn't have." He turned his head, called to his partner. "See what Sweet Cheeks has in her purse."

Kira took advantage of his momentary distraction and brought her knee up hard between his spread legs, doing her best to relocate his balls. Letting out a hoarse cry, the man clutched his crotch and fell to his knees.

Kira took a deep breath, and released a scream loud enough to wake the dead.

"Did anyone ask Hammer if he wanted to ride along this trip?"

Jaxon Law studied Zander Cole's profile as the dark-haired man guided the Mercedes SUV through heavy traffic on the Strip. True to his nature as a Healer, his best friend was always thinking of those who were broken — and how to fix them. Not that Hammer was necessarily broken; the big, quiet man was just . . . scary different. "I did. He said he wanted to go to bed early and read."

From the back, Aric snorted. "Jesus. Is he going to do his knitting, too?"

Beside Aric, Ryon piped up. "Quilting."

"What?"

Jaxon craned his neck and eyed the pair, snickering at Aric's puzzled expression. The big redhead was frowning at Ryon as though he'd uttered a foreign word.

"He doesn't knit — he quilts," Ryon said slowly, as though speaking to a three-year-old. "Says it calms him. He's pretty good at it, too. You should see the detail in his designs —"

"Calms him?" Zan interrupted, brows lifting. "God, if he was any more laid-back he'd be dead."

Jaxon put in his two cents. "I think what we see on the outside of that guy is a carefully controlled mask. Wouldn't surprise me if he's the most dangerous dude any of us know."

On that point, he got no argument. Jaxon, Zander, Aric, and Ryon had been together since they were Navy SEALs — a promising career cut short years ago when their unit was attacked by rogue weres, more than half of them slaughtered and the rest, including the four of them, turned into wolf shifters. But Hammer, along with their new boss Nick Westfall, had only been with Alpha Pack for a few months. Those two were born shifters, a fact that had the team and the doctors and scientists at the Institute of Parapsychology completely fascinated.

Nick, a rare white wolf, had replaced the deceased Terry Noble and brought Hammer with him to the team when they both left the FBI, and Jax had to admit the newbies were working out pretty well. Nick was tough-as-nails, but fair, and knew how to laugh at himself when the situation called for it. Unlike Terry, he wasn't above having a beer with the guys, and he sometimes joined them when their wolves needed to run and hunt. He had their backs, always.

Hammer was cut from the same cloth as Nick, though he was more of a mystery. The huge gray wolf preferred to keep to himself and remain ensconced with their leader at their compound deep in the Shoshone National Forest rather than make the trek to Vegas to blow off steam and get laid.

"Quilting," Aric muttered with a short laugh. "Man, I'm gonna give him hell about this."

Zan shook his head. "Probably not a good idea to harass a guy who can kill you with one blow from his fist. Ease up, Savage." Zan made a right, toward the Bellagio, and grinned. "Here we are. Reservations are under my name. We've got four nonsmoking rooms with king-sized beds and the weekend off, boys. Don't do anything I wouldn't do."

This prompted a round of cheers and whistles.

As Zan found a parking space, Jaxon addressed the group. "Keep your cell phones charged and handy. Is anybody besides me going off by themselves?"

Aric laughed. "Are you kidding? I don't know about these two," he said, indicating Ryon and Zan, "but if I don't find a hot woman with loose morals PDQ, I'm going to self-combust and torch half the Strip." Considering his particular Psy gifts, the man was only half-joking.

"No shit," Ryon eagerly agreed.

"I'm going to hit the casino for a while, just relax, maybe play some blackjack," Zan put in. "There's something to be said for going slow and anticipating the ride."

"I'll go slow the second time. Or maybe the third.

Let's go, ladies." Jaxon got out of the SUV carrying his duffel bag, scenting the air. His blood thrummed hot in his veins, his cock already half-hard at the prospect of burying himself between a pair of silky thighs, sliding deep. Fucking all night long, in every position. It had been weeks since they'd been able to make it to Vegas, and like his friends, he was feeling the burn.

Inside the hotel, Jaxon and the others checked into their rooms and dropped off their bags, but didn't linger. Zan had booked them all on the same floor, so they rode down together again and then split up. Zan went looking for the blackjack tables, Aric and Ryon heading for the front doors and disappearing into the night. Jaxon skirted the gaming area and strolled to the nearest bar, ordering a Jack and cola. He sat with his back to the bar, sipping his drink and scanning the crowd, waiting.

She'd be here. Right on the dot, like before.

Jaxon wasn't one to waste valuable time searching for a "date" when he had only two nights off, and Alexa had been not only reliable on their two previous weekends together, but extremely talented in bed. The blond call girl had taught him naughty things he'd *never* considered doing or allowing to be done *to* him, and some of those tasty memories had him squirming on his stool. Damn, the woman loved her job. *Lucky me.*

As if he conjured her, she stepped around an older couple and came toward him wearing a wide smile, a little black halter dress, matching heels, and nothing else. He knew that from experience. Her long blond mane tumbled over her shoulders, full and teased, in a dramatic style that never failed to call to mind an eighties rocker. But the fluff framed a pair of nice full breasts, the nipples even now peeking through the thin material of her dress and awaiting his tongue. Her face was overdone with makeup in his opinion, and she had the hard look of a girl who'd already seen too much of the crap life had to offer. But even so, she was still attractive.

"Hey, hot stuff," she greeted him in a sultry voice. Stepping between his knees, she twined her arms around his neck, pushed her breasts against his chest, and captured his mouth with hers.

Her tongue slipped inside and dueled with his, seeking and tasting. Her nipples grazed him though his dark T-shirt, begging to be appreciated. Wrapping an arm around her waist, he broke the kiss. "My room."

"Not yet."

He frowned. "Why not?"

"I have an idea." Her eyes sparkled with mischief. "Let's go for a walk."

"I'm not paying you to take me for a stroll down the Strip, gorgeous."

"There's plenty of time to play in your room, but this is different. Just trust me."

He hesitated. Inside, his wolf growled suspiciously, not trusting her or any situation that was "different." The man, however, was ready and willing to be led by his cock, especially if she came through once again with her love of the daring and kinky.

"All right." Sliding off the stool, he offered her his arm. "Have it your way."

Raking him up and down with her eyes, she ran her tongue over her lips in an exaggerated come hither gesture. "If you insist."

Pushing down another ripple of unease, Jaxon let her pull him away from the bar and through the front doors, outside. He wondered what game she had in mind as they walked in silence, away from the Bellagio and down a side street to the next block, leaving the hordes of people behind.

He didn't have long to speculate. Tugging his hand,

she led him across a dark parking lot dotted with only a few cars, toward the back of small abandoned building that used to be a club or something. At the back wall, she pulled him around the corner to where the side of the store was shielded from view of the neighboring business by a tall wooden fence. She backed him against the brick, attacking the fly of his jeans. Which, admittedly, was bulging with excitement.

"Alexa," he began, shaking his head.

"Shush. This is gonna be so good." Expertly, she freed him, stroked his erection. "You ever had public sex? It's quite a thrill."

"Yeah, but who's going to see us? There's nobody around." There was something wrong with her logic in this, but damned if he could think what it was.

Because at that moment she sank to her knees and manipulated his aching balls with clever fingers tipped with bloodred nails. Swiped the head of his leaking cock with that pretty pink tongue. Began to lick his shaft, laving him like he was the last ice-cream cone in the Mojave Desert. He moaned, burying his fingers in her hair, not caring about the gallon of hair spray making the strands stick to his palm like a damned spiderweb. All that mattered was her mouth, sliding down over his rod, the heat, the suction, taking him deep—

A scream ripped through the night, shattering the mood. Jaxon straightened with a gasp, disengaging himself from his date more abruptly than he intended, pushing her back. He listened, ignoring the hooker's muttered protests. Another scream went through him like a bolt of electricity, the sheer terror in the female's voice calling to something primal within him.

Quickly, he tucked his flagging erection into his jeans and zipped up, and then pulled Alexa to her feet. "I have to see about this. Go back to the hotel, where it's safe."

"Oh, come on," she began, pouting. "It ain't your problem. Let someone else deal with it."

Spinning her around, he gave her a push toward the corner. "Go, now, and don't follow me. I'll call you." In that moment, he knew he never would, but the reason eluded him.

Digging his iPhone from his jeans pocket, he took off at a jog, wincing at the stab of pain in his mangled leg. In human form he could walk with barely a limp, but more strenuous activity such as jogging, running, or sparring with his teammates still caused the injured limb a great deal of agony.

Ignoring the pain, he scented the air. *Fear.* The unknown woman's panic clawed at his chest, more than a stranger's should. He had to get to her, make sure she was all right. Following the scent, he slowed long enough to ring Zander. Thankfully, his friend answered right away.

"What's up?"

"My hookup, Alexa. You've met her."

"Right."

"We went for a walk, but something's going down and I had to send her back. She's coming your way." He gave Zan her location and the intersection he'd just passed.

"I'll call the others and send them as backup. After I make sure she's safe, I'll head there myself. What's going on?"

"Not sure, but I heard a woman scream twice."

"Be there soon."

"Thanks, man." Ending the call, he stuffed the phone into his pocket again and picked up the pace. He didn't understand this driving need to hurry, to get between this woman and whatever threat she faced. He ran full out, knowing by the sweet scent that must be hers that he was almost there. She was nearby.

His route took him farther from the Strip, across another parking lot and past more darkened buildings. Not an area where anyone should wander alone. What had brought the woman to such a desolate part of the city? He'd learn soon enough.

As he rounded another building, he spotted her. The woman whose scent would likely drive him mad if he had a few seconds to savor it. The petite blonde was struggling in the hold of a man in a dark suit, fighting like a rabid wildcat, biting, scratching, and kicking. A second man rose to his feet, gun in one hand, cupping his crotch with the other, and Jaxon felt a surge of pride knowing she'd put him on the ground. Then the first man slammed her against the side of a car and delivered a blow to her face that snapped her head back and made her cry out in pain and terror.

Tear out his fucking heart and feast on it while it beats.

Jaxon's beast rose with a vengeance, burst from his skin without conscious thought. His roar shook the earth, brought the tableau before him to a complete standstill. He stripped off his shirt, was barely aware of the rest of his clothes falling away as skin became fur, muscles and bones contorting and reshaping, the usual pain little more than a whisper in his mind. Hands changed to paws, fingernails to claws, man to pure, raging gray wolf.

All zeroed in on the man who'd struck the small, pretty blonde.

The soldier in him knew the smart move would be to go for the man with the gun; the beast demanded blood from the one with his hands on *her*. The one who'd hit her.

The one who now let her go, twisted around to confront the new threat . . . and stared at him in horror. The predator in him felt a surge of satisfaction. His wolf wasn't nearly as hampered by his leg injury as the man.

The wolf sped across the distance, leaped, and the man screamed, the last sound he'd ever make. His forepaws struck the bastard square in the chest, knocking him backward, into the side of the car. Off-balance, the man stumbled and fell, and Jaxon took him to the ground. Lunging, he went for the kill, snapped his jaws around the vulnerable neck, teeth sinking into flesh, through muscle and bone. The man's scream ended in a rough gurgle, his hands grabbing desperately at the wolf's fur, trying to dislodge him. To no avail.

The struggles weakened as blood filled the wolf's mouth, rich and sweet, and he was hardly aware of the man's companion shouting in terror. The beast longed to linger over his prize, to rip into the savory meat and take his fill. To howl his triumph over the man who'd dared to strike his—

A muffled pop and a searing pain in his shoulder brought him around snarling, his kill abandoned as he faced the remaining threat. This asshole had also wanted to harm the woman, and for that he was fucking dead. The wolf launched himself at the second man, who backpedaled with a yell, pointed the gun and fired again. His shot went wide, and Jaxon took him down as easily as he had the first goon, tearing out his throat. The urge to feed was strong, almost unbearable, now that they were no longer a threat to the woman.

The woman.

Again, the scent of her invaded his senses. With the danger past, he let his limp prey drop from his jaws and finally took stock, letting the aroma of citrus and vanilla fill him, the crisp, clean essence of her imprinting on every cell of his being. A strange rush fired his blood, as though the man inside the beast had mainlined a load of coke, a comparison he could honestly make. A much younger, more reckless Jaxon had flirted with the edge of no return before he'd gotten his act together and joined the Marines.

Instinct told him that the effect of this woman's scent had the potential to be twice as intoxicating as any drug, and much more dangerous to the man *and* to the wolf.

Turning, he saw her. Edging around the front of the dilapidated car with her hands on the hood, eyes wide with shock, trying to put the vehicle between them. The predator in him tensed, focused his attention solely on the woman, and he moved forward slowly. Began to stalk her—but not for the reason she might think.

She was slim and small, fine-boned, with a delicate face that was all angles and dominated by big sky blue eyes. Almost an elfin face, especially with the shoulder-length pale blond hair framing those sweet features. He doubted her head would reach his chin, and all things considered, she'd tuck against his chest and mold perfectly against his much bigger body.

Mine.

And why the hell would he go all possessive over a woman he didn't know? His irritation with himself emerged as a growl.

"N-nice puppy," she stammered, stumbling as she kept moving backward, around the car. "Good puppy. Aren't you p-pretty?"

The wolf snorted, which came out like a sneeze. He'd been called a lot of things, very few of them complimentary, and certainly never pretty. But from her? He could live with that.

She grabbed for the passenger door handle and tugged, only to find it locked on that side. Eyes round with fear, she stared at him, and he recognized the moment she realized she was trapped. There was nowhere to go, no escape.

The woman was his.

Also available from

J.D. Tyler

Wolf's Fall
An Alpha Pack Novel

Alpha Pack commander Nick Westfall isn't sure he's fit to lead—especially when he meets the one woman he can't claim without reliving the torture he endured at the hands of a rogue vampire.

Vampire princess Calla Shaw has seen her own share of heartbreak, but she can tell that the wild attraction she and Nick feel for each other could turn into something significant—if only he'd let it. But Calla isn't about to give up on her mate without a fight.

<u>Also in <u>the series</u></u>
Cole's Redemption
Hunter's Heart
Black Moon
Savage Awakening
Primal Law

Available wherever books are sold or at
penguin.com

s0557

Also available from

J.D. Tyler

Cole's Redemption

An Alpha Pack Novel

Healer and black wolf shifter Zander Cole has survived horrors that would have broken a weaker man. But when a battle leaves him deaf and his powers dimmed, Zan is devastated. Believing himself to be a burden to his team, he sees only one option: leave the Pack forever.

White wolf shifter Selene Westfall knows pain—she is certain her father was responsible for her mother's death. And she lives to exact revenge. So when she is challenged by a savage black wolf, she puts up a vicious fight—only to become the black wolf's Bondmate as a result of his bite.

Two damaged souls—one filled with hatred and one who's lost his reason for living—are forced together as they come to terms with their unlikely, turbulent bond. A love neither expected may be all that stands between them and a killer trying desperately to keep the past dead and buried....

Available wherever books are sold or at
penguin.com

s0557

Also available from

J.D. Tyler

Hunter's Heart
An Alpha Pack Novel

Wolf shifter Ryon Hunter is visited by a beautiful spirit
with an urgent message: "Help me...I'm alive." It's wildlife
biologist Daria Bradford, using a rare Psy gift to call for
help. Finding her mortally wounded in Shoshone
National Forest, Ryon knows that she is his destined
mate but is afraid of what she will do if she finds out
what he is —or what he had to do to save her life.

**"An exciting series that will have readers
glued to the pages and wanting more."
—Fresh Fiction**

Available wherever books are sold or at
penguin.com

facebook.com/ProjectParanormalBooks

s0525

Also available from

J.D. Tyler

Black Moon
An Alpha Pack Novel

Ever since he saved Dr. Mackenzie Grant's life, Alpha Pack warrior, panther shifter and sorcerer Kalen Black has had trouble keeping the beautiful doctor out of his thoughts. Their mutual brush with death awakens an intense passion between them, one that for the first time has the notorious loner letting down his guard—and placing Mackenzie in the path of a deadly enemy...

"Readers will fall head over heels for the Alpha Pack!"
—*New York Times* **bestselling author**
Angela Knight

Available wherever books are sold or at
penguin.com

facebook.com/ProjectParanormalBooks

s0493